ONLY VISITING

THIS PLANET

STORIES FROM THE NEW SOUTH

ONLY VISITING THIS PLANET

STORIES FROM THE NEW SOUTH

Dorie LaRue

Dedicated to Lynn Rafferty Bettis, the Irreplaceable

Contents

Preface

The woman characters in this collection do not wake up from their southern belle roots and make one long uninterrupted ascension to the status of modern feminist. For the most part, these sixteen stories reflect a bumpy ride, like all human experience rooted in reality, on the iffy evolutionary roads of time and history. The collection is divided into two parts and in the first section, *Women Transforming*, age has sometimes little to do with the stage of enlightenment. In "The Once and Future Soap," for example, a college student from a small town, attending the state university in the capitol, is impressed with her peers' progressive ideological standpoints, but is unable to figure out how to make the leap into the new world. A teen, in "Witnessing in the Kare Krishna Tradition," embroiled in summer church camp politics, courageously goes against her whole community's religious unconsciousness. Some of the women in the beginning of the collection seem stuck, unable to come to terms with the fact that their roles are not only unrealistic, but crushingly lonely. In "Only Visiting

This Planet" a widowed mother continues her controlling parental duty for her adult daughter, only to have her daughter suddenly break free of expected confines, though in a dangerous way. In "She A Hard Woman" a beauty shop full of women dutifully continuing the demands of cultural beauty standards, summarily fights off a gun-toting criminal, but remain clueless to their own independence and strength. In "Foreign Travel" a young woman, to the horror of her mother, defying all conventions by hitchhiking through Europe, indulges in her weakness for passionate romance, and its inevitable resulting failure is ameliorated not so much by self-awareness as by her own vivid imagination. Still, she survives. "The Recurrent End of the Unending," written in the second person reminiscent of Edna O'Brien's *A Pagan Place,* breaks the mold slightly. The narrator, though independent enough to leave a loveless marriage, falls right off the bat for a weak narcissistic man, and her buried selfless instincts almost do her in. In "The Not-So-Chinese Wedding" a middle-aged woman from Georgia, displaced for a few days in New York state, gains insight into her own needs, and realizes wisdom comes from unrelenting observation rather than her usual research on the Internet. And finally, in this woman's section, "One Day in the Life of a Good Ole Gal" provides a setting for a traditional southern wife to throw off all her culturally imposed limits, including the taboos of adultery and miscegenation. She is nearing the final product of evolution, a woman profoundly in touch with her own needs and who sees with clear eyes. She is neither important, rich, nor postgraduate educated, but she is authentic.

And what of the men? In the second section, *Men Dealing*, the characters are men who are affected by women's starts and fits to act out their new roles. To be sure, the new roles are sometimes stabs in the dark, fraught with ego and unrealistic aspirations. Yet, the women in the second section do awaken the men in varying degrees, sometimes kindly, sometimes clumsily, but always fueled by their desire to break free of the way it's always been. All the stories in this section are told from the point of view of a belabored man, and the women catalysts are sometimes major characters and sometimes wisps in the background, yet none of them act as expected, and all cause at least a promising blip in the men's consciousness. Thus, a retired major in the Air Force, in "Carrying the Fight," is forced to confront old wounds by his wife's abandonment, and she, as a self-realized personage, albeit in the few paragraphs she inhabits, is fully aware of her boundaries, and knows who she is. In "Are You Decent" a husband refuses to acknowledge his wife's compassion and grief over his own needs, but at least he realizes something is changing. Another ex-soldier in "Tabby's Blues Box" witnesses his date's courage to eschew racism, and though it doesn't fully sink in with him, her breaking role is at the climax of the story, thus underscoring its importance. And in the last story, a woman entranced with her new career in psychology, wreaks havoc on a post traumatic stressed ex-combat soldier, who tells the graphic story. Does the experience inadvertently cure him of at least one fear? I'd like to think so. The last three stories, "Vaporizing Cassini," "Fishing Trip," and "Even in the Dark," continue the evolution, until the final story, "Southern

Landscaping," a mother's words reveal a daughter, "[who] knows what to do."

In all, the men are dealing with a new kind of woman in their once familiar southern milieu. The women vary in their stages of enlightenment, and they are major, flat, or minor characters, but their common thread is their conscious embrace of change more or less to some degree. It is not for nothing this place is called the New South. Can the men take it? I believe they can and will in the future. They are not unkind, they are more in love than not, and they observe their own feelings sometimes even relentlessly, and even if at this point, they do not know exactly what to do with them.

Perhaps one day "southern literature" will disappear into the giant cauldron of "literature." No one can exactly define "the South" even as "the New South" adds a dimension but still resists category. Larry Brown, the quintessential southern short story writer, has a story "Sleep" which has no discernible north or south setting. Perhaps this should be all southern writers' goal. To be sure, we cannot depict "southern-ness" by geography, yet there is still a kind of literature in which familiar traits of southern fiction can be discerned: loss, racial guilt, eccentricity, family bonds, and yes, place. It is in transition, and a rapid transition at that, so perhaps our old name place genre can be held onto a little longer, at least until we all, men and women, reach the promised land of racial, sexual, and economic equality.

Part I
Women Transforming

The Once and Future Soap

At the end of the semester Lenora came home from her state university, leaving without regret the damp, disrespectful faces of the two sections of freshman English which had been relegated to her teaching talents in the spring semester. But turning the Mazda convertible her father had given her for her sixteenth birthday into the cold safety of her parents' driveway, she knew there was no denying something. She felt as stuck now in Hollyville for the whole summer as she had felt stuck for the whole term at State.

"Hello, dear," her mother called to her after Lenora came in. She must have heard the front door open and had her ears pricked for the Mazda's rotary engine grrrr. Lenora's mother came in from where she had most likely been working on one of her interminable A donor (generous) or B donor (extremely generous) lists on the Duncan Phyfe sideboard in the formal dining room. Lenora's mother was a formidable volunteer and charity organizer. She did not waste her time any more with C (stingy) lists.

"How was your semester?" her mother asked, as though she did not see Lenora every four weeks with her dirty laundry, as well as the two stacks of freshman compositions she brought home to grade in peace.

"Fine," said Lenora, making her voice overly friendly and obviously phony, as if to hide a clinical depression, a practice she'd adopted for years to discourage detailed conversations with her mother. Her mother does not cotton to friendliness, either real or fake.

Lenora was a graduate teaching assistant at Louisiana State University majoring in British literature with a specialization in William Blake. Holding any kind of conversation with her mother about her studies was always a conversation destined for failure. In fact, talking to her mother was a little like talking to a freshman about their papers, a task which Lenora was finding increasingly difficult, not only because of the enormity of the assignments, but also because of their poor quality.

In all fairness as far as her students were concerned, at one time Lenora had taken great pains to analyze distortions in logic or syntaxial error on the paper as suggested by the University's course outline; toward the end of the second semester however, something had snapped and she'd read them more hastily, her comments deteriorating to notations like "wake up," for particularly dense papers.

"That's very good," her mother said, severely. She was long past delving into Lenora's depression fakery. Her mother was frowning, "Do call Pearline and give your laundry to her right way." Then she went back to the dining room where her

A or B lists waited.

Lenora dragged the fat bag to the laundry room and left it beside the washer where color-coded piles of her father's shirts lay on the floor. Pearline was nowhere in sight which was just as well. Despite the newfound political consciousness Lenora had cultivated at Louisiana State University, Pearline sported a look, around Lenora, of pre-emptive umbrage. Having a black maid should be embarrassing, Lenora had learned last year. If any of the intellectuals at LSU had known, they would have looked down on Lenora. And the feminists would have her drawn and quartered. And despite all Lenora's friendly overtures Pearline reacted to any exchange with subterfuge and brick wall looks.

Her mother, banana republic totalitarian that she was, got along a hundred times better with Pearline than Lenora did. She just blithely went ahead, like it was the 1950's in Hollyville, Louisiana, instead of the heady 1970s, (which Lenora herself had yet to fully grasp) and would be that way forever. And Lenora's and Pearline's cold war barely made a blip on her mother's radar.

"So," her mother said, as they were seated in the cheery sunroom, the gladioli and late azaleas and tiny border flowers emblazoned by the afternoon sunlight outside and creating a kind of overly perfect garden effect. "What are you planning to do all summer, dear?"

Lenora sat as though she were contemplating the difficult answer to a deceptively simple question, but in reality, she was considering doing nothing more than sleeping late and lying by the pool at the Hollyville Country Club of which her father was president. One talent that Lenora did have was that if she were left alone long enough, without people snidely referring to the damaged ozone layer, she could roast to a lovely, gold-dusk hue. Except for that one physical attribute, though, Lenora had the tall, square body, the large bones, and the round face of a sumo wrestler.

"Oh, research, reading," Lenora said, sighing a bit, and squinting her eyes the way she thought an overworked genius might. Though sometimes Lenora resented the fact that her mother had nothing but the vaguest idea about graduate school, sometimes she capitalized on it.

Pearline swung out onto the patio balancing a huge tray with iced tea for Lenora, a teapot for her mother, and croissants ordered from Maxwell's Bakery, for both of them. Lenora was paralyzed between jumping up to take the tray from her or sitting in the wicker chair like a despot. "Hello, Pearline," she said in a tone as horribly cheerful as her mother's.

Pearline scowled and sat the tray on the wrought iron table. "You want some lemon, Miss Lenora?"

Lenora's mother took off her glasses and slipped them into a gold lame case. She poured her tea. "I heard about something that you might be interested in from Myron." Myron was her mother's hairdresser.

"Oh?" said Lenora idly, wondering what possible thing Myron could say that she would ever be interested in. Her mother and her friends saw him something of a guru.

Lenora's mother pursed her lips meditatively over her cup. "There's to be a television show filmed right her in

Hollyville. It's for one of those soap operas."

Lenora had long given up pretending she was not interested in soap operas to not being interested in soap operas. "Oh," she said.

Her mother was determined that Lenora consider her news interesting. "It's *By the Heart's Last Throb*. They're looking for extras. And an old courthouse. And a southern mansion to film." She sighed. "Antebellum," she added. Their house was big, but all modern glass and new brick.

Lenora knew her mother was afraid that she'd spend her days lying around in her sweats like she had last summer, and that she had looked long and hard for this tidbit of activity. Her mother looked upon Lenora as a good, obedient, sluggish child who needed direction toward the social intercourses as well as a more lighthearted approach to life, though she herself rarely displayed lightheartedness. She was forever trying to prompt her into what she considered fun things. Though her mother never watched soap operas, or TV at all, the fact that she was suggesting something so declass was an indication of her incipient desperation.

Lenora tried to soften the dubious look she could feel materializing on her face. "Interesting," she said. But Lenora was so tired with the boredom of classes and teaching and the long bland days of study, that not only was she planning to lie around the pool, she, in the spirit of thorough vegetation, hadn't even bothered to get any of the reading lists for the new fall semester from her teachers. Somewhere along the line she had discovered that she loathed teaching with its uninspired students who lined up outside her office at the end of the semester to suck up for grades, and the research with its endless bibliographies and convoluted literary theory. Of the two thorns, she did not know which she disliked the most. The students were intense, caught up in their pathetic lives. They told her long, personal stories about their love lives and families as excuses for missing classes. And at the end of the next year, Lenora would have to start her dissertation, the thought which depressed her with a special power.

"Who knows?" Who knows was her mother's favorite rhetorical device. "It may be a hoot." She looked at Lenora, playing the modern mom, hep to jargon.

"Interesting," said Lenora. "I should check into it."

"Have a croissant, darling," said her mother, satisfied.

The next morning Lenora wrapped her hulk in her pink dressing gown her mother had given her when she had her tonsils removed, while she waited for Pearline to deposit her clean laundry in her room and went downstairs to have a late breakfast. Pearline was squeezing lemons and watching the little countertop TV her mother kept in the kitchen especially for her.

"Good morning, Pearline," Lenora said, looking hopelessly at the bandana Pearline had wrapped around her head.

"I done cooked," Pearline said, her eyes on a couple in a clinch to the tune of an organ crescendo in something that looked like a recording studio.

"I'm just having toast," Lenora said. She wished she'd skipped breakfast today or eaten at the club. Yes, that's what she should have done. Had an English muffin at the club, before stretching out in a chaise by the pool. But it was too late. She had already committed herself by coming into the kitchen.

The couple on the screen swayed and clutched, then the camera panned in on the woman's face. She had extremely big hair and diamond earrings. Her face was passionate and tearful. "But Derrick," she said, a note of protest in her voice, "you mean I won't see you again until after your tour?" An organ's crescendo rose again.

Lenora peered into the breadbox.

"Ain't no white. Have to eat brown, Miss Lenora," informed Pearline, not taking her eyes off the screen.

Lenora pulled the whole wheat from her mother's hand-carved walnut breadbox and dropped two slices into the toaster.

"Leave, leave, leave. You're leaving just like all the others," the woman wailed.

"Your mama left you a note," Pearline said, nodding her head without taking her eyes off the screen toward one of the plastic strawberry magnets on the refrigerator.

Lenora read the note without taking it down. *Gone to folk art committee! Back at two! Tried to wake you!!!* Lenora's mother always wrote notes and letters in telegraphic sentences with many exclamation points. She wrote the way she probably thought, and this is why her father found it difficult to ever argue with her, and her concoction of deliberate obtuseness and vulnerability. Her father treated her mother with a kind of indulgent deference and worked long hours.

For the summer, her mother would be engaged with Hollyville's Folk Festival, various philanthropic deeds with her friends, and preparation for an endless number of formal summer suppers. If she were not careful, Lenora, also, would be one of her projects.

"I'm going, but I'll be back," the man's voice said from the clinch. Pearline started whipping something in a bowl. Her whipping arm blurred. "Humph!" she said to Derrick.

Lenora zeroed in on the man as another crescendo rocked around him, and a prophetic screen of smoke ensued as though he had already spiritually left. He had on a rock singer's tacky, glittery outfit and it flashed sporadically in his cloud. "Rock on, Babe," he sang. "Rock on, oo oo."

Pearline snapped off the TV just as the credits and the theme song took off. It was *By The Heart's Last Throb*. She started banging pans and dishes into the sink.

Lenora shook the percolator to see if there was any coffee left. So, this is what Myron and her mother were touting. *By the Heart's Last Throb*'s storyline must be taking Derrick on a tour of the Deep South. She could just hear Myron talking to her mother, "Be a soap star, dahling."

Lenora tried to imagine herself tiring of the pool and becoming a soap opera fiend. Actually, the mindlessness of it rather appealed to her. Maybe she should find something to do besides sunbathing this summer. Absolutely nothing cerebral. Something that looked cerebral, preferably, but was really plebian. Maybe she could stop by the bookstore on the way to the club and get something light to read. Something very light.

She remembered shopping for a birthday card last summer in Mary Ann's Bookstore on Main when a seedy, bearded instructor from Tulane had come in. He was taking the summer off for research and was staying with his mother. Mrs. Atkins. Yes, Old Mrs. Atkins, a member of their church. Her son, who'd gone away to school at Vanderbilt, then on to teach at State before his book made him famous and he'd been hired at Emory. He had come in as though he were in a state of agitation. "Trash," he'd gasped, rubbing his hands together, wild-eyed like a dope addict. "Trash—got to have some trash." Mary Ann said that that happened every now and then. He'd get fed up with intellectualism and have to cool his brain with something like science fiction or detective novels. Lenora understood now.

At Lenora's last bite, Pearline turned and swept her dish into the sink as though she had eyes in the back of her bandanna.

That afternoon, Lenora tucked a Harlequin Romance inside her William Blake anthology, and lying in one of the woven plastic chaises beside the country club pool read long, impassioned sentences like, "Jennifer watched, wide-eyed, as Randall slowly unbuttoned his imported silk shirt, exposing his tanned, virile, well-honed chest," and "Claudette felt Dunlop's rising manhood as she surrendered, losing herself completely in wave upon wave of unbridled passion." The books have much in common: the covers all have pictures of women with unnatural cleavage spilling out of their dresses, they spend quite a bit of time having their cleavage crushed up against their hero's well-honed chests, and the heroes are always rich and slightly nasty before the women turn them around. But it worked. The knee-jerk passion spirited her as far away as she could be from Blake, the nineteenth century, and that spirit of intellectualism at the University that Lenora hasn't quite got the hang of yet.

As for herself, Lenora has only had two affairs in her life. One was with a thin, overly cerebral graduate student when she was an undergrad, who spoke of their sex as assignations. That always reminded Lenora of the words assignment and resignation. During the last year Lenora had met a married French professor on Tuesday and Thursday afternoons from three to five and once a month on Mondays from six p.m. until ten p.m. At first Lenora had high hopes for the relationship. She thought his urbanity and international sophistication might rub off on her, refine her edges, so to speak, for the day when she might have a more suitable lover. Unfortunately, Renee spent most of their time complaining about his wife and their life together. "Mon Dieu! The woman is mad!" he'd say to her as way of greeting. "Thees time she cuts up the Hugo abstract to leetle bits!" Renee's wife had a habit of taking the scissors to his things whenever she got angry. All his socks were toeless, and the last time Lenora had seen him, to say good-bye (and that it was all over), he had taken off his tweed jacket and his vest, and his shirt had been mangled until it resembled a dickey. Lenora had left him with his head in his hands muttering curses at his wife. She had not even been able to pick up any useful French phrases as she'd hoped, except a few perhaps pertinent to a monograph on misogamy. She had hoped at least Renee, if not Adam, could have rubbed some of their intellectual savvy off on her.

Two days later, when Lenora came home from the club,

she went into the kitchen and saw Pearline standing by the sink, rinsing dishes, and loading them into the dishwasher and talking with a young woman.

"Hello," said Lenora. She felt her smiling turn from slightly friendly to apologetic as a fashionably thin woman in African dress lifted her chin haughtily. "I'm Lenora."

The woman tilted her chin sideways in a way that seemed oddly familiar to Lenora. "Nroka Shrahlinka," she said, and immediately turned back to Pearline.

It took a second for Lenora to realize that she had introduced herself. Nroka Shrakhlinka?

"Hmph," said Pearline, not even glancing at Lenora. "Even change your name. Sin. That what it is." She arranged the goblets on the top shelf to make room for a mixing bowl.

"I changed names from one given by a slave holder to a name from my—from your—from our heritage. Heritage. You know what that means?"

"How you even say it?" said Pearline. "Nikki Linkletter? Nookie Lahlinkie?"

"Well," said Lenora brightly, and she was horrified to hear herself sounding exactly like a garden club hostess, "I'm going to have a lemonade. Would anyone care for one?"

Nroka Shrahlinka stared at her for a second as if Lenora were a Martian who had made a temporary emergency landing in her mother's kitchen.

"No. Thank you."

Lenora plunked her gear down and opened the refrigerator. She moved the Tupperware and covered dishes around, forgetting for a second what she was looking for.

Nroka Shrahlinka suddenly threw her arms into the air and began pacing the kitchen. Lenora, too startled to move, saw that she was wearing leather boots with a wide fringe down the sides.

"A soap opera! A maid! Isn't it bad enough, what you do—but you want to actually appear on television—as a maid? A maid! Billie Holladay! She never would take a part like that!"

Once as an undergrad Lenora had been ill and missed a few days of her Modern History Lecture. When she returned, the professor in his attempt to reach his disaffected students, was presenting a lecture dressed like Aristotle, transported mysteriously to the twentieth century to make commentary on the modern state. Lenora felt like she had then, suddenly fallen into another world. Was it just minutes ago that she was on horseback galloping with Claudette and Dunlop across a sunlit hillock in anticipation of an afternoon tryst? Mon Dieu! She was really getting into those paperbacks.

Nroka exploded again as Pearline pushed her glasses back on her nose and peered at the dial on the dishwasher. After a while Lenora, standing stupidly with a pitcher in one hand and its lid in the other, finally caught the gist of the woman's words. Pearline had been spotted in her uniform at the A & P and had been offered a role as an extra in the soap to be filmed in Hollyville. The director had needed a black maid to walk in and out of a southern mansion. She was going to get a few hundred dollars. Nroka claimed that any role like that was an insult.

Lenora set the lemonade down carefully on the kitchen island and took a glass from the cabinet. It occurred to her that she could be to them no more than a piece of furniture. She could leave without being at all obvious. She could stay practically unnoticed. It also occurred to her that she had an odd, expectant, hopeful feeling not unlike the one she had in the beginning when she had first met Renee.

Pearline went into the pantry and came out holding an armload of sponges, paper towels and a bottle of 409. She trudged out, as though Nroke was no more than a fly.

Nroke stood, unmoving, like a carving of an African goddess, wrought from some deep, mysterious mahogany. She looked at the door, which Pearline had taken and for a moment Lenora looked into her eyes and fancied that she saw something tremulous and flashing in them that she had seen before.

Lenora stared at Nroke's histrionic, frozen pose and despite the dozens of braids looped and pinned up, the colorful dashiki, and leather necklaces, she was reminded of someone she knew, but could not name.

And then she stared past the wild patterns, the exotica glowing in her mother's kitchen like some strange sacred bird poised for flight, and she knew whom she was looking at. It was her old playmate from childhood—Mattie Mayfield. Pearline's daughter. Of course. One of her mother's previous maids had been Mattie's aunt and she had brought her niece along with her to work all one summer, when Pearline had a hysterectomy.

And then Lenora was whizzing back in time and they were ten and had played paper dolls under the china berry trees and fried ants on the sidewalk with a magnifying glass.

She could almost smell the sharp honey smell of their tiny deaths, see Mattie's skinny legs dancing over the concrete, her eyes glowing with a touch of that flash. Mattie taught Lenora to play poker, and whistle through her fingers like a boy. She taught her to steal pastries from her mother's own kitchen right under aunt's nose. She told her the facts of life, and graphically demonstrated with Lenora's Raggedy Ann and Andy as stand ins. Then Lenora tried to relate the image of little Mattie with the red and green and blue and the braids to the plank-straight figure who had become this wise and lethal person. What had Lenora been doing in the same time it had taken Mattie to learn all that she had learned? And it seemed to Lenora that since she had squatted on that sidewalk with Mattie Mayfield, she had not done anything else significant in her life.

"Mattie!" Lenora said, and her voice cracked, unexpectantly, and she had to swallow. "Don't you remember me?"

Mattie looked at Lenora from that kind of heritage that only she possessed, and the layers of know-how that she had acquired somewhere on earth to enable her to pace and protest and wear a wonderful red and green and indigo dashiki and she said, "My name is Nroke Shrahlinka."

And then she walked to the back door, opened it, and disappeared into a square of bright air and azaleas.

For the rest of the summer Lenora lay in the arty macramé hammock on her parents' patio and stared off and on at her anthology for no other reason than to ward off her mother. She completely stopped going to the club. Her romances never amused her again. She began to have headaches, which ironically served to prompt her mother to respect her privacy when she took to her bed as though she were some distant relative, some terminally ill genius. Her mother also instructed Pearline not to play her TV at those times, and she hustled her father and his suggestions of new car shopping out of Lenora's room. She dragged Lenora to a doctor once for a prescription which Lenora threw in the bottom drawer of her bureau.

In the fall, Lenora continued to make the straight *B* average necessary to stay in graduate school. She met her classes and blinked at the intimate stories her students excused themselves with and gave most of them A's, so they would go away.

She did begin to take copious, uninspired notes for her dissertation, obsessively reading and rereading William Blake, willing a kind of adequate, surface understanding, which, coupled with her preoccupied demeanor, served to salve her dissertation committee's worst fears. Her roommate deepened Lenora's depression by writing on bell hooks and expressing scorn over Lenora's choice, as she put it, of a dead white fruit loop.

Once she fell asleep after reading "Songs of Experience" and on the line that she'd inadvertently memorized: "Whose ears have heard the Holy Word/That walk'd among the ancient trees."

That night she dreamed a tangle of trees and shadow, and a resplendent green and red bird's flash of iridescent blue plume. When she awoke, an image of Nroke Shrahlinka appeared in her mind, and she thought of her briefly, and never again.

Only Visiting This Planet

Because of her penurious nature, Mrs. Griswald always waited until she heard her daughter's gravelly footstep in the drive before she flicked on the porch light, which gave the effect of a sudden floodlight on a prison's grounds. Tonight, upon signal, after she had touched the switch, she peered through the navy voile curtains and shamelessly spied as Janice trudged by the azalea beds, her head bent, her back rounded like a lumbering fattened bear. It was three o'clock in the morning.

Janice disappeared from Mrs. Griswald's perspective for a second as her steps turned, skirting the sidewalk, and became muffled in the newly seeded St. Augustine. Another second and Janice's arrival was announced by the glowing tip of a cigarette as it shattered on the porch and went skidding into the flower bed. Mrs. Griswald hated her daughter's habit, but because of Janice's excess weight, she had lately forborne mentioning it. She had read in *Ladies' Home Circle* that smoking deadened the taste buds and was hopeful that

Janice's taste-buds were slowly dying out. Janice paused under the yellow bug bulb that Mrs. Griswald faithfully screwed into the porch socket every summer and gave her shabby macramé bag a shake, peering in almost perfunctorily as if she expected her mother to open the door, which Mrs. Griswald did. Met with the sullen expression on her daughter's round face, flanked as it was by strands of greasy dark hair badly in need of cutting, Mrs. Griswald, despite her outward calm, had the sudden urge to reach out and shake her daughter. Unspeaking, Janice gave her no more of a glance than if she had not been there and walked directly towards the kitchen as was her habit whenever she came home.

Following her, Mrs. Griswald saw that she had already turned on the top burner of the stove and was obviously planning to reheat supper. Taking the aluminum foil off the peas and shutting the Frigidaire with her foot, Janice sniffed the pot thoughtfully and half-glanced at her.

"Don't start, Mother," she said, distracted, as she set the peas on the stove and began adjusting the flame. She took out a boiler for the rice and one for the shrimp sauce, from which she had already earlier in the evening shamelessly picked out and eaten all the shrimp.

Mrs. Griswald sat down in one of the chairs of the lime green Formica and chrome dinette her husband had decided to buy five years ago, the same year he had died. Despite the conspicuous gleam, she stroked the tabletop for invisible crumbs and immediately felt calmer. She folded her hands, glanced over the countertop at the clock shaped like an old-fashioned teapot with a spoon for the hour hand and a fork for the minute hand, and said, "It is now five minutes after three."

"Do you know where your children are?" mimicked Janice, stirring the shrimp sauce with her finger and slurping it off.

Opening the ancient, temperamental dishwasher, Janice lowered her bulk down to a hunkered position. With her still possibly sticky fingers, she ruffled through the dishwasher, then carelessly yanked out a small mixing bowl. "I am twenty-three, Mother," she said.

"That's just the point." Mrs. Griswald was anxious that the conversation not pick up a familiar ring, but nevertheless heard her own voice say with almost the same timing as their last conversation, "You should know better. Last night you came home at ten minutes till two. The night before that at sixteen after one. We *do* have neighbors you know."

"And what will they be doing up a two a.m.?"

Mrs. Griswald did not answer. As with all conversations with Janice, this one, too, was going nowhere. The thought of her neighbors aroused at two in the morning because of her recalcitrant daughter was only mildly upsetting compared to the other things Janice did to annoy her. Janice slept until noon every morning since she had flunked out of Louisiana State University six months ago. Janice wore big sloppy T-shirts winter and summer with offensive slogans on them such as "So many men/So little time." She wore old beat-up moccasins, not the preppy kind with the crepe soles, but the ones with no soles at all, making her tread unbecomingly suggestive of bare feet. And Janice was obese—so huge Mrs. Griswald had sent her to a health farm in Atlanta for her high school graduation present, but Janice had only lost fifteen pounds and had come back with what seemed to Mrs. Griswald to be a decided contempt for dieting. Too, the whole enterprise had cost Mrs. Griswald ten thousand dollars of her certificates of deposit. And because Mrs. Griswald had scrapped a plan never to touch the capital, this useless endeavor to Georgia had cut her monthly income almost eighty dollars. Once she had calculated that Janice's weight loss had cost about six hundred and thirty-three dollars a pound and this thought had the effect of depressing her in a way no other thought could. (She had always been too much of a coward to calculate what the compounded interest per pound would be.)

"Mother," said Janice, "I'm in no mood to argue." She had put everything—the peas, the rice, and the shrimp less sauce— into the mixing bowl and was actually going to carry the whole steaming mess to her room.

"I don't want to argue, either," Mrs. Griswald said, her eyes remaining a second on the bowl. She knew she would find the gook-encrusted dish on Janice's dressing table the next day. "You sleep all day; then you are gone all night. I pointed out the hour because you are my daughter, in my house. And there is a thing called decorum—courtesy—if not downright decency and discretion." Mrs. Griswald was hinting at her own responsibility in the protection of her daughter's chastity, but even she had to admit privately, staring at the enormous, bulbous breasts stretching this night's T-shirt message to an almost illegible state: "Only Visiting This Planet," this *was* a little far-fetched. "Besides," she went on, a thought coming to her, "some man has been telephoning all day." Actually, he had only telephoned twice, but Mrs. Griswald was gratified by Janice's huge behind turning suddenly to catch the swinging door she had elbowed open.

"Oh?" she said carelessly, but not moving.

Mrs. Griswald fumbled among the Kleenexes in the pocket of her second-best chenille robe. She held out a folded note card on which was written "Manuel Felipe Ferrah."

Mrs. Griswald did not mention that she did not like the sound of the name "Manuel Felipe Ferrah." She did not tell her daughter that, because of the man's accent, she could barely understand him. Instead, she said slowly to prolong Janice's interest, "He said he will be in town at six tomorrow evening or rather," her eyes swept the fork and spoon of the teapot clock, "this evening."

Janice glared at the note, balancing the rice bowl in one hand.

Taking a deep breath, Mrs. Griswald said, "I simply thought it would be advisable if we, you and I, would discuss dinner, since-uh-your friend will be arriving at the dinner hour." (On the rare occasions when Mrs. Griswald and Janice entertained, Mrs. Griswald called the meal dinner — otherwise, when it was just the two of them, supper.) Hurriedly, seeing that Janice was frowning and stuffing the note with much difficulty into her tight jeans and elbowing the door open again, she went on, "I thought Mr. Farrah might dine with us. We have so few guests, and if he is from out of town, it might fit in with his plans. And you know I have always encouraged you to bring your friends over..." Her voice trailed off; but Janice, the frown sliding from her face, suddenly, surprisingly laughed, and said, "Oh sure—why not?" and slopped out, leaving Mrs. Griswald alone with the dirty pots on the stove.

Mrs. Griswald got up, turned on the water in the sink, and picked up the copper scrubber. After the second phone call today and after recovering from the sheer displeasure of the foreign accent, Mrs. Griswald, falling back on some long-ago article from the *Southern Family Magazine* decided her tack should be *understanding*. But as she squeezed the water from the sponge, Mrs. Griswald made a long rusty sound in her throat, suddenly tired. Not only did she not *understand* her daughter's psychological make-up, but she did not fathom even the everyday behaviors concerning her, which Janice chose not to explain, and which Mrs. Griswald knew were useless to question. Where, for instance, did the money come from to buy the new instrument, known as a balalaika, lying, even as she scrubbed pots sans decent dishwasher, in her daughter's closet? Mrs. Griswald rarely gave her money; despite Janice's surviving taste buds, Mrs. Griswald was too thrifty to allow much money spent on non-nutritive substances. But Janice bought cigarettes by the carton, and caches of Benson and Hedges packages were in every room of the house. And where did she go at night? And now this new mystery-who was Mr. Ferrah?

Finally, Mrs. Griswald finished Janice's dishes, hung the towel, and went to bed.

Mrs. Griswald had been surprised at Mr. Ferrah's promptness and equally surprised at his late-model car. She had half expected a delivery truck or a motorcycle. And Mr. Ferrah was older than she had imagined, too, with a sort of unctuous attractiveness. He wore a diamond ring which flashed when he gallantly presented Janice with a bottle of wine.

"How do you do?" he said to Mrs. Griswald, and with a gesture so similar to a bow, it made Mrs. Griswald almost forgive him for the liquor.

He was dark, of course, if not swarth. His face was slightly fleshy, but not unhandsome with thick, black eyebrows. His hair was an uncontrollable tangle with a sleazy shine to it and he was wearing a white shirt, open at the neck, from where a gold chain gleamed from the shadow of his dark chest. In another age, Mrs. Griswald might have been forced to call him cheap because of his jewelry, but she knew that young men wore such things now, even in the best families.

Despite the fact that Manuel stuffed in too large mouthfuls and that his hair was shabbily cut, and he wore no tie, Mrs. Griswald felt her mind slide into a slightly calmer state than she had known all afternoon. A strange phenomenon became gradually evident to her consciousness—to have another person in the house was a novelty. Mrs. Griswald realized with a shock that if nothing else, it was good to have someone else's face over the table, besides Janice's, contemptuous looking, in an odd light, something like her father's.

Though Janice and Manuel seemed content to enjoy the meal, Mrs. Griswald fished around in her mind for a conversation starter. Mrs. Griswald was reminded of the early dinners after her husband had died when she had met this same problem with Janice by insisting she give her an itinerary of the day at breakfast and then a thorough sketch of her accomplishments at supper. This practice had long since died out.

Mrs. Griswald laid her salad fork down. "And where are you from, Manuel?"

Manuel seemed surprised by the question. He flashed a brief smile and took a sip from his wine. His eyes skimmed her appraisingly. "I am from the East Coast."

At Mrs. Griswald's words, Janice had stopped her fork in mid-air and was staring at her. She was wearing a clean T-shirt and had her hair plaited into two fat braids and pinned on top of her head in a heavy-duty babushka fashion.

"He's from everywhere and nowhere, Mother," she said in her mockish way. (She was obviously enjoying the wine and Mrs. Griswald wondered if she had been spending her evenings at the Bayou Thunder Saloon, the sole local tavern in their little Christian town of Ruston, Louisiana.)

Actually, Mrs. Griswald had been hoping for a clue to Manuel's nationality: to her there was a big difference between Spanish, Mexican, Puerto Rico, or Cuban. Ignoring Janice's remark, Mrs. Griswald persisted, on a new track, "And how long will you be in town, Mr. Ferrah?"

"Please" he said and waved his fruit compote which was serving as a wine glass, "call me Manuel. Unfortunately, I only have business here for one day. But I will return in perhaps a few weeks. Perhaps sooner if I am lucky."

Janice dropped her chin as if something she had been speculating on had been affirmed. "Next question—your occupation, please, Manuel."

"I'm a salesman." Manuel squinted into his glass

modestly.

"How about a drug salesman-for-r-r, for Eaton Laboratories? Okay?" Janice squinted into her glass.

Manuel laughed. "Mrs. Griswald, I must compliment you on this wonderful dinner."

Mystified by the ease with which Janice teased the man (almost as if they were old friends), Mrs. Griswald was nevertheless gratified by his show of manners and felt the man's occupation was honorable enough. Certainly, it must have taken some education. "Thank you," she said, wanting to add something to that effect, but Janie broke in, the wine without doubt affecting her, "Or was it Libby Laboratories?"

Manuel leaned forward, confidentially, to Mrs. Griswald. "Your daughter is not a sudden person, Mrs. Griswald."

"Subtle. I think. Mr. Ferrah, you mean subtle," said Janice.

"Subtle," the man corrected himself, looking at his watch as if he were becoming bored. "I think such women are indicative to this country."

"Indigenous," said Janice.

"Thank you."

Mrs. Griswald watched this exchange as if she were watching a foreign film in which the subtitles had been mixed up. She had no idea how to get from the subject of her daughter to the occupation and whereabouts of what she really wanted to know: Mr. Ferrah's family. Janice's affected manner was beginning to make her lose her grasp on the small amount of tolerance she had worked up.

And even more upsetting, after dinner, the couple did not

sit on the porch amid the summer smells of sweet olive and wisteria to eat the dainty fresh fruit concoction Mrs. Griswald had laboriously produced that afternoon. Instead, Janice stood up, like a burlesque of an old movie, and said, "Shall we?" and they went straight up to Janice's room and shut the door.

Mrs. Griswald sat, dumb as a cow, a wave of shock descending upon her, leaving her staring dizzily after them. Then thought after horrifying thought came to her. What if this man were a rapist or a perverted murderer? What if he were an escaped convict? Who knew how long Janice had known him? Despite her superciliousness, she was still young. Then another thought struck her, causing a wave of nausea if not abject terror: what if their neighbor, Mrs. Littlejohn (whose daughter had been in the same class as Janice and was now married to an accountant in Omaha) came over on one pretense or another to nose out the strange car as Mrs. Griswald would have done in her place?

The house seemed so quiet that Mrs. Griswald could hear the wild beating of her own heart. Gradually, though, it slowed, as she took the long deep breaths the *Ladies' Home Circle* had advised to prevent stress-related heart attacks. She gazed around her and the familiar walls and quiet emptiness gave her a curious underwater feeling. As literal-minded and ungiven as she was to metaphor, she was beginning to be reminded of the evening as a slow drive down a gentle hill, the vehicle she was in imperceptively picking up speed until she realized the uncontrollability of it, the imminent crash.

She put her hand to her throat. Suddenly her head became very clear. It wasn't herself she had no control over, the evening, or even the stranger in her daughter's bedroom. It was Janice. Finally, inextricably, Janice had reached the point where she would do just as she pleased.

Mrs. Griswald was no fool. She knew the thing to do was to salvage what she could from the situation. It was the only plausible thing to do. Cut losses, as her husband would say. She also knew that she had been wronged. She had given Janice a nice home and all the love and respect any child needed. She must think. She must think.

Mrs. Griswald closed her eyes. She swallowed hard as if there were an unusually large pill at the back of her throat. She knew what she had to do. Not in vain, in Piggly Wiggly, had she peeked (with almost mystic prescience) into the most risqué columns of other magazines than the *Southern Family* such as *Cosmopolitan* (with titles like "What's Hot/What's Not," and "The New Morality"). If she were not to lose her daughter completely, she must become (here Mrs. Griswald shivered) broad-minded. The bitter pill hit the bottom of her stomach and she almost retched, but her eyes gleamed with survival and slyness.

And too, the same feeling, a not unpleasant feeling (like when the dentist pulls the dull, throbbing decay from one's mouth and the emptiness is startling but relieving) appeared as it had initially at the dinner table: the limbo was gone, that awful waiting for Janice to do something. Something obvious, something outrageous so that Mrs. Griswald could relinquish. Relinquish.

In her new-found, last-ditch philosophy, a thought surfaced, recoiled, surfaced again. Maybe this is just what

Janice needs, she presented to herself, trying the words on. Eons ago, an interracial courtship would have been met by her with abhorrence, but now, what could be worse than to watch the years pass as Janice became fatter and more unsocial. What was that old movie, *The King and I?* And what about the princess of Monaco? Grace. Mrs. Griswald had no high hopes that Manuel was of royal descent, but it was how you looked at it, as her husband had often told her. With supreme effort, she pushed *Breakfast at Tiffany's* and its doomed southern little lady out of her mind.

Watching the absurd fork and spoon move around the teapot clock, Mrs. Griswald saw that it was half past the hour when footsteps on the stairs caused her heart to jump again. The door swung open, and Manuel appeared, in the same peculiar underwater that Mrs. Griswald still occupied, and looked at her almost respectfully. Indeed, if he had had a hat Mrs. Griswald could imagine that he would have held it in his hands and twisted it.

"I weesh to thank you for the splendid dinner," he said, with what came close to another bow, and then with a flash of diamond ring, he was gone.

"Good-bye," she said faintly, thankfully, to no one.

But with the slam of the front door, Mrs. Griswald's strength was shocked back from oblivion. She left the kitchen and went to the stairs. With the man out of the house, she felt shades of her old self. Perhaps she was not as powerless as she had felt. She went up the stairs, and suddenly an incipient anger fueled her steps, and she climbed faster and faster. No matter how close to wedding bells, or how palatable the idea of Janice's romance was beginning to be to her, decorum must be discussed. Maybe when Janice saw how broadminded she was being about the man and even the man's race (heaven! he was probably Catholic), but how insistent she was on etiquette, Janice would appreciate her, her position. Mrs. Griswald, within her justifications, was beginning to feel pleased with herself. She had come a long way. It was so good to know when to cut your losses. To be broadminded, yet still have some standards. She put a hand on the knob of her daughter's bedroom door and righteously pushed it open.

Janice, her moccasins firmly planted in the middle of the hand crocheted heirloom bedspread, sat cross-legged, surrounded by what appeared to be the entire contents of her underwear drawer. By her foot was an opened suitcase, overflowing with more nylon, and in her hand was, and Mrs. Griswald peered closely, an ordinary Baggie with oregano, like oregano perhaps. Like unground thyme. Perhaps. Like...What was Janice possibly doing with...Now where had she seen that before? A wavy picture, like bad television reception, appeared in her brain, coming clearer, slowly focusing on...Hundreds of Baggies in an important...scoop. Baggies in hollowed out T.V.'s, Tide boxes. A bust, the paper had said. The second obstacle of the evening floated towards her, loomed, leered at her—the single Baggie, the utter tangibility of it - for Mrs. Griswald knew she was looking at A Dangerous Substance. And as if to verify the efficacy of Mrs. Griswald's (accurate though limited) streetwise repertoire, Janice looked up, like an enormous Buddha, and waved the thing gaily. "Oh, don't worry, Mother, I don't smoke "theese" stuff. I sell it."

Now Mrs. Griswald sank into the cheery chintz printed chair she had had covered to match the room's curtains. She watched with unblinking catatonic eyes as Janice heavily got up from the bed and placed the substance beside others just like it, in the suitcase of underwear. It dimly occurred to Mrs. Griswald that Janice was packing.

"What... What are you doing?" she breathed.

"I'm leaving this house. Leaving." Janice paused to pluck a Benson and Hedges from the pack on the cluttered nightstand. She rustled through the debris for a lighter, which she found and, after lighting up, threw the lighter toward the macramé purse on the floor.

"So, you don't need to worry. Just relax, for once."

"Where? Where are you going?" Mrs. Griswald's underwater sensation had increased, and she thought she heard Janice say, "Blubble, blubble. Houston, Dallas, maybe. Blub." Janice blew smoke, which surfaced.

"Houston. Dallas." Mrs. Griswald repeated stupidly.

"And I'm taking your car, Mother." From the nightstand drawer, she took the second set of car keys which Mrs. Griswald had so long ago carefully hidden. She swam toward her chair.

"Did you think you could really hide these from me?" She shook the keys in Mrs. Griswald's face. "You hid them in the same place you used to hide the baking chocolate when I was little. The china cabinet." That thought seemed to remind her of something and she knelt by the bed and withdrew two unopened cartons of Mallomars. She stood up and pushed the underwear and drugs around in her suitcase, making a place for them. (Are all the clothes she is taking underwear, thought Mrs. Griswald, and was absurdly relieved when Janice scooped up a pile of dirty tee shirts off the floor and threw them into the bag.)

Then the thought of Janice driving off in the night made Mrs. Griswald less stupid. Suddenly a dark cone of terror descended upon her and already she felt her absence, dreaded it, despite everything, everything falling, dissolving in front of her eyes.

"I had thought," Mrs. Griswald began to lie, "that we might take a trip this fall together. To Houston. Or New Orleans. Or even Florida."

Janice opened a drawer from her bureau and grabbed a pair of her outsized jeans.

Mrs. Griswald licked her lips. "Or perhaps...perhaps you might try State again."

Janice picked up a pair of jeans, dirty, from the floor and wadded them up. She put them in the bag and closed it. She picked up her balalaika and purse. "Good-bye, Mother," she said, and hefted up the suitcase. Then she walked out of the room, down the stairs. The screen door in the kitchen creaked.

"Or a car." Mrs. Griswald said softly to the unmade bed. "Perhaps you would like your own car."

Below her, in the drive, Janice revved up the motor of her mother's *Consumer Reports* approved car, put it into gear, and backed it onto the street, her left front wheel rolling over the curb.

At the noise, Mrs. Griswald stood up and walked out of

the room. She found herself at the end of the upstairs hall where a small window was open, and the worn screen was being gusted in and out by an unusual breeze. When she leaned against the window casing, against the old, yellowing paint, she could see the sky lowering over the cul-de-sac, hollowing shadows here and there as the streetlights began to tremble and flicker on, one by one.

Somewhere down the live oak bordered street, under the vault of leaves, she imagined a person walking, passing each streetlamp, becoming briefly illuminated in the dusty milk sheen of the globe-lights. She did not know who the person was; it was unimportant. She watched the figure grow closer, shadowless, come to tell her what to do next.

She A Hard Woman

She a hard woman. I works all week and comes in early on Saturday for twenty years 'cept one year when I at Lonzo's. Like washing these lady's heads be fun. Like every Friday night Aaron don't be shit-faced and come lookin for trouble. Last night he shit-faced. He say woman, don't look at me cross-eyed cause I done took enough shit today.

I be having three ladies' haids to wash before I even get through the door and then to sweep up cuttings and rench them curlers. They all come to get they hair curled just like on the other side of town at Lonzo's they come to get they hair straight. I work for Lonzo but Aaron make me quit. Say that chap's a queer. Lonzo let me curl and keep half the money. He all right.

Here I just another ole colored servant. Say yes'm and nome and thank-you-very-much mam. I has to stand up all day cause the boss lady has a big sign IF YOU GOT TIME TO SIT YOU GOT TIME TO CLEAN. By end of the week back's out so bad 1 could scream.

Some of them ladies be coming in and they ain't be doing nothing all day but watch them some TV or shopping or drive them big cars around. But some be coming and they ain't got nothing but trouble. One lady, Miz Ferguson, she little and blonde, have them big eyes like those toilet paper Charmin kids. She real nervous like somebody 'bout to jump her all the time. Twenty years ago, she say she went to get her a job, but her husband made her stop. Huh, I wouldn't a minded that. She come in once a week and get just a wash. Blow dry. Condition, sometimes.

She got her hair cut like a little boy. It become her.

She never needed no job no way. Always got a good car. They be getting along okay as of late. He done bought her the biggest rock ever walk in this here shop. She wear it all the time.

He won't let her take it off

Her big problem drink. I smell it when she walk in. She got this little way of talking.

"Ah Rosa Bell," she say. She look like she goanna cry. "Have you got that rinse I use once a month? You know it's time."

"Well, hey, Karen Ann," say Bossy. She take this big sniff and smile. "You losing weight again? You going to go up with the window shade, girl."

Miz Ferguson laugh. Sound like squirrel chatter far away. She rub that rock on her neck and say, "Clemson likes me skinny, Marlene. You know that."

She say once she tried to leave Clemson. He had took all her clothes away, leave her buck naked, and lock her in the bathroom. The he turn all the heat off. Say "Freeze, bitch, freeze." It November. She go back cause she found some maid job but couldn't figure out how to get a house cause it a month before she got paid. Sitting here now with this big diamond, car paid for. She do worse.

Last night Aaron done take the car and bust a rod in it. Boss lady have to pick me up and take me to work. I could see she thought she done me a real good turn. She come driving up and honk and I has to hurry out cause Aaron wake up and say, "Tell that honky Bitch to shut up or I shut her up. "

Next thing I do is have to wash Ole Miz Beall's hair. Miz Beall is this real ole' white lady that gets around on a walker. Her hair so fine like a thread or something and she get it washed.

Put Autumn Ash on it. Then she get it dried and comb and up in little ball on top of her head. She look the same coming in as going out. Her son that drives her has an outstanding loan at the bank and she be done paid his loans off twice but he won't learn. Her daughter-in-law sorry too. Run off with her two grandchirren and won't even send her a picture. She got a second mortgage on her house just from her boy's tricks. Say she wont call in the loan. He go off too and then where she be? Besides who drive her to the beauty shop? Oh, there be trouble everywhere.

Today I be having a sore shoulder cause Aaron done pushed me up against the wall last

night. He so drunk and mad cause he has to push the car home and then them chaps what helped him push won't leave and they drink beer all night and I so tired this morning I don't think I can make it.

Saturdays so busy I has to go in every one. That Bossy is just looking for a chance to say I ain't dependable. She be done say it one time I were late. I had to bring Aaron to his Probation Officer cause he wasn't sposed to be driving for six months. His brother usually take him back then, but he be in court hisself. Forget why.

All these customers real old. I been knowing them for years. This place not like them fancy places downtown with them young skinny girls and who works at the Kut and Clip or Hair City. This beauty shop be in this world longer than me almost.

Some of these folks be here talk about their problems just sound like a story on T. V. They granchirren be having wrecks and costs them money or somebody be pregnant and not sposed to, or somebody's kids always thinking about divorce. Or they be done going off to Maplewood to get the treatment. Maplewood this place in Mobile to take off the lard. Seem like most of the trouble be with they granchirren—women with men worried to death how to keep 'em or how to live with 'em once they got 'em. And some of these customers, those that still got they husbands, be having alcohol or cancer at home.

They's one young girl, Sarah, come here though. She been to Maplewood twice but can't keep it off. She get her hair braided in one of them old timey fashions and wind it around her haid. I say it make her look old. She ought to get it cut short and with them fluffy bangs.

Today she come in and say she flunk out of college. She say her daddy don't know it yet and when he find out shit gon hit the fan. She want to do somethin' crazy. She want to go off to St. Louis. She want to work in a fancy riding stable she saw in a magazine. My kinfolks be having hosses and works at Fairgrounds in New Orleans. I could tell her bout hosses.

"Look at this," she say. She be having this soft little girl voice like she don't be weighing

two hundred pound. She show me a ticket to St Louis. She say she charge it on a credit card. She say, "Maybe you won't see me anymore." She say she send me a postcard. I hate to see her go. She be coming here since she be a little girl and her momma bring her, back when her momma still alive.

Bossy have to chime in. "Honey, you be careful. I don't know as I'd want my daughter to go off alone. "

Then a few other beauticians look at the ticket and shake their haid. They think she should get married she flunk out of college. They's one of them, new, younger than Sarah, Renee, just laugh. She sing for this band at the Cock-Eyed Lizzy's. Ain't got no man at all right now. She say, "Go get 'em, honey." She be getting off in a few minutes cause she say she be having a gig. Only got one permanent to do anyway, and just as I thought that, the timer ring, and she start to rench the haid. Marlene goanna roll and style it for her.

Sarah give her a big grin before Renee be out the door. Like when she smile she be all pretty. She don't need to go off. She tole me once after her momma die when she was little her daddy fuss at her all the time. She say he mean and used to make her finish every bite of food. One time she order a Triple Sundae Delight at Dairy Queen and couldn't finish it and he make her eat the whole thing. And she say, that was the beginning of her fat life.

Just about the time Renee get gone a man be coming in the door. He got this big shopping bag. He hold a gun.

Everybody that see him sort of scream. Ole Miz Beall just sit and look.

"Just sit tight ladies," he say, and wave his gun around so ever body see it except Miz Landry under Dryer 6. Outside a siren come up and then be off agin. He pull the blind down and turn the closed sign around just like on TV. He say don't nobody move and nobody get hurt. Just like a movie.

Sarah look at him curious. Not like she be scared. I scared. He be wearing this stocking on his head. Real skinny. No meat at all. Little guy. But I scared.

He look at Sarah. "You," he say. "Pick up all them ladies' purses." He point to the counter where Marlene be and she take a step back. "Dump 'em here." He reach over and punch the cash key on the register. It ding open and he pick out the bills and drop them into his A & P bag. Sarah don't move. Ever body else look like they be froze too.

And then he say real fast like he getting' nervous. "I say, you, Fat Girl. Get them purses and dump 'em out on this here counter." Sarah get up and pick up the purses. Miz Ferguson be getting this strange look in her eye. She reach up slowly and unclasp her necklace under her blouse and drop it in her purse. I don't know why. He never even be seeing it. Sarah be hooking purses on her arm but she done got this sly look. Miz Beall hold on to her purse. Sarah pull, Miz Beall pull back. "Over my dead body," She yell. Her towel fall off and hair dye start to go ever where. Deep Summer Auburn.

Sarah say, "Don't mess with him, Miss Beall. Just give it—
"

Just about that time Miz Goree, deaf as a doornail anyway, push the dryer off her haid. She look up from her *True Confession*. She say, "Marlene, am I dry yet?" Then she sort of realize and she take in that man, she take in that gun. She scream, "Lord, Lord, a gun!"

Man yell, "Quiet or I'll waste all of you." He walk over and put the gun right in her face. Then just like she done it a million time Sarah pick up Miz Beall's walker and shove it over the man skinny shoulders, down to his elbows, quick as a cat could lick his ass—gun fall right on the floor—and then she grab up a can hair spray and let him have right in the eyes. "OW," he scream. "Oh, shit" and he fall over in Miz Goree lap and she scream and proceed to whump him with her *Confession*. Then she pushes and he roll over onto the floor.

Sarah sit down on him so hard he make a sound like a throwed calf. Bout then I come to life and pick up my broom by the sink and whop him side the haid. He shut up. Sarah holler, "Help me tie him up." Marlene wake up too and grab his hose and pull and pull and what comes up but panty hose. Just right to tie with. She reach around Sarah and through Miz Beall's walker and together she and Sarah tie his hands up tight. I jest stand there with my broom, ready.

"Hit 'em again." Miz Beall got this big grin like she watchin the funnies on TV or somethin.

Sarah be still sittin on him even though he be tied like a goose. She say, "Fat Girl, huh."

Marlene think to call the Man. In the meanswhile I got my

broom and Sarah ain't movin.

On the floor he don't look so big. Young, white fellow. Need to be in school. Out playing robber.

Then the Man come in. "Lord, what have you ladies done?" say the one. The other young one snap out his handcuffs but they can't get Marlene knot out. It done be wrap around so tight they be having to get Marlene scissors and cut it off. They pull him up and he groan, out of his head like, "Don't nobody move. Don't nobody move."

I got just enough time to sweep the floor and get out by closin. That A & P bag that robber have remind me I got to get Aaron's six pack and somethin' for supper. That youngish blue policeman be givin Sarah the eye. Maybe she be cashing her ticket in. She get her hair cut right she get a man. Get her a nice fellow take care of her. She won't have to go nowhere.

Foreign Travel

This sidewalk cafe at 88 Herengracht in Amsterdam is jammed with tourists and businessmen who all seem to know what they are doing. Pamela sits in one of the spindly-legged chairs at a small table for two and nurses her second cup of coffee, trying to make it last as long as possible because already, with the remarkable prescience that European waiters have for the less affluent tourists, hers has her number and is ignoring her. Pamela takes another pretend sip from her coffee, which is cold, and scans the crowd of pedestrians. She is looking for two young men. She knows at any moment they will come, and the one wearing the expensive three-piece suit and the thin black tie will leave his friend in the background and draw stares from all the women patrons. His friend is dirty looking and Portuguese and speaks only his native tongue.

"Ah," coos a man's voice suddenly behind Pamela, then mutters something unintelligible. But Pamela recognizes the undertone. "Vie via," she returns, not because she guesses that

42

the owner of the voice is Italian, but because this is the only phrase she knows in a foreign language that means "go away." She turns to face her accoster. (His face has a sallow tinge and he wears a huge gold crucifix studded with fake jewels.)

"Go away," she says in English, and he fades before her eyes like an apparition. Pamela is becoming adept at handling encounters such as these. Already her thoughts are returning to Michel Cozeau.

Pamela is very pleased with the story-book manner in which she and Michel met. A sudden cloudburst had begun to drench the crowded Dam Square. Suddenly, the rain around her had stopped and she realized that she was being sheltered by a huge umbrella held by a young, well-dressed man with an olive complexion. The man had turned his head slightly, eyes still on Pamela, to address in French a smaller, shabbily dressed man beside him whom Pamela had usurped and who was unperturbably pulling up his collar against the rain.

"I have just told my friend to forgive me but a delicate flower like you takes priority." His voice was as cool as the rain and the sheer urbanity of his slight French accent transfixed Pamela. He addressed his friend again, then translated for her benefit, "She is beautiful, no?" His eyes darted at her to measure her reaction.

Pamela, who had never been called beautiful before and who believed that in Europe anything could happen, had shivered, knowing that this was the stuff that dreams (and movies and books) were made of.

The waiter catches her eye and raises his eyebrows in mock solicitation. Pamela demurely shakes her head and pretends to peer absently into her cup. Actually, she could easily have a go at one of the broodjes or croquettes, or even the raw herring sandwiches she is beginning to acquire a taste for, but Pamela is on a budget. In her room at the International Youth Hostel, in her backpack is a ragged book: *Europe on Twenty-Five Dollars a Day*. Pamela figures that this book is written for normal, reasonably well-off people, not one who has been reared in abject poverty on her mother's telephone operator salary for most of her life. By visiting mostly freebee landmarks, and by buying bread, cheese, and wine to avoid expensive cafes like the one she is in now, Pamela has so far been successful in sticking to her stringent budget.

In addition to the book, Pamela hauls a pair of khaki shorts, a bikini and one Dacron and polyester miniskirt which can instantly be transformed from a small messy ball to wrinkle free dancing attire in one fell shake. She also carries a black diary wrapped in Saran Wrap, and an enormous paper-thin seashell which she picked up on the Italian Riviera (and which will be broken into a million pieces by the end of the summer). Strapped on to the outside of the backpack is a pair of cowboy boots which Pamela wishes she had not brought. Already they have caused trouble. They are heavy and take up precious room. After wearing them only one day she has a huge blister which will not heal. Also, she has been accosted by two very dark provincial French boys in Paris, who followed her for hours trying to buy them. They did everything to get them but upend her and pull them off her feet. Now she barely remembers why she brought them. Her mother had discouraged her. So because of her mother, she can't throw them away.

Her mother has just given her a flowered bag filled with various plastic bottles in which Pamela may put lotion, face cream, soap, and sea-sickness pills. Her mother laughs nervously, "In my day the farthest trip a young lady took was over to Vicksburg to picnic in the park. Of course, we were only looking for husbands. A silly bunch of office girls..." In the imaginary conversation Pamela replies, "But I am not looking for a husband. I'm looking for a lover. An adventure. An *amore*. Or two, or three." Actually, indeed, Pamela had decided that three lovers for the summer was the acceptable number for an adventuress. Not enough to put her over the invisible slut-border, but enough to make her feel daring. In reality, Pamela had not replied, but had discreetly turned her back to dump the flowered bag into a box marked "Things to Be Stored," after thoughtfully removing the pill box for her birth-control tablets.

Her mother had tried everything but faking a heart attack to keep Pamela from going. She had telephoned in the middle of the night with phony dreams of air crashes, she had reported mystical omens that had begun to crop up daily, she had counted all the instances of terrorist violence in the news. She was convinced that Pamela would be kidnapped. She believed that letters from her would never reach Pamela by America Express. She had been certain that Pamela's savings (which Pamela had conveniently multiplied times three for her mother's peace of mind) would not be sufficient. She inventoried Pamela's clothes again and again, always finding Pamela's dearth of clothing untoward. She affixed a curse on the boots.

At one-week intervals, Pamela drops a postcard to Shreveport, Louisiana, USA, with brief comments on her adventures with the two older, imaginary schoolteachers she is traveling with and their charming European relatives who cordially accommodate them. According to her postcards, Pamela and her friends are driving a rented Renault and have attended Mass twice.

Pamela is happy with Amsterdam. She is collecting interesting anecdotes to tell her friends at St. John Berchman's Catholic School where she teaches modern literature when she is supposed to be teaching grammar and composition. She holds a running conversation with them: the time she put her backpack in a hostel in Paris, went sightseeing all day and then forgot the address of the hostel, the horsemeat sandwich she accidentally ate in Sardinia, the night she got on the train in Freiburg, traveled all night and awoke in the same train station instead of Luxembourg. Pamela is anxious to have a story about Michel.

At the end of a week, with Michel and his mysterious friend, Fernando, Pamela has seen much of Amsterdam, its quaint shops, its canals, 17th century churches, the Rijksmuseum, the Stedelijk museum, Anne Frank's annex. Michel has insisted upon showing her the sights by electric line, by canal, but mostly by foot. But today, Pamela, when met by Michel and Fernando, will drive to the Hague via the

Zyder Zee. She (who cannot afford film) has constructed an elaborate philosophy about the tourist-ness of cameras and hopes to sketch a windmill to add to her other (rather bad) drawings.

Michel and Fernando know all the small exotic restaurants unavailable to most tourists. With the exception of one trip to McDonald's, each restaurant has had commonalities: they are small with smoky interiors and few customers, and those present are dark and quiet and of indeterminable race. Pamela has learned to use chop sticks. She has developed a taste for curry. She has learned to eat cous cous, obtainable only by a long cellar stairway. (This restaurant especially struck her fancy; it was run by a family of Arabians and could accommodate only one party at a time. Sipping ouzo, Pamela had dropped her eyelids languidly and luxuriated in a feeling of worldliness. She had made a mental note of the name of the street, 10 Geldersekade, to drop to her friends.)

The waiter whom Pamela is avoiding all eye contact with is standing before her. Pamela knows she is taking a whole table in a crowded restaurant and experiences a twinge of annoyance. What could have detained him? Yesterday Michel had been looking for a gift for his sister; perhaps he was shopping and had forgotten the time. The waiter stares down at her unrelentingly. (He is very handsome in an obviously lower-class way, but his lip is curled with contempt.) "Your friends do not come today, no?" He is probably French.

"They come," says Pamela in the abbreviated way she has

adopted in this foreign place where she can be anything her whims dictate. "They come."

The waiter snorts and moves away, his pockets rattling with guilders.

Pamela scans the newest surge of crowd but to no avail. She wishes every day that when Michel comes, he would leave Fernando at the hotel. Pamela is convinced this is part of Michel's old-world charm and is reminiscent of decorum requiring a chaperon.

Stephen an American teacher at the hostel with whom Pamela chats each evening had suggested Fernando might be a body guard. Pamela thinks not, but the idea has possibilities. The American, Steven, is interested in Pamela, but she has had enough of everyday people at home. Steven looks like the typical young man she dates. He teaches high school math in South Carolina and Pamela knows that at home he probably wears Hush Puppies and carries his pens around in a plastic protector in his shirt pocket. But she can't resist chatting about Michel. He was actually born in California but was reared in France. He is a model for a furrier in Paris and has a sister who once had a minor part in a film at the Cannes Film Festival. (Michel has actually shown Pamela a picture of his sister, Monique, who looks disconcertingly like a young Catherine Deneuve.) Pamela cannot help throwing in a few more items for Stephen's nickel. Michel's father had been an international spy before the war, Michel's sister knows Julie Delpy in a social capacity, and Michel's brother has had brushes with terrorists. Also, Michel wishes Pamela to resign her job at St. John's and live in sin with him in his apartment near the Champs Elysee.

"It would kill my family." Pamela lowers her eyes modestly.

"That bastard," storms Stephen, who is lonely, and more than intrigued with Pamela. "To ask you to risk everything—that French bastard—" He is overcome.

"Such is the European male," says Pamela wisely. "Ask everything—promise nothing."

Stephen is too thin and weedy looking, but very intense. "Don't go," he pleads, as Pamela carelessly scans a guidebook for American schools in Paris which might give her a job, enabling her to maintain her liberation. Stephen wants her to go to England with him instead, using their Eurail passes for discounted ferry tickets.

Pamela lays her hand on Stephen's arm. "I can take care of myself," she says bravely.

Pamela becomes aware that a cluster of waiters are staring at her and talking. She realizes that Michel is very late and suddenly feels depressed. For a while she forgets that she is an adventuress, twenty-four, and has the opportunity to give herself to the most attractive man in the world. For a brief second, she wishes she were with Stephen, who is bicycling alone to the Zyder Zee to see the Dutch fishing fleets. She knows she has not misunderstood. She was to be here, at the Cafe Oude Rai, 88 Herengracht, where they have met every morning this week, at nine o'clock. She gasps as she looks at her watch—11:30. She begins to go back over the day before, searching for clues.

Yesterday they had taken a ride on the canal. As they boarded the boat, the owner snapped their picture. During the ride Michel pointed out the historical significance of seemingly every important edifice on the route. He had chatted about the art world, giving a discourse on the *Mona Lisa, la Gioconda* he called it, digressing, but so eloquent, so touching, that Pamela felt privy to a new analysis never before known to the world. (The only problem was that she could not remember a single word about the painting. She had meant to repeat it to Stephen.) And at the end of the journey, the finished photo was handed to them—Michel in the center as if he were posed, Pamela, on his arm, her eyes unfortunately washed out by infra-red, like Orphan Annie's, and Fernando, lurking in the background, slightly startled by the photographer.

Pamela could hardly conceal her disappointment when Michel put the photo in his breast pocket. "It might be used for advertising," he'd said, and noticing her dismay, added, "I'll have a copy made for you." Pamela, who was already envisioning the photo on the bulletin board of her office at the Academy, nodded, hoping her flawed eyes would disappear in the reprint.

Then it was on to the shops. Michel was looking for the just-right present for his sister, about whom Pamela felt oddly jealous. Michel was so picky. He handled delicate delft, glassware, velvet, silks, and was always dissatisfied. And always in the background was Fernando, who did not speak English, with whom only Michel could communicate. Fernando, the mysterious chaperon, the bodyguard, the eternal fiddler on the roof.

Suddenly yesterday, in the middle of the street, Michel remembered he must pick up an engraving. He checked his wallet, he needed to cash a check. "Do you have enough, Pamela? It comes to about 750 guiders. I will reimburse you, of course when we get to the bank."

Pamela had blushed. In the little strap-on pocketbook over her shoulder was a mere five guilders, ten dollars in American money, her allowance for the day, of which with luck, she meant to spend only about two and a half guilders. She had shaken her head, stammering—"I need, also, to cash a check." Her traveler's checks were in the backpack, locked in the hostel, a penurious habit that she had cultivated so that she would not even be tempted to go over her budget.

Michel had stared at her briefly. For the first time Pamela had noticed that Fernando had disappeared, and she felt oddly alone. Suddenly Michel seemed to be in a great hurry. He looked at his watch, a thing Pamela never remembered him doing before, made an exasperated click with his tongue against his straight, white teeth, and said, "I'll meet you at the usual time. The Cafe Oude Rai. We'll rent a car and do the Hague, perhaps Rotterdam."

"I'll be there, Michel," she replied, but he was already disappearing into a crowd of backpackers.

But now, as the waiters move in and out of the tables and decorative jungle fronds, steering clear of Pamela, she begins to feel, rather than see, little details of the past three days that she did not know she remembered. Michel has worn the same suit for three days, as well as the same shirt. She knows it is the same white shirt, for in her mind's eye she sees the familiar fraying around the cuff. She remembers Fernando, who only speaks Portuguese, watching her face intently as if he understood every word she had said. She remembers their frugal dates, the fact that she is always in her room by ten. Suddenly she knows what the waiters are whispering about. She knows that especially her waiter has already deduced things about herself that would have saved Michel a lot of trouble. She knows that the engraving shop would have taken Michel's checks if he had had any. She knows Michel kept the boat picture because he did not want her to give it to the police. She knows that Monique is not his sister. Suddenly Pamela tenses her whole body as if she is a spy and has an important move to make. She slides her whole day's allowance from between the pages of her passport and leaves it under her cup. Then quickly, not waiting to see if her trick has worked, she bolts through the crowd, as if she has remembered an appointment, a lover stranded at the wrong address.

Pamela is sitting on the bed in the hostel, her arms around Stephen's thin neck. "Michel is gone," she weeps.

Stephen makes deep, sympathetic noises in his throat and pats her back magnanimously, but righteously. "I told you so," he says (despite himself).

"No, no. You don't understand." Pamela's sob catches in her throat. "Michel's brother, who is a member of the Contra Cause in Chinandega, has been taken hostage. Michel must fly to console his brother's wife, who is pregnant, and even as we speak, is threatening to take her own life. Michel then flies to the Republic of Nicaragua to offer himself as an exchange for his brother."

"How monstrous!" growls Stephen, "You must never take him back. He is leaving you stranded and unhappy."

"I won't," promises Pamela. Blowing her nose, she agrees to go with Stephen (who is beginning to look a little Russian) to le Havre.

Witnessing in The Hare Krishna Tradition

Just about the time I decided I'd never get the hang of love, never even want to go out again with any of those boys at Crowville High School, much less make out with them in the back of their parents' cars, my luck changed. I had spent a whole afternoon one Saturday mostly watching my mother and the rest of the Crowville Missionary Society tidy up the Methodist parsonage, wash curtains and windows, wax the hardwood floors, while outside one of the men of the congregation mowed the yard in long, neat strips around the magnolia and pecan trees. Listening to the talk I learned the new preacher had five kids and one was a boy in high school. Even if he were a dud, I thought, having five new kids in church should liven things up. The parsonage was right next to my grandfather's cow pasture. In fact, the left fence along the parsonage lawn was barb wire and post he'd put up himself. I was keeping my horse there that summer. I had a small pasture nearer our house, borrowed, but once out riding I'd visited my grandmother for some cold water and then was too tired to ride home, so just turned Thunder, that was his name, in with my grandfather's herd of Herefords and caught a ride home with one of my uncles. Then I decided I liked to have Thunder in my grandfather's neat, clipped pastures. My own borrowed pasture was overgrown, the owners saw no need to bush hog it, and ever so often I'd come in the little barn for my saddle and see a slithery flash of snake tail, which I thought had my name on it.

Before that summer, before the new pastor and his family had come to town, I'd spent a year giving up on everybody I'd gone out with. Not that I'd had that many dates, but the few I did had turned me off. They all talked a lot about hunting and fishing and football signals, and they all broke off in the middle of a sentence apropos of nothing and planted big blubbery Plumber's Helper kisses, while surreptitiously starting a hopeful hand in the direction of what was known as first base. And they all had brand new copies of the New Testament in their shirt pockets, the little red ribbon bookmarks sticking out of the tissue pages like a lizard's tongue. It's not that I wasn't interested in kissing, I was, it was the incongruity, of being sandwiched together with a kisser and a Gideon Bible. I thought I had their number on that religion stuff.

At the beginning of the summer the youth in our town had experienced a return to Jesus like the community had never seen before. All of them except me and one other renegade, Mitch McCloud, had been saved. They were all witnessing right and left, attending revivals, and a few, in the run-down Pentecostal Church at the edge of town, were speaking in tongues. Even the Baptist and the Methodists were lying down with each other, so to speak, attending each other's revivals and Bible schools. Not me, boy.

My best friend Dagney Scott, normally a Baptist by parental insistence, had caught the bug. Dagney was the smartest person I knew. She made straight A's, had a knack for to-the-quick observations, and was the first person in class to get a driver's license. She was even teaching herself Spanish, lying in the hammock under the sweet olive trees in her parent's back yard, drinking iced tea and lemon and dragging one foot of painted toenails in the dust. "*¿Cuánto me amas?*" She should have known better. Why, she'd even done it once with Daniel Simons, a well-kept secret.

One afternoon we had it out. I accused her of succumbing to a fad, the "in" crowd pressure, something a few weeks ago we'd both shunned, and were in complete agreement of their lack of general worth to the world. Actually, this had been my year for dropping out. I'd dropped out of band, and at the end of the year I'd resigned the elected, coveted membership of the annual staff, to the great disappointment of my teachers and my mother.

My teachers didn't bother too much about it though. They thought I was going through some kind of identity crisis, or that I had some dark, psychological reasoning for my behavior that it'd be best not to tamper with. My mother came right out and said I'd been reading too much.

I didn't mind them thinking this. I even tried to encourage it by "not wanting to talk about it" and scowling and trying to look mysterious when anybody mentioned it. Actually, underneath I had perfectly good but mundane reasons for my quitting epidemic—I hated the marching part of band. While it was one thing to sit in the cool, vast interior of the band room playing my flute in arias of Tchaikovsky and Schubert and having the only solo in the spring concert, it was another to face the long, hot summer ahead pounding up and down the football field learning the drills to make a CHS or a football helmet or whatever struck the band director's fancy, to the tune of "Hold that Tiger!" To say nothing of fall and the hated football games and the cold and school spirit and the ridiculously old band uniforms that made us look like Jiminy Crickets complete with white spats.

As for the annual staff it hadn't taken me nine months to figure out what a lie it was—all that stuff about getting elected, and the secret joys that went on behind the closed doors of the library after 3:00 on Tuesdays and Wednesdays. It was nothing but the most menial, boring of secretarial chores: typing and filing and cutting and pasting. I had already made a fatal mistake choosing the business route through high school rather than the home ec route. Even though both were equally noxious I'd begun to figure I could have slopped together a sewing project better than I was handling a profit and loss sheet.

But as far as being a drop-out, the only problem was that it was right at that beginning time in high school when people need to belong to stuff. I didn't figure this out though (until it was too late, and then I didn't care) and I kept wondering why each decision I made that made me feel gut-right also made me feel more and more like an exile.

Dagney Scott got religion for almost two whole weeks before it passed, and she came to her senses. It was disconcerting for me because I considered her the ultimate in taste. She had nothing but sarcastic comments when the whole cheerleading squad showed up at school wearing Arline Frances type fake diamond heart necklaces. She hated the same teachers I did and loved the same ones I did. She was in the Beta Club, and with her grades could've had everyone eating out of her hand, but she'd do weird things like, on a dare, jump out of a window during class, and not care what anyone said. Also, she dated boys from other schools, which made some people mad. That could only mean one thing according to our high school's philosophy: she thought she was too good for CHS boys. But Dagney just laughed. Looking back now, I remember she looked exactly like a teenaged Barbara Streisand.

I was glad when she got over her psychosis because I had things I needed to talk to her about. Later I would warn her to stay away from those mesmerizing visiting revival preachers who, by their very newness, as opposed to the old familiar faces might, hold your eye. I had more important stuff. I had taken one look at the Byronic brow of the only son of our new Methodist preacher and fallen madly in love. He was thin and English looking with a modest mass of raven curls that some prosaic old haircut had failed to completely snuff out. There was only one problem, he was a year younger than me.

"Why are you sweating that?" Dagney waved her Spanish book in the air as if wiping out my stupidity. "I say go for it. It's kinda cute anyway."

"Maybe I can rejoin MYF." I began to scheme.

"I miss being in love," Dagney said, like she was a million years old and didn't fall in love again every week. Her eyes got that distant look they could get.

"The thing is." I said, "He's already seen me riding Thunder in Grandaddy's pasture and asked Mitch McCloud—get this, 'Who is that blonde?'" I *was* blonde, with a little help from Revlon's Summer Streaks, but I'd never been *called* blonde before. It made me sound different and better. Decadent.

"Get Mitch to help you then. Tell him you're interested, and he'll see if—what's his name anyway?"

"Billy," I said. It seemed back then as if it were the most unusual, exotic name in the world. "And—he loves horses."

I wonder if kids still use that third-party system. You get someone to ask the prey what they think of you, and if they don't say anything negative, they tell them that you like them. It's a pretty good system.

I can never remember two words Billy ever said to me. I fell in love with him strictly on his looks. Thanks to Mitch, MYF, and Coach Warren, my grandfather's neighbor who let me borrow his pretty bay quarter horse, Mulligan, for Billy to ride, our romance took off fast. My world righted for the first time in a long while. To have someone beautiful cantering a horse beside you down a deserted dirt lane seemed more than was right to expect from life.

Mitch McCloud had always been a friend of mine. He and I had suffered through the Sunday Services at Crowville Methodist from the time we were babies. He was a good person to keep tabs on Billy because he was the same age and was in our same church.

The funny thing about Mitch was that he was an albino. He had wild platinum hair that looked like it might glow in the dark, its length close to flaunting school rules. His skin was as white as a painted China plate. His eyes were spooky, palest blue, and red-rimmed. To entertain myself in church, I used to sit and pinch his arm gently, watching the orgy of colors I could make: pale pink, mimosa pink, pink-red, dark red. And another funny thing about Mitch was that, if you didn't let his lack of color put you off, he was really good looking. He was tall and well-built. He had a straight nose and a good jaw line. Of course, he did have a reputation for being a smart mouth. In class if the teacher said something like, "Why don't you all shut up and get to work?" Mitch could counter with something like "What a novel idea," a real wildcat remark in that day, where good behavior, at least on the outside, good grades, and fitting in, was the credo. Mitch was the first person I ever heard say, *what a novel idea.* He also owned a skateboard before anyone ever knew there was such a thing as a skateboard. Pretty advanced for someone in a town without sidewalks.

Mitch had a real interesting past too. He was abandoned by his mother when he was about three months old. His father, who worked on an oil rig one week on, off the next, came home to find him, two days hungry, dirty wet, and screaming bloody murder. He took him to his own mother and father and promptly left, never to return except infrequently in a Daddy Warbuck's fashion.

Mitch's grandfather was a big passive man who sat in the Crowville Methodist on the third row from the back, pretending not to doze most of the time. His wife, Audie Mae, Mitch's grandmother, had a stern Old Testament wildness in her eye, and a rasping, harsh man's voice that was fascinating but scary, especially because it carried over everybody else's in the church when we sang. Hearing her bang the piano with strong if not accurate fervor, listening to her belt out "When the roll is called up yonderrrr," was enough to frighten the most hardened sinner. She also taught Sunday School to the adult women. Even my mother had a subdued respect for her.

Mitch sat quiet enough in church, with my pinching his arm, or reading something he's sneaked in, or answering my sarcastic notes. I'll never know why he and I never turned on to religion. Perhaps he was caught by the incongruity as I was. By come curious inductive reasoning I had worked out that having no blacks in church meant that religion was a farce. I didn't have to go to Sunday night services which my mother decreed optional, but I still had to suffer through Sunday morning. For Mitch, maybe, having his staunch, Christian grandmother scream at him so often that he was no good, just like his mother, turned him off.

Or for me, maybe it was my father who in my life I never saw in church but twice, and one of those times he was dead. The other time was at my first wedding.

The fact that my father eschewed church, not only that,

but kept his grocery store open on Sundays, was a source of embarrassment and shame to my mother. She also saw it not only as her stigmata, but as an ever-flowing source for her own victimization.

She used to grill him now and then, tearfully or dry-eyed angry depending on the moment, "Am I to be the only woman to sit in the church without her husband?" and "The seventh day, on the seventh day, now, He rested."

"Wellll," my father would say slowly, in a satisfied way, "those Christians don't mind buyin' from me on Sunday."

He had her there. Everybody flocked to our little store two miles out of town in the community of Longview right after church on their way home. It was the only store open.

But it was his contempt for the Bible Belt establishment that must have played on my unconscious—"Oh yeah—that deacon sittin' in church owes everybody and his brother. Hasn't paid anybody—includin' me in years," and other dark hints about something so awful that my mother would tell him to hush. But whatever my father's philosophy or religious ethos, I think it was the hard straight-angled church benches that kept him away mostly.

Sinner that he was my daddy gave out more credit than anybody in town. Even Billy's daddy started a charge account in our store. His mother used to bring his four younger sisters to shop, but not on Sunday.

It was quite unusual to have that many children as a preacher. There was a lot of jokes and secret talk before they were accepted. A few years later, I found out why. The newest Methodist preacher, who'd replaced Billy's father, with his young wife and newborn, had confided in one of the older boys at MYF that communities didn't like to be reminded that preachers did it.

Billy and I double-dated a lot that summer with Dagney and whoever she happened to be dating. She might have the captain of the football team from nearby Central High, or some baseball player from Winnsboro. I ignored her choices of men.

They might drop us off at the Bijou in Delhi to go "park." Billy and I would sit in the darkened theater holding hands, sneaking dry kisses during the fifteen-year-old newsreels or even Frenching, turned on by Elvis Presley's bootcamp suffering after love.

Later we might park with Dagney and her date beside some moonlit cotton patch. Once all four of us squashed in the cab of a Dodge pick-up were shot at by some irate farmer. My life unwound as exciting as any 1960's movie plot.

Finally, in somebody's parent's backseat of an Oldsmobile, we were sufficiently turned on by its plushness or something for Billy to advance the hand on my knee upward. I literally held my breath for that slow-motion creep, the marvelous, excruciating journey which culminated in coming to rest on my rib cage, and never moved much further all summer.

"Give it time," Dagney finally advised, mystified too. "*Asi est la vita.*"

By August I was looking forward to school and having somebody to sit with at lunch and recess and pass notes about. Never mind the marching band, or the annual staff, or Beta Club from which I was eternally excluded because of my abhorrence of and subsequently straight <u>C's</u> in math. For once I looked forward to the fall.

The summer was to culminate with three days at the Methodist church's camp at Lake Bruin. My mother packed my flowered TG&Y suitcase with my swimming suit, shorts, new underwear and a tin of sugared pecans. I added my newest novel by Ayn Rand and a pair of A&P sunglasses.

The girl's cabin, like the boy's cabin, was built half over the water. At night we girls all rolled our hair on giant sized brush rollers or orange juice cans and went to sleep listening to the lap-lap of Lake Bruin against the beat-up piers.

During the day we ate and splashed or swam out to the nearest dock and listened to someone's plastic wrapped radio and the latest Chuck Berry tune. In the afternoon we raced through the lakeside wood to Bo's Grocery and Boat Dock where we could see live white-tailed deer penned behind the store. At night we wandered out pretending to snipe hunt, sometimes pairing up and away until we were summoned by one of the chaperons for bed. Ours, a huge, strong-armed member of the congregation who supported her alcoholic husband by working in the town's only meat processing plant, laughed at us for rolling our hair for the thirty minutes we'd be curly in the morning before we plunged back into the muddy tepid water.

It was that last Saturday afternoon at camp when it happened. Only a few hours before we were to go home, we were all standing in waist deep water around an atheist the MYF had discovered swimming in their very own Lake Bruin.

Someone had tried to witness and was met by an out and out rebuff. And they had met their match.

Gradually everyone paddled over to see what was happening. The guys whose Gideon Bibles were permanent unread fixtures in their shirt pockets back on shore stood, their hands on their hips, unmoving, their scowls clouding the Christian air. The girls stood by their men. Billy, bored, was already edging off. He motioned me to come, but I was as fascinated as if it had been a Russian, or a Martian who had fallen out of the sky.

"Well," said Lester, the president of MYF who was also the champion towel popper of the football team, his sunburn flushing even deeper, "if yuh don't believe in God, whut do yuh believe in?"

"I don't disbelieve, I just don't believe," said the outsider, who was older than us, maybe twenty, and who had calm, blue eyes, deeper than Mitch's, and a dark, neatly clipped haircut.

Lester's best buddy, Russell, snorted, "I'm saying', sinner, yuh either for the Lord Jesus Christ or yuh against him."

"Oh, I'm for his teachings, but who's to say whether a miraculous birth really happened or not? Or is it that important?" he added to that solid, immobile wall.

There was a low gasp from the group. "It's important if yuh think goin' to hell is important!" someone from behind said, and there was appreciative laughter and a murmur of assent.

"Well, ah never," said Linda Jenkins, who had started the Arlene Frances necklace craze, and witnessed regularly at Sunday night services, I'd been hearing. Her brother was a crop duster and a part-time preacher. She touched Bobbie Jean, her best friend, on the arm, and the two of them, who could lead the rest of the cheerleaders and the whole pep squad over the cliffs of Gibraltar if they'd wanted to, left, trailed by the other four girls.

Somehow their running off left me the only girl standing side by side with the crew-cut Judas, facing the three guys, but I didn't think about that until later.

"I don't believe in hell," the stranger was saying. "If there is a god and he is good and not evil, he wouldn't have any use for hell, anyway. Besides, how do you know God *is* a he?"

There was loud, relieved laughter—obviously they were dealing with a harmless lunatic.

Russell White lay his hand on the stranger's shoulders kindly. His neck and wrists were a dark tan, but his belly was red from too much sun that morning and looked painful and weirdly vulnerable, "I'll pray for you, brother."

But Lester asked him how he was going to feel in Hell with his hair blazing, his eyes stuck with hot coals, his mouth, his ears on fire.

"Shut up, Lester," I said, impatiently, without thinking. I wanted to hear what the man had to say. "What else do you think about afterlife?" I asked him.

Lester glared at me but shut up. It was then I realized that the only way I got away with that is because they didn't believe I, the permanent drop-out, was a real girl anyway.

"Well, I don't believe any honest, intelligent person can say for sure what's going to happen. If he, or she does, they're either lying or deluded, or both. Read Spinoza," he said, looking at me, "and *The Quest of the Historical Jesus* by Schweitzer is fascinating stuff."

The rest of the group began to edge away. "Don't come crying to us, son, when you burnin' in hell-fire," they called over their shoulders.

I stayed and talked for another hour or so before he had to leave. It was as if this guy had been speaking to my secret self, had made me realize I wasn't an atheist after all—I just didn't like God, that big, invisible phony who created hell, and who'd probably preferred people like Linda's and Mitch's grandmother to me and Dagney. Now I was an agnostic because Claude—that was his name—said that an atheist had to have just as much faith in atheism as a believer had in belief. I was eager to get home to the library. The whole new school year stretched in front of me like a pleasant dream.

After I got home it wasn't long before I realized Billy and me were through. We'd had a fine time on the bus home. I'd sat and admired his Prince Charles nose, his hair that was growing out from the awful crew cut he'd gotten after he'd come to this town and realized that was the style. We sang "Ninety-nine Bottles "and even managed a kiss behind one of the seats of the old painted-over school bus.

But he never called me again. I rode Thunder round and round in big circles in my grandaddy's pasture waiting for him to come out, hopping painfully and cutely on his bare feet, to lean on a post and talk to me. But no one came out, except one of his little sisters, the youngest, dangling a one-armed Barbie that was naked except for high heels, and on my near arc, yelled, "Bubba can't love you no more." Then she ran banging back in the house.

I couldn't figure it out. I had to rely on Mitch who dutifully said he would call Billy, then call me back. I waited, drumming my fingers on the receiver until it rang. "I've got bad news," Mitch said, a strange note in his voice. "Billy's folks said he couldn't see you anymore. Because of the atheist. You were talking to an atheist."

I spent the week before school started sobbing inconsolably. My distraught parents begged me to tell them what was wrong and when I did my father snorted, "Is that all?" and went back to the store.

To my surprise, my mother was furious with Billy. "That boy! Oh, I'd just wish you'd never met 'em," giving her own answer to the ancient question to have loved and to have lost, and patting my head buried under the chenille bedspread. I was so upset she'd completely forgot her mounting anxieties about the growing time Billy, and I had been spending together that summer and her own earlier complaints ("Are you going out riding again with that boy!") and wished him back or to have never existed, one or the other. "And they haven't paid their bill since they've been here, either," she added.

It was a while before I accepted Billy's parent's objections to me, and my staying and listening to that agnostic in the middle of Lake Bruin. Taking my head out of the Chenille bedspread, I realized the atheist as they called him was the talk of the town. I had to go it alone too, because Dagney's parents—they both worked for the same insurance company, driving their matching Volkswagens 60 miles a day to Monroe and back—had decided to move closer to their jobs. I didn't even have Mitch anymore either, because before Billy's body had even cooled good, later that day, he had phoned me again and told me he wanted to go out with me, that he'd been in love with me for a long time. I'd just never considered Mitch McCloud. I didn't think I could ever love him except like a buddy. He was too familiar. Besides, he knew too much about me.

I never saw Billy a lot after that—lucky he was a year behind me in school and I didn't ever have classes with him. Except I saw him at church where he never talked to me or even looked in my direction. When he got his license, he started dating a girl in his own class who got elected cheerleader by a nose. Once I ran into his oldest little sister in the drug store and she told me he was eating bananas all the time, trying to get heavy enough to try out for football.

Mitch never spoke to me much after that either. He sat away from me in church too. When I was a senior, I heard that the new young zealous principal, whose daughter got elected Most Beautiful, had the Ag boys grab him and hold him down while they cut off his too-long hair. I saw him later in the week, between classes. His hair was choppy and awful, his mother-of-pearl pink neck shiny in the hall like a glow worm, as if I'd been pinching it in church. He wouldn't look at me. I was sorry because I wanted to tell him how mad I was and how I hated Mr. Riegal.

I had long before found Spinoza in our own school library. He was in a set of philosophers someone had donated to the school still in their dusty box. "Try over there, hon," the busy, oblivious librarian had said. She was too busy to help, counting and arranging the annual box of Gideon Bibles the Lord inspired to have donated every year.

Years later I heard Mitch had gone off to California and gone wild on drugs and crazy living. It was common knowledge because Audie Mae complained bitterly all over town. Then I heard he'd joined a Hari Krishna religious group and had shaved his head. I tried to picture him in a long billowing robe, wearing an earring and handing out literature at airports, and it wasn't hard. Some people thought this was finally what sent Audie Mae to her grave.

Finally, I heard he'd given that up and even gotten respectable and married, but then his wife had left him. After that he had moved to Monroe, back to Louisiana, and had started a good business in the copy field.

My second marriage I lived on a farm in a small town near Monroe. I looked for his name one day in the phone book and sure enough it was there. Every now and then, in a mood, I'd pick up the phone book and run my finger down the M's until I found his name, Mitchell K. McCloud. But I never called him.

The Recurrent End of the Unending

You always see yourself starting the story in the same place; his elaborate plan to leave your car at the Pack-N-Save, that mad dash along the prophetically named street, Pandora. You were about to begin a great adventure after three years of divorce's silent wound licking, should it be womb licking? womb-wound licking—you sweep down the street like a spy, in your spy-fever left over from a misspent childhood reading Rex Stout. Notable: the way your high-heeled boots click against the concrete, the long, upturned-collared coat, the conscious slide of new silk underwear, age-old signaler of an incipient affair. And that wild permanent hair, curling in the damp southern mist of Louisiana. Was it always raining?

You read the numbers on the houses and with each step come closer to a euphoria that will last two-and-a-half years. At first, passing the look-alike houses, you believe he has fallen on hard times, but the yards become less run-down, less filled with toys and junk. You stand before a respectable house of medium size. The door should be unlocked.

Later you will find out he has not taken a wild chance leaving it open to trashers and thieves in order to savor the pleasure of your company. He has lost his key. His has lost his wife.

But first, because you have mirror sickness, you find the mirror. Your mirror sickness hits you at odd times, before class, after class, in the middle of the night, at a red light, leaning over the frozen food counter at the supermarket. You are a mirror junkie constantly called to get your fix of self-inspection. Even though the fix itself is merciless, one arrested object peering into another passive object, grasping at some ideal neonatal model, gradually dissolving by the forces of gravity, you can't pass up a mirror.

He won't be home for hours, but you apply more make-up, your eyes squinting critically, you are not looking into a mirror, but a microscope. Your eyelids are a peculiar blue, your lips are frosted, your lacquered nails flash as you smooth your unnatural brow.

In the past few months, you have proven the thesis of a book on the Ph.D. reading list by the diligence with which you have pursued your beautification. Sacrifice has paid off to the point that you have risen above your genes. You have dieted, plucked, permanent-waved, and otherwise rearranged the molecules of your body. You have fed narcissism with Puritanism. Max Weber should see you now.

Zsa Zsa Gabor says, "There are no ugly women, just lazy ones."

After this ritual, this mandate from the mirror, you go through his house looking for clues, but because of some museum quality to the air, not touching. The whiff of sophistication emanating from his things feeds your euphoria. Inside the cupboard are exotic items that you would only speculate about: Carr's Water Biscuits, perhaps antique servers, wool sweaters, ancestral gems. You are afraid to open them. Perhaps his wife's allure resides in there: interesting scarves, expensive oils, a forgotten bottle of *Joy*. Perhaps she herself will materialize, wearing something floating, watching you in a winsome, childlike way.

Outside the closed-door a massive Chinese mahogany table gleams softly in his bedroom, a gentle reproach to all you lack in taste. The black lacquer of the dresser satisfies something latent in you. The nineteenth-century keyhole desk, its eclecticism backlit by the approaching dusk, holds pictures: one of two boys, his sons, the elder holding the cuckold sign behind the younger. Another is of an older relative, perhaps his father, who wears a strangely cut coat, oddly exotic, and unplaceable in time. The smallest frame holds a boy (holding a fish) whom you think is the older son taken later, but you find out it is he, twenty-five years ago. But that comes later.

Your boots have squished designs on the carpet, and you sit on the edge of his king-sized bed and pull them off. You are glad it has taken so much trouble to get here, the car-hiding, the long stretch to walk, the rain. Now, the wait. Perhaps all this bother will discourage other unscrupulous graduate students, who have set their hearts on him.

Your pantyhose glides on the silent carpet like a thief, a thief who might have passed the unlocked door. You go from room to room, window to window, note the shadows sequestering the back yard, the rain-slick streets. From a front window you see the blinds drawn tightly on the house you are to be most careful of, the house of an Important Person from the Department. You draw back when a light comes on—you feel three years of boredom slide away and a strange pang begin. Your heart thumps in careless rhythm.

You slump on a chair in his study, but carefully so as not to flatten your hair. You read the titles of his books, feeling inferior. You recite poetry, long difficult lines in rare meter, divide the foot, count. You are a likely riddle, sitting there. The walls begin to hide in shadow. The waiting begins to smother, like being caught in a too-tight bottle.

You are on his agenda. He is at the gym, now, somewhere he is lifting weights, jogging on a treadmill away from fat and middle age to get to his wife. The last one. You contrive scenes in which his labors are interrupted by young intellectuals in leotards, older divorcees who evaluate life wisely.

You indulge in self-pity, the blonde head of your child, who is with your ex-husband—probably drinking, feeding him lies— flashes in your brain. You remember his footsteps when he came home to you, the way he called your name, as though you might have left. Finally, you did.

Then you think you must be doing something, not found this way, caught in reverie; you must be reading something intelligent, found oblivious to the situation. You return to the living room, flip on a lamp switch. You check your watch. You have an hour to go, so you turn on the tiny TV on the breakfast bar, flip through sitcoms, but just to be safe, settle on a dry documentary. You turn off the sound.

You are stung with dread and anticipation. The rain comes down so hard you can hear it. It comes and goes in flurries. Other travelers, their headlights flashing false alarms, turn on the street, then glide on by.

You return to the mirror, adjust your mask. You think of all the times this mirror has held his wife's image. You have heard she is very young and very mad. You think he will be wild in bed.

In an hour and twelve minutes a tight, high-idling motor surprises you. The window is filled with light, then silence. You jump up, turn off an African scene where a gazelle is running in soundless, erratic circles with something as its heels. You pick up William Blake, like a shield, then abandon all plans and run to open the door. It creaks open like a coffin.

You say, your door creaks like a coffin's. You had the presence of mind not to smile in relief and show gladness that he came home. You both pretend embarrassment. He asks if you found the place all right.

He raises his eyebrows in a mock quizzical look. His arms are filled with papers. You follow him to the kitchen and don't know what to do with yourself. He puts things away. His student papers on a table. His gym stuff on the washer. In the kitchen, he takes out a ham and inquires if you have eaten.

He takes off his London Fog and muffler. He tells you about some opera he had seen earlier in the week. He says names you don't know, and his words conjure brightly painted sets and women in callous fur coats. He says that opera is his passion. He asks, have you been studying.

You hedge. You study eight hours a day, like a job, but if you fail, then there is not use in his knowing that. He frowns at your hesitation and says, in his brilliant litotes way, the exams are not un-difficult. You lower your eyes, then pretend bravura. He prepares dinner and you listen to his talk—a long story about the dean.

Your mouth is stiff and unhungry, but you eat anyway. You have heard that his wife is anorexic, and you don't want him to be needlessly suspicious. Your face is heavy with make-up. You can feel it when the bites go in. He asks what you have done to your hair.

Afterwards you sit on the carpet and he seems shy and vulnerable as though he has just realized a graduate student whom he barely knows had called earlier in the week and asked if she could seduce him. You don't like elaborate games.

He looks sorrowful and polite and refuses to touch you. You sit between his long legs and imagine them pushing weights up in the gym, the elongated muscles flashing along the hem of his shorts, for other people's eyes. He says to tell him all the latest but instead all you can see is the culmination of this amatory pursuit. The long hours of waiting dissolve.

You ask him to show you his medieval lyre and he goes to get it. It has four strings and you know he once played it in front of a huge audience in a prestigious university.

He strums it, no more talented than any man. You want him to sing, from memory, in oral formulaic, but he declines. You take the thing and strum; my dog has fleas. He takes it from you.

He puts it down and fiddles with his stereo. He chooses

something German like a drinking song. The broad vowels float lusty into the room. He turns it down. What is that funky stuff? you say. He pretends to be insulted.

He tells you about Vietnam, his appointment as captain. You see the steaminess, the jungle fronds. You remember he has been to West Point. You think he will be wild in bed.

You see him lifted from battle by a helicopter, handed a jock strap and tennis shorts to be transported to some general who has looked up credentials until he has found a tennis partner. It is a good story. But you are in cahoots with the general, even now you are lifting him from the battlefield of his marriage to your pleasure, with no preliminaries, no long seductions. More of an appointment.

Nothing goes on.

Finally, as though exasperated, he laughs and touches your hand. Something flurries inside you. You were beginning to think all was lost.

He is still talking about Vietnam. You brazenly kiss him between sentences as though his touch has released you. You touch him back. He moves and lifts you up. He says he has a bed you know. You follow him to the king-size bed.

You undress first while he does last minute things. In bed you watch him, by lamp, take off his clothes. He is perfect. You check as you do with all men that he does not fold his clothes or hang them up neatly.

He gets into bed with you. You kiss. You have to force your tongue into his mouth. You touch his face, his chest, but he does not touch you. He moans again and you give in to pleasure.

Suddenly, you believe he is the sensitive scholar who has been dumped by two wives. Suspicions you didn't know you have, flee.

He kisses you, his hands lying motionless on your arms. The fact that he does not touch you makes you more excited. Like those novels shimmering in adjectives with no mundane mention of foreplay. But you wish to be his lyre.

It is in vain.

You are beside yourself with guilt and desire. You have set him up for another failure.

You come up for air and push him kindly over on his back. You work diligently the Protestant Ethic.

His almost-failure makes you garrulous, reckless. You do not say you love him, but keep kissing him, repeating his name. Finally, he sobers you up, by saying yours, sarcastically.

Suddenly, he says he has to call his wife. He gives you the choice of the bedroom or the living room but doesn't move. You get up. You feel your rear flashing indelicately in the same lamp light you watched him undress.

You are cold and wrap up in your oversized jacket and curl on the couch. You are undone. A well, in the dark.

A conversation goes on. You wish you had the energy to eavesdrop. You drift off in agitated slumber.

He comes back and wakes you with noise instead of his hands. He says she threw up seven times that day. Eat and puke, eat and puke, he says.

For a second you don't like him. He sits beside you, dejectedly.

You pretend to be understanding. You put your arms

around him and think stupid, ah, don't be unhappy. He wants to know if you know what *bulimia* is. He is as detached as an amputated limb.

He eats another ham sandwich and you go back to bed, but it is better this time. You wake him two times, like a construction worker waking his acquiescent wife.

In the morning you ask, as a test, can you stay another night. He says not. Hurt, you let him see it. He touches your hand and says another time will come.

Encouraged you arise and perversely do all the things for him you never did for your husband. (He says one of his wives wouldn't and one of them couldn't). You fry eggs, squish oranges, and ask to iron his shirt. He declines but you insist. You want to think of him at work all day in creases you have pressed. He gives you the shirt and tells you where the equipment is. Inside one cupboard, there are no water biscuits but four cans of spray starch.

When he leaves, he wraps the London Fog and muffler in a dashing way. You feel wifey and dumpy in you K-Mart gear. You get giddy and kiss him too profusely good-bye. Show time, he says and leaves.

You make the bed and fish in the pocket of his tossed shirt to lay his pens in a prominent place before throwing it into the hamper. You tidy the kitchen and fix the garbage disposal whose growl has rattled when you turned it on. It renders two fruit pits and some undistinguishable muck. You leave your dissertation by the pens. You dress, put on your still-wet boots and leave.

You are at home in the red house in the woods that was the whole of your property settlement. The clouds have been swept from the heavens by the mid-day sun. It is a primitive place and needy. The weeds bow in the heat over the once-cut places. The fences nag gravity. For three years you have stayed there alone, keeping your small son safe, feeding animals, grading papers by the fires of wood you split. Now you have this small longing in you that won't go away.

At night across the fields badgers and rats and foxes let out their springing cries at each other. They add dimension to your dreams. But now flooded by sunlight, the gates loose on their pivots, the rich grass choked by weed, there are no night cries and your thoughts despair this other dulled world.

In a few minutes your son will rattle over the cattle gap with your ex-husband. He will be overwrought with his pleasures and grievances. His father will have performed tricks for him, juggled, taken in the matinees. He will have been complimented and shouted at. Teased, and ignored. In a few days he will be back to normal.

In the past three months you have become a demon lover. Three times you have packed the flight bag, kissed your son good-bye, left in the hands of your ex husband, driven two hundred miles, upon one pretext or another, to the university that will give you a degree soon, and to your great love.

This last time your great love has said your name and brushed the hair back from your face. He has said an incantation against the dawn. You will think about those gestures a long time from now, when you are trying to remember if he ever did anything hinting of love.

He has what you call an ironic smile. A smile which gives an edge to what he is saying, a secret objectivity. But what of this imperfect lovemaking? The one sidedness, the existence which is due only to your inventiveness. Your hands are never still in bed, they move obtaining as much pleasure from the touch of his skin as you wish to give him. Reassuring, too, delivering him. You say this makes up for lack of passion on his side, the way normal loves go, when both of you should be disturbed by each other, rocked in a mutual longingness. When his formalness, his lack of interest sometimes speaks sense to you, you will not abide it.

Last night he talked about his first wife of whom you are inordinately jealous because she has history on her side, the sons, and economics. She left him two years ago, you surmise to find herself, then became sorry. He said that she is beautiful and spoiled. He calls both his wives Japs. And before you remembered you'd read Phillip Roth your eyes widened, and he'd explained: Jewish American Princesses. His faults only guard against other predators.

The second wife who left him last year you oddly think of as the Other Woman, feeling her position temporary, in danger of usurpation. You see her less of an obstacle than a temporary barrier. How long could his long-distanced marriage last with one, however exotic, was bulimic, and alcoholic.

In bed with him you think the right word will be said one day, the shades fall from his eyes, and then he will see you. He hasn't seen you yet. After lovemaking you position your legs around his, the sweet taste of him clinging to your lips, for this is the only way he can have it, and inhale his various smells, which remind you of nothing, as though the newness of him was some rare compound. If you had to say, it might be fresh wool and thyme, or mint and sea-wind.

The way you came to know him was prosaic, sitting at the translation table with the other students listening to his rich voice, read, and wax wry with his understated joking. Old formulaic: student falls in love with teacher.

Once he likened the study of Old English meter with the mystery of the second law of thermo-dynamics and you looked that up in a physics book. After studying, the most you understood was that heat went out, never came back and you disregarded the metaphor and said the second law was why we wear clothes in winter. You notice if you can make him laugh, and if you memorize bits and parts of poems and old lectures you have an edge.

A strange quirk of mind he calls it. He charms you, but he has a different ploy, straight story telling in that cultured, litotes way. When you come back the third time, he tells you something is wrong with your dissertation and asks if you are a man-hater.

He says, obviously, from your writing, you have been hurt. His words are like salt on the edge of a razor. He points out one poem as evidence. It is about him, uses the persona of Sir Gawain, posing as someone who has been tricked to risk his life for honor. You like to think it is honor keeping him responsible for the certain party. He points out your Robinson Crusoe poem, which is about him too, his impotency cleverly disguised as isinglass, the politics of an island disturbed by the arrival of another person. You make your face go bland and study his. It is unaware, but cocky. You relax. He just needs to stir. You say to let it be. The hours with him begin to taint. They are both published, you point out. He seems overjoyed at something.

Finally, you smash the distance with your hands and mouth, and he comes back to you. But it is more difficult that time until your own ardor releases you back to your illusions. But first your trembling snags his zipper and sticks it and when you go flying at it, he moves your hands. Come, come, come, he says and moves you to the bedroom. Then he undresses casually and scrutinizes a place near his mouth in the mirror. Your passion presides in your stomach and you are made to wait. There is no scope for you here. You despair. But then he brushes your hair back and says your name and the evening light at once catches on some object and separates itself like a prism might across the room and the tumult begins again.

You are used to grievances when you leave. No mention of the next when or where. You drive home calming yourself, then you remember the sound of his belt buckle clanging on the dresser, the flash of his buttock when he removes his shorts, and how unlonely it all remembers.

You cry sometimes. The way it looks later in your mind when he buckles the belt snappily and proceeds to class. The way he didn't look at you once but lay doubled up and said it was warm for May. It sounded as though May flower petals were drifting over the world. You cry when you remember how you cling, pretending that is what he needs. I'm dangerous, he says. But who but an impotent man would say that? Besides there is nothing you will not undo.

The thought of your comprehensives looms like a heinous affair. You are to pass four exams given all day for four days and to somehow pull it off with him. You forget sometimes if you are working to possess a terminal degree or to possess him. You did not know which will be worse, if he allows he does not want you this time, or if he allows he does.

You were ready to dig in where you had to. You sit in his office playing the do-you-want-me game. You have long become used to games. His office is dark when you walk in, his head in his hands. The other person has needed him four times since you saw him last, to help her prepare for her own studies at some far away prestigious place and he has driven the distance at each request.

You've come in grateful of the speeding ticket you've just received. An interesting story. It falls flat. You see he has new shoes and you feel oddly uninformed. You sit giving him five minutes more to want you, then you leave, taking it well. You return to your small cloister in the campus hotel and study. Clear head, you think of nothing but the best of what is thought-and-said and how to arrange it in your mind. Then you go to sleep.

You are woken up by the telephone. You sit in pitch dark knowing who it is.

You can't think, your brain clogs with darkness, chockablock with the pitch. Let me turn on a light you say, but he tells you you don't need it. Just listen.

The dark presses insufferably. His voice has a strange

edge. He has a distance to drive but he will be back in two days to supervise the comps. He says do you want to stay at my house.

You begin to dither. You digress. He says do you, impatience bursting, impairing.

You consent and end up alone at his new house for the next two days. You have thrown yourself into an arena, but you buy groceries and line your books up and lock the doors like someone might during a siege. You deny. You refuse to invoke. You survey the new house like a building inspector. Your grievances pass. The old-fashioned transoms, the high ceiling, falling down wainscoting fires your imagination. You are in a novel again, and outside the story is a long and dull day.

You think perhaps his travelling will do her in. You look for signs that this is so. Nothing seems propitious.

Your next visit coincides with your dissertation defense. He has a new place and this new house is larger, and now you see things you had never seen before. A guitar in its case and you did not know he played. A carved wooden box on the lacquered dresser. A new microwave gleams in the dining room on a sideboard, a stranger too. And new plants. You realize the huge stretches of his present life that you know nothing about.

You can hear the seconds tick when you look up from your books. You imagine his choosing this house and signing the deed. Talking with the neighbors.

There are no curtains and the houses cram together so you can see the inhabitants to the east. That house is like the one you are in. The one you are in is an ancient, sprawling farmhouse, built, then gradually surrounded by other houses similar but not so big. It is the oldest house in town. He said that it has character. That is your word for houses, and you fretted that you did not say it first.

The studying seems clueless. You read "The Wife's Lament" and because it is known as a difficult poem with layers of ambiguity you feel stupid because it speaks truth to you. You are obviously missing something.

At dusk, you rustle through the kitchen which is a shamble of boxes and stray unput-away things. You pull the bread from the bag you brought, open cheese. You cannot find the silver, so you take a new putty knife from the top of a can and wash that. It slices the cheese in perfect, tantalizing squares. Perhaps he will be amused by your ingenuity.

In the living room you twiddle with some dials and find some lonesome love song. You listen for a few minutes, then take umbrage. You turn it off. You sink into the wide, sectional sofa one of his wives has probably chosen. You can see the street from there.

You have begun to wait again, even though it will be close to eighteen hours before he comes.

The view from the window, Carencro's main street, looks like a movie set for an old Southern scene. Perhaps the exteriors are fake, props. Across the street is a general store, queued on both sides by more old houses. His front yard is fenced by white pickets that are climbed by premature roses struggling in the cold. A shadow of a man passes. The incendiary tip of a cigarette arcs and splashes sparks into the street. He walks faster as though he has just remembered something.

You imagine yourself picking some stray off the street and being caught. But you can't imagine his Byronic brow even slightly confounded. He would probably introduce himself.

You pretend you are married to him and his divorced wife, the insane one, returns and shoots you at close range. Fortunately, it is only a flesh wound and you handle it all with humor and aplomb.

You imagine his sons and you and your son together. You imagine reading to the younger ones, and taking care of them all, unselfishly, when they are beset with childhood fevers.

Then you hear his phone jangle in the bedroom, but you don't move. He has asked you not to answer the phone, after earlier saying you could give his number to your babysitter. You have marked that, and you plan to use it when you are through to help forget him. Another thing will be tentativeness.

The sound persists an inordinately long time. You want to answer just to make it stop. Finally, there is abrupt silence, one ring cut off in its plea, like something choked to silence.

The silence of the room seems a censure to your presence, as though the person on the other end of the phone had suddenly realized you were there. You get up and walk up and down the long floor. In the light of the window next door, you can see two people talking but cannot hear their voices. You have a sudden, wild desire to know what it is they say. Perhaps they are discussing politics, or art, or what to have for dinner. Maybe one of them is not amendable to love tonight. That one moves out of sight and you lose interest.

Your limbs feel heavy and a small headache is beginning at the back of your head. You tell yourself that you are in his house alone, and that he has gone to visit his wife. Even to you these two facts are incongruous, but you cannot fully give them the appreciation they deserve. You decide to hang towels in the windows of the bedroom.

The phone starts again. This time you steel yourself. You count thirteen, fourteen. Fifteen. If it is not the crazy wife—he is with her—it must be the first wife. Amazing that she should hold on after two years. You snort in sympathy for her. Or perhaps it is some graduate student from the university looking for adventure. Whoever it is, is determined to smoke him out.

After the ringing stops, you go into the other room and crouch on the sofa—your ears seem in danger of bursting. It is almost dark, and you've forgotten to put a light on. Your imagination rises to the occasion: What if it is he and since he'd told you not to answer the phone, was trying to signal you that he had changed his mind, needed to talk to you.

You turn on all the lamps. You pick up one of your books but inside everything blurs, the words give up their spacing and jumble, black lines start to appear. They begin to smash into each other and if they could, would render a low noise like the rattling of gravel. You put it down.

Later you try sleeping to make the time pass. You turn down the coverlet. You despise colored sheets and you mark that too. You decide to sleep naked, with make-up. You check the dresser's mirror. A foreigner's face peers back at you. You ask aloud what it is doing there. Inscrutable oriental face doesn't speak. You inspect your breasts flattened by birth control pills. You are too old to take birth control pills. You inspect your thirty-six-year-old rear, hanging like two minuscule hams. The studying has taken it out of you. The pills alone have made you amenorrhoeic for nine months. Perhaps you are turning into a boy.

Later when you are almost asleep the phone begins again. You burst out of the covers, spilling books, paper. Perhaps he has another lover other than you. You speculate. You see her not like the young intellectuals you usually torture yourself with, but your age, and capable of saying brave, astute things. Bringing him to his senses. The ringing is a mating call then and takes the edge of confidence when before it was hysteria. You pull the covers over your head in opprobrium, like a child, but see his legs there intertwined with another, like some fulsome cave in which you are a spy.

Then again, the thought that it is he, the urgency of this caller, impels you to reach a hand and put it on the receiver. You are in Ann Frank's attic, the call which persisted so long the families gathered around it grievously. Was it the gestapo or a warning from a friend? Perhaps it is he, then, needing to warn you to clear out, that he is bringing his wife home. But you can't make yourself pick it up, the receiver trembles electricity in your palm, ready, but there is not life in your fingers.

This silence you sit up and lean against the wall. Outside the streets glow, as if it has been raining, which it has not.

Toward dark the next day you take your post at the windows willing him home. Every car that turns the corner shines hope by its headlights only to hit you, broadside, and dissolve into nothingness.

It is the last of winter or the beginning of spring. Outside, the roses coaxed to life by a few false suns shiver in the deep air. Someone is frying a spicy meal and its domestic smell wafts through the open window. You try telepathy, wishing. Release magic and close the window.

Last night you dreamt of him for the first time in your life. It was an occasion. He was back with his sylph-like wife and they were roaming in floating motions around the bed. You are taking this well they say. Her skin of milk glowed, her frailty, her long golden hair spilt past her waist. He held her arm protectively, (of you) and kept turning solicitously toward her. He wears the shirt you ironed. You recognize the creases. Brooks Brothers, the little buttons like eyes. You shout his name, but he refuses to look at you, or doesn't hear. She pulls his arm and they disappear and appear in odd scenes around the house, which you get to by out-of-body travel. They are seemingly uncaring that your body is in the bedroom completely nude. Once an artist told you the difference between *nude* and *naked*. He said that nude was that state you want to be seen, and naked is an accident. You are nude. He is making coffee, and she is sitting on a bar stool. He is repairing the tile and she hands him his tools. She is strumming the guitar (of course, it's hers) and he takes it from her and tunes it perfectly.

When you wake, your heart is thumping in falling trochaic, no joy to listen to or to waltz to. You begin to think of fierce things that happened to you having nothing to do with love.

You remember your mother waiting for your father, in his cups, to come home from god knows where. When you went to sleep, she had been fretting in the kitchen, finding fault with her life, and she was there in the morning when you woke up. In the light she had become disheveled, slightly hysterical. She had started in on you, since your father wasn't there yet. She said your manners were atrocious and that she spoiled you with all her sacrifices and giving. She cooked your breakfast and remembered your report card from last six weeks and drew a parallel from that to the condition of your underwear drawer. She said to straighten up, and would you ever straighten up? And tell me how you will ever keep a man if you worship a god of sloven. You knew she was about to point out the way she had to beg you to do chores around the house, and with a mother working too. She said the bottom line is that she has to beg you to do chores around the house, and her working too. Then she looked at your cowboy boots and said that your personal appearance was one of a slob and you had not thought of that.

Your father came in a way that accomplished drunken totter and dash. She said an amount of prayer had been wasted on him. She began to sob expansively. She wanted him to account for himself. He tried to light a cigarette but forgetting to close the match cover, it burst into flame. He howled and dropped it, then your mother stamped it with her foot, howling too. She said for God's sake you could have burnt us all up. He said enough of this. To spite her, he took out a whiskey bottle curved to fit over haunches, from his back pocket. It was the hair of a dog.

She exclaimed when she saw it and began to list her grievances. Lack of money, small house, no help. On this last she shot a pure look of hate to you. Work, work, work, and now this one drunk for my reward. Her hysteria made him thoughtful. He pulled out a wad of money and calmly tossed it on the table, not far from your own egg-on-toast. Then he asked was this what she wanted, and she wailed louder, knowing that he had been gambling. She said she was not long for this world, was death itself. He said to get him coffee. He turned on the gas stove, took one of the bills, a hundred, and ignited it, then lit a cigarette. She was catatonic, then she erupted.

You were frightened of sitting there, but more frightened to move. He solved your problem by kicking the leg of the chair you were in. He said vamoose. You flee, your mother's yells reverberating like yodels.

Later what you thought about was not the novelty of the flaming hundred, but the idea of your mother waiting it out all night for him, while you were sleeping. Waiting had multiplied something in her, and the lack of sleep. Waiting, you know, intensifies your wants.

You have lost all sense of time. You move back into the living room. The street before you has long flickered off lamps and you are sitting in a dark-shadowed house. You doze off and awake to his crashing into the unpacked boxes in the kitchen. He makes no secret that he is home, his footsteps loud on hardwood floors, as he looks for you. He chuckles to see you sitting up sleepily. Your joy is short-lived. He says he must make a phone call.

You use the time to put on make-up and tidy up. You put on your pajama top and shorty robe, even though it is not much past eight. You get in bed, with your glasses on, and train the tensor light on the novel you are reading. I bin there before, says Huck Finn. You begin reading with alacrity, even though you normally loathe Twain. You escape into the terrible waters. They take hold of you, and you attend to the problems of the floaters. The self-same pang that curdles in run-away slaves, curdles in you.

He returns, twiddles in the bathroom, and comes out naked. He pulls the book from you and turns off the light. You lie side by side, not touching. He says to take all this stuff off and pulls on your robe. Then you lie, stalling. Something curious in you has started. You want to make him wait. But your body betrays you. You begin melting. All the waiting hours, the incessant telephone, and the place where he's been before too, seem unimportant.

You furl around him. Your fingers go to a *pas de deux*, your mouth mingles with his. He is a delicious boy.

He lies flat, his arms as light as a ghosts on yours. You want to touch every inch of him, the shape of his nose, his brow, throat. A little less handsome now, without his glasses, and this pleases you, makes you tender. His eyes, myopic and vulnerable, hollowed, induces something in you to unloose the dark zones within him.

How in a matter of inches downward the moleskin hollow of throat could your hands, mouth, be turned from the gentle art of dance into despair? You had come to bed, and become overflowing, fecund as a rain, and he had come with thoughts of the impossible, of dark cares. The damper occasioned by the voracious wife who knew him in the morning. You have never felt as separate.

He said if someone had told him yesterday he would be capable of lovemaking he would not have believed it. You still didn't. He asked what your weekend was like. Your weekend has nothing to go with anything. You look at him directly and see the details of his wife's person in the reflection of his eyes.

In the morning you try to remember what you had gone to sleep reciting. The Age of Johnson, The Restoration, other neat categories in which you have mnemonically crafted lists under. Sometimes sleep obliterates it. You dress together like husband and wife. He says good luck. He kisses you. It is a dry peck. You say Show Time. You leave first.

The thing you must be is clear-headed. You drive to your exams remembering Chaucer, his Nun's Priest Tale, Arthur, swords thrusting through water. You study one last time in the library.

A conference room had got turned into a classroom. There was a long table and forgotten dissertations crammed the bookshelves. Two other students are there already. You eye each other, calculating. The one woman had failed the thing last year. The other you didn't know.

He was addressing the test-takers. He said read the exam first and if there are any questions, he would answer them. The failed woman across from you looks up from her exam and asks what *salient* is. There but for the grace of God. He says watch your time and leaves.

You make your mind go shrewd. You see the answers roll off the tip of your ball-point pen. You write essay after essay, informed, slightly informal, and all for him.

Afterwards when you knew you had passed one day's test, you drive in the direction of his house and spot him ahead of you. At a light you honk, but he takes off suddenly, passes an old pick-up, and a Camaro in a fell swoop, speeding. You follow him, seventy, seventy-five. A line from one of your poems comes to mind: "Oh how you fly, you fly." You both are untouched by mortality or speed limits.

You pull into the driveway after he does. He says what timing. He is convivial. He fixes lunch and putters in the kitchen. You hit the books.

You sprawl on the bed surrounded by a sea of old tests, notebooks. You see how convenient it would be for him to push them aside and join you.

After lunch he connects the washer-dryer in the kitchen. You ask if he didn't need a nap. He says not at all. He abandons his repairs and goes to the grocery store. You go to the eighteenth century.

You have no power to tell if he wants you there or not. His key in the door rattles into your consciousness, floats you out of the eighteenth century to this other band of time. His arms are laden with groceries. His manner is distracted.

There is a persecution of delays. First, he puts away the food. Then you eat supper sprawled on the bed awash with your notes and books. At any other time to sit there, just existing, sharing food would be felicity itself. But his quietness, his withdrawnness which had seemed diffuse at best now grows to full scale. It seemed a presage of some substance less disaster.

Then he gets up and twiddles in the kitchen as though he were procrastinating. Despair flows up in you like the coming of evening gloom. It moves you to the edge of a great deep, it draws you closer, floats you up and down and winds you around so that your backbone quivers when you look at him.

Finally, he comes to the bedroom with a drink in his hand which he puts beside his bed. You send books, paper flying. The gloomy hue of the evening dispels. You undress quickly and slide between the sheets. He undresses grimly, like a man who was being directed by some contrariant influence. He sits on the edge of the bed.

He says you are a very intense woman.

You study the decor and note that you have it memorized. Years from now, you will be able to envisage it, describe it to the last detail. The opposite wall has the door with its high stained-glass transom. The glass stained an eternal rose. You know the wainscoting, the high ceiling, the Casablanca fan above your heads. The black lacquered dresser holds the huge, shadowed mirror. The closet is in the corner of the room built after chifforobes but before someone thought of closets. He has already painted the bedroom an embarrassing pink.

His wine sparkles in his glass. You look at the person on the bed, the other thing you have always wanted.

He begins to slosh his wine as though he were a connoisseur in an attempt to see its fullness. Your silence makes him fidgety as though he expected you to protest, to let loose a barrage of protest.

You sit up and put your feet on the floor. Your home-ec teacher in high school once, the shrunken-headed one, said feet on the floor was the best means of birth control. You stare into the mirror but can't find his eyes. You are getting old and most of the years seemed to have taken place recently. You tilt your chin a little but can detect no sign of wantonness or other appeal. Without your lenses, the image in the mirror is substance less and your eyes blurry with myopia. Nothing intense there, the intensity resides inside, and you know it is a fault.

He finishes his wine in one gulp as if he has given up on something. He jerks his head toward the pillow, and you crawl in. He snaps the light and the streetlamp takes over. He has taken down all your towels. The odd thought of voyeurs floats into your head, oddly entices you to the moment. His presence, the shadows, releases you to access. Your displeasures converge into forgetfulness.

Now, suddenly, there is an end to his passiveness. He smothers you with kisses as one determined. Your surprise hovers, your joy self-sufficing, becomes his. Something trembles out of abeyance, eager, like one who has returned from a journey and finds home strange but lovely in unexpected ways.

Enough at first to experience his ardor, all interinvolved, his opposites. You half sit up, half cancel the magic by your desire to please. He is a gift without condition. The unreserve seems too perfect to believe. You run your tongue from his mouth, you seek the penetrative of his whole existence. You want to find some concavity to let you into his very body.

A discovery is insensate, still fed by that first magic. That half of you that was unaware that he can touch you springs like an anger, passes to perplexity, then gives you leave to slide into a new joy. For here it is not, like the earlier encounters, all strung out in wanting and not wanting, but the very vividness of the constraint, proffered and a genius from where it came. It is more whole through a winning back its own. His mouth finds yours.

To feel the light after ten months of oblivion. To be warm, content. But in time it was as though that which wells up in you had passed to take reflection, then came back, became a strait, and separated out. The place was between two levels; the immeasurable poured into measurable, then back again. Your interiority encompasses, flows, seeking what it loses, embraces what it never had. You both begin to lose ground. Now when you go from lover to helper all is lost. Despite your will to seek, the surface welling and unwelling, something in you gives up, as if a glimpse of what you thought you could have, dispelled by its immediacy.

There should have been a heart-sinking or a retreat. Instead, you become mechanical, a desperate woman. The boundless was nothing to you, all to your flesh. You want it to be over.

Then it rang and the nothing in you grows larger. Three short rings from that object near his bed, near the wine glass, the closed lamp. You hesitate, ready to act, for acting's sake.

He doesn't move. For dark reasons of his own, he lets you hesitate, relax again. He says then, you know I have to answer that. He says, I have to. You sit up.

You want the only way he could have stopped you was the thought of her suicide. But you knew it wasn't that. You wanted him to at least curse once, to whip back the covers, explode them. Gotten angry. He got up as one skulking.

You sit in the empty bed, and something begins to be reborn in you.

You get up and dress, the plan has taken an infinitesimal second of time. Your fingers fly with your buttons, the actual in your life seems to reside in their hardness. The beauty of your books gathered seem glorious in their almost forgotten promise of a new life. Your bag is almost ready, you having lived out of it. It is an unearthly hour.

Outside you leave the trunk open, you make trip after trip for the mountainous books. Your recovery is almost sacrilegious to the religion you have been living lately.

You move out quietly, non-dramatically.

You have forgotten your purse. Nothing makes you feel more feminine and stupid as to lose your purse. It is preventing a perfect exit.

A conversation is short. He asks what you are doing. You say I am going. He says no. It was the answer to the question of if he had wanted you there or not. The answer seems unprofound. You are fully clothed, and he is completely naked except for his glasses. You say, its ok. And because you understand nothing, you say, I understand. You walk over, rub his stomach twice. You leave.

You get in the car and rev the engine. You drive through his backyard so that you won't have to go in and ask him to back his car up. You bump some yard hole and a few of your books bounce out the open hatch back. You get out, retrieve them, and close it.

On the way to the campus hotel, you are stopped by the passing of a train. The cars speed by so fast you can't count them. The gate lifts. You're out.

Before you lies no clear and happy prospect but the two remaining exams. In the remaining hours before the sun breaks you cram, but you have slept fitfully. Reality is not a fit bed partner.

The Restoration gives you headaches, the powdered wigs, the fops, brocaded gowns, the follies. No comradeship between the sexes, like creatures facing backwards. Too much like the present age and outlook.

But you are eager to regenerate yourself through expatiation. To take rejection well must be a sign of maturity. Perhaps he will remember you, one day, in fondness and admiration. Perhaps you will tell him that.

The sun is up. You, unkempt, fettered by your learnings, move forth to examination. You think he will smile fondly, sadly at you.

You make your way to the faded red brick examination building, stepping over crushed early blossoms, berries, pine needles cushioning the sidewalk, the air edges in warmth from a sun unwilling to give up trying. Only your good sense could part you from him and it had. The Restoration facts float inside your head, line up.

He is standing at the end of the table like a sacristan. His face is hard-boiled. At first you think you are late, then you see that this countenance is reserved for something else. He explains the directions to you and the salient woman, whose demeanor seems to have heartened since the last test. You ask him a question just to check your fancy and he explodes and at the same time uses an economy of words. Listen up, the directions are on the test. The questions are clear.

A door opens in your mind. You are an exiled flower, exiled by your own hand, and he is livid.

You think it is love.

Once you had seen him doing something incriminating you were back to page one. There is a skeleton uncloseted. You had read, written, allowed your mind the peace of vacancy once or twice, and written again. Then when you dragged the examination up to his office, where he was waiting, (they had no monitor for these tests, a fact which disturbs you. The salient woman could have cribbed from your paper, you could have seen fresh perspective on hers, uncluttered by your own brand of private symbolism) he comes out of his office, turns on his heel, stops, turns back to get your paper. He goes back into the office and shuts the door.

His closed door opens the door in your mind wider. Your

thoughts smack against each other and become heady.

You reach him by phone but by this time your matter-of-factness toward your own rejection has sobered him. He tries to apologize for the interruption. You say I won't let you. I should apologize for my abruptness. You say you have no regrets. He tries to outdo you in magnanimity. It was your magnanimity first and you wish he would leave it alone. You are too cowardly to ask him if his anger meant something. You prefer your own fantasies. You say good-bye. But he hasn't seen the last of you. Better to leave this way, time to enjoy a little of your new-found knowledge.

At home your half-finished dissertation flows from your pen. You write poems touched with dramatic irony, tough love, un-love, and unrequited love. The few times you can get him on the phone your dissertation director emits subdued approval. Keep writing, he says, you almost have it.

At home the wind rustles through the stove pipe in the last remaining days of cold. You play Monopoly with your son. His head bends, hair fit for an angel child, studying the board. You read to him, loving the complexity of children's books. You make a book for him from typing paper in which he is the main character and cut pictures from magazines. Something in you has tipped, smacks of peace.

The peace is short-lived. He has called once officiously, has said that it is an officious phone call to announce you have passed your comps. He says that other phone call in the middle of love making was a traumatic experience. You ask, for me, or for you? He says, for you. You say, oh. You forbear to point out that he is the one who is impotent.

You mull and think lucid thoughts. You use the time resting from writing your dissertation, and judging events and a man, to fix up the farm. Your son follows you carrying his plastic hammer and screwdriver. You tighten wire and clean long-unused stalls of their dried manure, petrified lumps but lighter than air. The unridden horses buck with pleasure. One spring day you put the finishing touches on your dissertation and mail it south. You hold your arms up in the air, you breathe in your country kitchen. You plan to cook homey things; you plan to read everything you've ever wanted. Your son laughs at your extravagant movements. You dance with him, plan to make cookies and not burn them.

Because of a guest you repair the floor of the old bathroom; the plywood near the tub has rotted out due to your son's uninhibited splashing through the years of his babyhood. You have plans to put the house on the market and to get a job, far far away. You are applying everywhere, and also to a prestigious university near his. Let fate have it.

Your mother is with you. In a fit of magnanimity, you've fetched her. Traversed the ground that separates her from you fretting the end of her life away in a nursing home. As always, she ignores your child, talks of your sister and her family. Your sister is the one who wears the diamond. The diamond was the family's only treasure, a crazy grandmother had left it. Your sister put in on a hundred-dollar gold chain. Your mother gave the house and money to her as well. That ounce of attention from a man has made you forgive and forget.

But the week was working out badly. You planned for her to get to know her grandson. You sit a chair under the garden tree, so she can watch you row the garden and plant after a boy comes and breaks ground. She is fidgety and doesn't see the beauty of planting, betting on the come. Your son drags his feet dangerously near the new seed waiting to get covered. He says why oh why can't we get our food from the grocery store like other people? Your mother says she is missing *Wheel of Fortune*. The deep magic of interminable rows of vegetables from your childhood dissolve before your eyes, the jungle vines of climbing beans, the collard's swish, the way you bit into filched tomatoes, the dust flavoring your mouth, and with a certain wildness.

They move inside, and you are left alone. You can never be sure of anything in your life.

Your mother comes out on the porch and calls you. She walks slowly and carefully. Inside are hundreds of bright green, pink beige, and blue pills which she takes according to the clock. Antidepressants, tranquilizers, blood-pressure ones. The tiny blue ones for vertigo. She calls them her dizzy pills.

She calls you to the phone. You know that it is a man from a way her face is set. Inside, she sits down near Vanna White and her face grows even more imposed upon. She shouts, No, don't buy a vowel, you idiot.

Your dissertation director's voice is on the other end. He says a member of your committee has lost your dissertation. Was using the back of it for typing paper at home, misplaced the rest of it. Your mind flies back to the oldest house in Carencro. You are trying to imagine his breaking out a typewriter from one of the unpacked boxes and in a fit of creative passion, working on something at home, ignoring the phone calls, the undone chores, the painting, the ancient plumbing. It is not possible. The director wants you to send another copy. A certain member of your committee thought it was his personal copy. You think it is, but not in that sense.

You imagine the director sitting at his desk with his boots propped up like two little hooves. You speculate on his speculations. You try imagining them both in cahoots. You fail. Perhaps this a ploy, the only way an impotent man can ask for sex, and not be rebuffed.

The wheel of fortune spins its clatter amid shouts. You hang up and dash with the phone into the bedroom. The long cord snags on the door but you yank in into the closet. You don't plan. You don't think. You dial his number.

You imagine the phone ringing in those same insistent tones it rang by the hand of his first ex-wife, or mystery lover, or whoever it had been when you had stayed there alone. You imagine his long legs striding across the hardwood floors. You imagine his picking up the phone with impatient fingers. Your heart compresses, in that split second you form the words that will tell him you are on to him, love him no matter what failure he thinks he is in bed. Kiss-kiss. You are John Stuart Mills' willing, intelligent slave.

When he recognizes your voice, he waxes displeased, strange. Becomes a berserk man, a flimsy excuse—all decorum, the lovely restraint gone. You interrupt, crazy yourself, that this is an officious phone call. He says he hasn't done any of those things. Forget it he barks. He will take care of anything. His end of the line clicks.

You have dumped a copy of your dissertation in the dissertation director's office. In the past few months you have been sustained by some influent freshness and the poems have flowed off your pen. You've tidied up the old stories, five of them, you'd been writing all your life and arranged them with a title. He peruses them, hurrumphs in affirmation. He comments, disposes, calm master of your life. He decrees a signature.

The signature is hard got. You step into the elevator; you float too fast. You are widely aware, warm, fragile. Your recent past dwindles, the life in the red house, the woods, the solitude, the writing, the planting, a shore left behind. You step out into the hall, toward his office, the open sea. The olive green of his door, on which all your solaces are projected, darkens and closes in.

When he opens it, your square of fixed belief poises for flight, forgetting stale recurrences, and at once the sight of him rises like a rich paradox. The light from his open window passes to and fro behind him, catches the objects of the room aslant, across, astray.

The face reflecting a thousand weary mysteries changes, becomes fixed into something, transmutes into loathing. He says he does not have time for you now. You wave the officious business under his nose. He says come back later. He says, for god's sake.

Thus, in a moment that which is despised is occupying a solitary desk left over in the hall from some overcrowded classroom. Other students come to and fro, and by craning your neck, you can observe their smug, graduate student conceit before they disappear into his doorway.

You twiddle, you thumb the stack of papers ready for legalization. You indulge in some grave scrutiny of his behaving. You busy yourself translating experience into systems. You beg the question, you paraphrase.

A young woman approaches, whose pleasing harmony of dress and face make you look. Her scrutiny of you is quick, as intense as yours. She smiles, deprecatingly nodding her head. You know that behavior. The rapid checking out, the measuring of your face against her own, the speedy calculating of age. You smile at the same time. She goes into his office.

They appear together. They leave.

Some rough promptings encourage you to realize that it is she. You ponder her raven hair, you urge doubts. You are pulled against casting the woman in that role at first, you are pushed toward the logic of it. The admixture intertwines like a loom gone haywire, casting the warp and weft in a wacky texture.

Later he explains his rudeness was the product of his wife's proximity. He says hang it all, she was in the next room. You say is this affair over or not? But you say it in your mind, coward. You say aloud, what is it you want from me? He says, listen now, I don't know what I want from you. Try to put yourself in my place.

You put yourself in his place. In his office, to which you have slunk back, is a miniature sandcastle petrified to paperweight. Perhaps some moon-eyed student has given it to him. His typewriter with its old English ball sits on his messy desk. Books, lectures, old letters are stuffed between them. His very essence caught by hours, years spent in this room was bitter sweetness crushed up to your lips. You imagine you are him, sitting at his place bombarded with the effrontery of your love. In your long banishment from her world, you have grown savage. You would eye you with due suspicion, a shadow eyeing the shadow-boxer.

After a second copy was read, after the paperwork was accomplished, you were due to graduate. Then you find a new job, in a prestigious university fifty miles from him.

All the cloak and dagger stuff persist. You think you are getting sterner with yourself. No longer do you call him on some trumped-up pretext or another. You wait for real reasons before you drive fifty miles.

Finally, it comes, a reading at the Woman's Center. The gathering was measly, but they were all there for you. Not like the Open Mike you were used to at your university sandwiched between the famous poets and the grubby graduate students.

The Woman's Center made a video of you all, sitting all *gemutlich* in a semi-circle. You licked your lips and read smoothly, all the usual trembling gone. Not because you were becoming more poised, but because you had read, and rewritten the stuff so much you would get half-way through and bore yourself. You give them a show though, your dress a little kooky, and read them all funny ones so they wouldn't have to think much. They like ones about sex and coming to terms with yourself.

Which hasn't happened. That's why after you finish reading, and chat and shake hands with the director—who grasps both your hands and says, tremendous—you use the phone to call him to tell him you could come over. The place you are in is a frame house and it is cold. Your fingers shake dialing his number.

He had never called you to come. He had never told you not to come when you called him. He did not tell you now.

There were changes. He had painted and installed a new mantel for the fireplace that doesn't work. The kitchen had been done over in black and white terrazzo tile. A kitchen island, spotless, divides the room and a new window takes up one wall.

He is wearing torn jeans and a Brooks Brother shirt. He'd been making homemade mead and offers you a glass. You sit on the wraparound sofa by the window you know so well and sip doubtfully. You are reminded of your mother's Black Draught, the cure-all which she dosed anyone who looked "funny."

His long legs prop up on the coffee table in a jaunty manner. He smiles in an unmoved way. The phone rings. He smiles again, this time forbearingly.

Watching his receding back, you call on the old arts. Nothing happens. You think of two lines of hexameter, by two different poets, same syllables. No magic comes. Your eyes drift around the room tries to trick it into consciousness. A strange thing happens: the ennui from reading, rereading you own poems come willingly back. Your mind wanders like in a dull class. You think possibly your refrigerator at home is devoid of milk. The fifty miles to drive later already seems tedious. He returns, his face for an instant tensed by cold iniquity. The gaze shrinks when he sees you, knocks away.

You sit staring at the coaster which held your mead a few minutes ago. You hear shouts of a battle, sword clash interspersed with your mother's wield of power in a small, potent bottle. It tastes like laxative. Your mind is cast, disabled from judgment and useless of thought. You are caught between two weapons ready to batter and breach you by ram-strokes of different and opposite consistency.

You go into the bathroom for ablutions of an unnatural kind. Earlier this week, your legs in stirrups, you have had a conversation with a doctor who listened to your tale of amenorrhoeic woe. You lost your freedom in the way of birth control. Now you sit in the newly tiled bathroom, still admiring the claw-footed tub, the marble topped lavatory he has completed by his own hand. In your hand is a foil-wrapped substance you have read that is only 87.5% effective.

You turn the box over, read, pull the instructions, and read again. You fumble, press and beseech the gods. You forge, digging for the field-gate where after nine months a baby will only have 11.5% chance of being. At the moment of conjuncture, you could not have said what affliction you are avoiding.

He has done nothing in the way of curtains. The street scene is as before, the lamp from the street will refract, bend over the bed in few minutes when he closes the light. You remember the qualities which have left behind those enduring impresses. You fumble for them.

He moves over to you and pulls your shirt over your head like one undresses a child. He kisses your breasts which have begun lately to hurt from some mandate long buried by chemicals. A shifting border runs inside you between light and shade. Life is suffered by interludes.

A confluence of wills begins between the sheets. There you always know yourself and him, the vain intricacy of your lives recedes. The limitations profound the effects. Now your hands did not pause in discovery. They are tactile rudiments for your profit, and for your loss.

The house is silent, the shadows sequester you from each other. The child's face at home flashes once, then is gone. The elemental superimposes habit. Then he kisses you in a way that disembarks both your pasts. You are in a sea that is strange, as though you have never sat thwart or held a tiller. This sea replaces the earth, but no break is felt. You are finally in a position for the marvelous. His hands are lingered perfection. He moves down. His mouth. You return perfect heed. It is your daily want to perfect these moments.

The unaccorded polar directions dissolve. And it is the same story. You know at once the old voids there were not yours, but some other spirits', his now parting the two of you asunder. A wild rage like fear encompasses you, but your body is too trained. You are an insane person with a disciplined brain. His contraries separate, transfuse with yours, you go down, downer to escape your own selfhood, exchange yours for his.

And then you find that void that is especially yours while at the same time, light years away, his pleasure, complete.

You move towards his face, you want to memorize it, like the wainscoting, the ceiling stared at for hours, waiting. He jerks his head, turns his face away, left, right. His pleasure humiliates him. He covers his face with his hands, realizes what knowledge is giving him away, uncovers, and pulls your face to his shoulder to stop your scrutiny. All your tiny knowledges of him pale beside the monumental.

You lie on your back and look up at the ceiling fan that he has installed with his own hands. He has it in reverse so that the angle of the blades on slow pushes the warm air down, its whirr the background music for complex stories. It reminds you of *Casablanca*, of Tennessee Williams. The place is a set, then; the fan, the stained-glass transoms, the high ceiling are props. There is a texture there that is familiar but unknowable. You think of him and his wife arguing in this room, of all the histories of husbands and wives arguing in this room (Lower your voice, the servants will hear), and those who will argue in the eons to come.

He kisses you like one who's trying to bring a drowned one to consciousness. You close your eyes. You can't get your mind away from the thought of sets and props. You see the dramatic composition then, the play that is all exits and entrances, and curtains rising and falling, and rising. You barely glimpse the denouements, years into the future, can't make out their natures. And the act you are in now has no socially redeeming value. Even to you, no thematic significance. Only new characters waiting in the wings, souls in recurring scenes fading in and out, and the performers, because of fateful, blundering exits, accidental entrances, keep hopelessly cuing each other.

The Not-So-Chinese Wedding

Coincidentally, on her fortieth birthday, Eunice Lynch, a late bloomer, was awarded full professor at her mid prestigious college in Statesboro, GA, where she had taught for six years, an event which slightly made up for having to live with a widowed mother who daily voiced her prehistoric fears that Eunice will die unwed. Eunice's college loans are not only loans with exorbitant interest, but also the bars on her prison. Over her mother's protests, Eunice was dating a medical doctor, Dr. Lui, from a nearby university hospital where Eunice faithfully donated her slightly more valuable than most type O universal donor blood every month. They had been dating for almost three years and Eunice felt for the most part the relationship was successful (her main evidence that he kept making dates), though at times, vaguely unfulfilling. Eunice tolerantly chalked this up to cultural differences, and though Dr. Lui was not technically an ABC (American Born Chinese) because he was brought to this country as a child, Eunice surmised that his parents' first-generation habits had rubbed off on him here and there while he was impressionable. Dr. Lui never said "I love you", for example. Googling cultural differences, Eunice read that it is difficult for Chinese men to verbalize love. Dr. Lui also sent the same box of 24 red roses to her every Valentine's, a couple of days early for wiggle room, from the same flower shop with the same message, "Happy Valentine's Day, Jerome Lui." Dr. Lui did not believe in holding hands either in public or in private. Dr. Lui did not believe in cuddling on the couch during Netflix movies. Dr. Lui did not believe in pet names for each other. He was opposed to enthusiastic hugs even after returning from international trips, and comforting hugs even after Eunice was mugged waiting for him in front of Barnes and Noble where they play Wei Qi every Tuesday. Or when Mr. Peepers, her fifteen-year-old French bulldog died in her arms one amber leaved autumn day.

Eunice's mother had no objections to Dr. Lui's race. In her eyes, Dr. Lui's medical degree trumped any and all flaws, real or imagined, he may have harbored. Her mother simply believed Dr. Lui should have proposed by now, and that Eunice should cut her losses and begin again.

"I shouldn't think," said Mrs. Lynch with her unwinking stare, "that Dr. Lui's family will receive you with any enthusiasm at all, since it is obvious you are still "just dating" after three years.

Eunice opened her mouth to speak but the habit of years made her shut it again. She was repacking for the third time the battered left-behind Samsonite suitcase belonging to her younger married sister, who had escaped daily family obligations to Fairfax, Virginia, several years ago. Jerome had invited Eunice to fly with him to New York, to his niece's wedding, and secretly she believed meeting his family was laced with promising, if cliched, implications. To share this speculation with her mother would be taking a grave risk, however.

Eunice had researched the topic and she was packing under the assurance *black* is the height of New York fashion for wedding attire after 5 pm. Her anxiety lay in the fact that the wedding was at 4:30, and, historically, in Statesboro, Eunice had never laid eyes, at all the weddings of her cousins and sister, on a black dress, morning, noon, or night. Of course, that was decades ago when everyone was young. She does have the pink sheath…The oatmeal-colored skirt and flowy top could be a backup… But there was only room for so much, the wedding dress (so to speak), the first night-supper-at-Jerome's-brother's-house-with-hundreds-of-guests dinner dress, breakfast slacks with the immediate family, and the last night dinner casual blazer and navy-blue skirt. Her new matching teal peignoir set was hidden away on the bottom, safe from her mother's observations.

"I am sure you don't intend to go on grumbling right up until I leave," Eunice said when she sensed her mother was about to extend her remark. She had learned life was better just to label whatever her mother was saying at the moment, rather than address the content of her comments or point out her mother's less than cogent logic. Normal people fish for compliments. Eunice's mother fished for arguments.

Her mother was not deterred. "I wasn't grumbling. I

know you think I know very little about anything outside my generation, but even today, surely there must be time limits on how long a thing can run."

"Run?" said Eunice. "Thing? That's slightly vulgar." Sometimes Eunice won by hinting that her mother had forgotten decorum.

"Not at all," Mrs. Lynch said, with her signature aggressive realism. "Sometimes there is only one way to construct reality."

Friday morning, Eunice rode in Jerome's little Toyota Yaris to the Atlanta airport three hours early for departure due to Jerome's reoccurring experiences with capricious international flight times. He spent a week in Guiyang every year where he honed his skills in Tai Chi, and at the same time, according to him and the AMA, prevented heart disease and pernicious mental decline. She was wearing her white blouse that wrapped and tied at the side and her flowing India skirt. It was as close as she could come to Asian themed attire, though Jerome informed her that his family was thoroughly Western, and so went the wedding. Eunice was slightly disappointed. Though she knew that her fleeting vision of red flowers, firecrackers, loud gongs, drums and long processions was a bit farfetched, she had hoped for Chinese food and a few touches.

They rode in slow, dead silence all the way to the Atlanta airport. Jerome would drive a gas saving 50 mph to the ER if his passenger had had both arms severed off. And though his phone dinged two times, he ignored it and concentrated on driving safety. After getting Jerome's car into long term parking, and getting the rental car business sorted out, they found themselves, thanks to Jerome's prudence, strolling almost leisurely and boarding a Hartsfield-Jackson train, in calm pursuit of Gate T-30.

"Please hold on. This train is departing. Please keep your belongings gathered. The next gate is Gate A, A as in Alpha," the robotic voice informed them with perfect if mechanical condescension. At Gate T, T as in Tango, Eunice and Jerome stepped off and were caught up in the swirling humanity of the world's busiest airport. Eunice clutched her sister's carry-on bag and her own big purse stuffed with frivolous novels and loped after Jerome. Eunice did not believe in tranquilizers or alcohol as an antidote for fear of flying. She believed in Jane Austen.

"Here," said Jerome, and "here," and "here" at each turn. It was almost the first words he had spoken so far, and though annoying on one level, Eunice felt her face soften just to hear his voice. She also patted herself on the back, for the millionth time, for her tolerance of cultural differences.

Jerome did talk, however, once they were stalled until the pre-boarders preboarded, to his son, who should have been waiting for them at Kennedy. "Such obtuse error," Jerome said, after an ambiguous conversation, punctuated by long silences, holding his cell phone radiation the requisite distance from his ear. The words, superior and haughty, were a bit shocking, though Eunice had caught a similar tone in the middle of the night, when she and Jerome had been awakened by a hapless nurse, confused by his written stat orders. It seemed, Eunice gradually gleaned, Aaron had missed his flight from Chicago, and would be unable to meet them. He would take a taxi from the airport, instead of joining them in his father's Hertz rental.

Eunice saw Aaron at Christmases. He reminded her of his father quite a bit, especially with his habit of instant disagreement with the slightest opinion. Like her mother, the father and son both enjoyed arguing. Last Christmas Eunice mentioned a video she had seen about a female lion who had adopted an orphaned baby gazelle. (Maybe her mother was right about some things. If Eunice was not married soon, she will be one of those hopelessly single women, sliding toward old age, and watching cat videos for entertainment. Eunice had gone from cat videos to lion videos, and from lion videos to videos about African prey who by courage, and some miraculous twist of fate, escape their predators. But she was not sure if her evolution had entirely eliminated the old lady cat video specter. Oddly she had been lately attracted to instant karma ones, mostly from Brazil, where robbers get their comeuppance and maybe more from potential victims who were both aware of their surroundings and armed.) Both men were appalled at the lion story, however, and flatly disagreed that the lion-gazelle calf duo could have possibly happened. After spending far too long on a subject that had been inspired by Eunice's attempt at small talk, the conversation finally waned, but by then Eunice was not quite sure she had viewed the video correctly. Perhaps the lion mother was not hungry and had adopted the baby for a later snack…though it had died, uneaten, and the video ended with the lion walking sadly off into the open savannah. At that point, according to the bowel deep over voice, the viewing audience was informed that the lion mother had lost a baby cub of her own recently.

Later, settled down in their seats, Eunice dug out her Jane Austin, and Jerome took his stack of medical journals from his carry-on. "Please fasten your seat belts," the flight attendant frowned as she whisked by them. Soon, another attendant began explaining, in that perky voice intended to disguise sinister implications, the life-saving apparatuses and emergency exits, and that their arrival at JFK was 3:05 and they would be flying an average altitude of sixteen thousand feet. Eunice opened Jane. *"Mr. Elliot!" repeated Anne, looking up surprised. A moment's reflection shewed her the mistake she had been under.*

It was a short but not unexciting flight. Midway through, a flight attendant came on the system and said, a slight rise in her voice, "Excuse me. One of our passengers has taken ill. If there is a doctor on board, could you please press the call button."

Jerome turned a page and smoothed it to make it lie flat.

Eunice looked at him, waiting for him to move. Maybe he had not heard. "Aren't you—"

"No," said Jerome without taking his eyes off, Eunice's glance revealed, 'Effects of Aspirin for Primary Prevention in Persons with Diabetes Mellitus.'

"But—"

"He will be ok. Or she."

"How do you know?" Eunice could see attendants

clustered around a seat several rows down, and another hurrying from the cockpit area with a hard-plastic case. Then, amid muffled groans, "Stand back!"

After what seemed like several minutes, Jerome looked up, but only as if he were annoyed with her eyes boring into him, and said, "I know I don't want an emergency landing, do you? How about an unscheduled stop in Charlotte with a Best Western voucher? Do you? I think not."

Jerome turned the page as delicately as if it were a rare antiquated first edition folio. "And practically speaking, I do not want to get sued for legal consent issues."

Eunice wouldn't have thought he could get more practical than the emergency landing litany. But he had.

It appears Jerome's all-suffering response had been quite appropriate when, so long ago, Eunice had asked if his family would mind if he were dating a non-Chinese. Collin, Jerome's brother, and father of the bride, was married to Janice, a tawny blonde woman who ran her own string of boutiques. Michelle was married to a surly realtor from Brooklyn, Matthew, who was making a fortune, Collin teased, in Airbnb with a number of brownstones. Both Dianne and Jerome were divorced from Chinese spouses. Travel *was* broadening.

"This isn't ancient China, Eunice. You need to come into the 21st century."

Sometimes Eunice wondered if Jerome's mock exasperated voice was really mock.

Now, Eunice felt a tad defensive, because Jerome had refused to discuss his family at all, and she had come empty handed, knowing nothing about anyone. How can you sleep with someone, share the deepest intimacy of intimacies, yet asking the birth order of someone's siblings turned out to be a huge *faux pas*? Jerome had stiffened, before laying down his Scrabble piece, with what for him was almost a flourish, to make "xi" and also "hypoxias" on a double point box.

"You will have to ask them," he said icily, toting up his points.

Eunice was reminded of their conversation when she heard Collin tell the story of how Janice had mined him for information about his family and by the time she met them, she knew their life histories, their tastes, their hobbies, even their favorite foods. "They loved her the first meeting!" Collin crowed.

Collin had the distinction of appearing on *Jeopardy* many years ago before the children. He was a hair's breadth away from winning $56K when he was stumped by "Civil War general who was recruited from the West and became Lincoln's favorite."

They were sitting amid family and guests, most of whom seemed to have a goodly number of hyperactive children, on Collin's and Janice's patio, and for the festivities, the converted driveway, and four-car garage, were alive with twinkling lights. The backyard sloped by way of stone slab steps that led down to the lake and the swimming area, and that part of the landscape where the wedding will take place. Craning, Eunice can make out from her vantage point the suspended stone dock for fishing and the waterfall that flowed over large natural-stone boulders. Eunice was told a small grotto had been created so swimmers could sit beneath the cascading water. The whole area was cordoned off while the wedding planners set up the arbor, chairs, banners, and ribbons. The flowers will come tomorrow.

"What did you guess, Collin? Your Jeopardy question?" Dianne was telling the story and now pressed Collin, engrossed in another conversation, for detail.

"I guessed Sherman," said Collin, turning, with a self-deprecating laugh. He mimicked his youthful voice. "Who is William Tecumseh Sherman? It was, who is Ulysses S. Grant. Lordy. I'll never forget that."

Like *hypoxias*, which turned out to mean oxygen deficiencies. Jerome even had an *s*. Eunice had learned never to challenge Jerome in Scrabble. And she will remember that definition forever, too.

Then Diane shot an exasperated look in the direction of Jerome. "What is wrong with you? You didn't tell Eunice I am a teacher and working on a doctorate? She has finished a doctorate. Hello? She is *also* a professor."

Jerome shrugged. Eunice could have guessed he would say that.

Collin gave Eunice a mock resigned glance. "Sometimes we think he is Chinese," he said.

Beside Collin sat Daniel, the oldest of the siblings, Eunice surmised, and the only one at the table who did not laugh at Collin's joke. He was an elderly bachelor, still working, and, she had learned over the course of the evening, was one of the inventors of public key cryptography and cryptographic hashing, and in his field a semi-famous researcher, if not a speaker, on molecular nano-something. Eunice couldn't help observing the cryptographer puzzling over one of the little boy's Transformers, turning it around and around in search of that elusive first step in getting it from robot to cop car. Eunice recognized one of the Decepticons. Her sister had three boys.

"Need help, Daniel?" Matthew said, a tad sarcastically.

It appeared all the siblings had attended NYU, except Jerome, who had gone to Columbia. Dianne, the professor, and Michelle, the film maker, who had an advanced degree, had none of Jerome's reticence when sharing at least educational background. Dianne was having trouble finishing her dissertation. She suspected her committee was ageist.

Collin, who ran a private prep school, was turning back around to resume a conversation with Matthew, who appeared minimally interested. "As I was saying, when, in high school, are you taught differential equations?"

Over the heads, Eunice could see Aaron, surrounded by his cousins and Uncle Jiao who was pumping his hand. Aaron had just arrived from a day of late flights. Jerome who had seen him pull up in the taxi, was getting up, and motioned to Eunice to stay put. He made his way through the crowd to his son. They shook hands.

Uncle Jiao was not a real member of the family. He was 92 and once married to a first cousin of the Lui's, whom he had outlived, but had been so fond of Lui family celebrations, the Lui's continued to invite him, and he continued to come.

Eunice got up then from the table too and moved to one of the little bars where Michelle and a small group of women were standing, as if posted, and ordered another martini.

"Lisa," Michelle caught the arm of the bride who was zooming by. "Uncle Jiao told me you should be wearing, correctly, a red wedding dress tomorrow. You know, for fertility?" The women giggled.

Lisa patted her aunt's arm. "Thanks for helping me pack. Mom is overloaded. OMG! You reminded me," she stage-whispered, "did I pack my Pills," then zoomed off again.

Eunice sat down again and allowed the talk to flow around her. The air was soft and cooler now, and a wind had sprung up. There were some concerns about the earlier rain showers, and the effects on the venue for the outdoor wedding.

Matthew, beside Eunice and across the table from his wife, had lapsed into gloomy silence. Differential equations seemed to have run its course.

Collin was imitating Lisa to his guests, "The only thing I've ever wished for, Daddy, was an outdoor wedding by the lake."

Janice said, "She forgot to wish, no rain." Janice seemed nice enough. She asked Eunice about the vicissitudes of teaching and lightly lamented her unused degree in early childhood education.

Michelle was looking at Eunice, speculatively. "Are you in literature?"

"Not quite," said Eunice. "Composition and rhetoric."

"Where did you graduate?"

"I graduated from Vanderbilt."

"Ah, Vanderbilt." Michelle's tone was neutral. She smiled remotely at Eunice over the top of her champagne glass.

"How exciting you are in film. What are you working on now?"

"A doc. A documentary. Rather pedestrian but pays well. A kind of how-to for a hospital."

Eunice was surprised. She would have guessed something more exciting.

Then Eunice made one of the biggest *faux pas* in her life. "Did you ever see *The Joy Luck Club*? It's one of my favorite old movies though I thought the book was much nicer."

There was an explosion of laughter from the table, even from Dianne, whom Eunice had warmed to over her dissertation woes.

Michelle laughed, "Well, that was quite a segue from documentaries to Amy Tan but since you ask, we all hated it." There was a kind of a slight pitying incomprehension to her tone.

"Why?" said Eunice, with an awful feeling caused by her transition gaffe, and the certainty Michelle was going to tell her exactly why hate was in order. Jerome complained about her penchant for using weak segues or none. It must be another one of those many gravely significant social conventions Eunice had missed learning…the ones she was always making. Her actual worst was at a dimly lit Japanese restaurant the time she bit into what she thought was some kind of egg roll in a white rice wrap, and it turned out to be a rolled up warm cloth for wiping the face and fingers.

"What's bad is the negative Chinese male characters and stereotypes the movie portrays," said Michelle with a genial smile but palpable disbelief in her tone that anyone could be so clueless as to miss obvious sexually charged cues.

"Good grief," said Matthew. "Are people still talking about that movie?"

Others around the table began to call out helpful explanations:

"Quite one-dimensional!"

"Women trying to free themselves from Chinese oppression—"

"—and reconcile with mainstream Western culture!"

"It's the husbands that are sick! A rapist, an adulterer, and a heartless cheapskate!"

"What about the China Dolls and the Gangstas?"

"What is this movie about? I haven't seen it."

"It's about Chinese females being beautiful and good and screwed over."

"And Chinese males being jerks."

"And white males being perfect."

"After thirty years in the States the stereotypical old moms are still speaking broken English!"

Some faces just looked struck by a lack of suitable epithet.

The filmmaker in Michelle asserted itself. "On the other hand," she laughed with mock bitterness, "you don't want to know how much it grossed. Instead of violins, buy your kid a video camera."

Eunice finally seemed to be learning about Jerome's family. "What about *Crazy Rich Asians*?" she asked timidly.

Much later, back in their room, in the charming lake side inn where the out-of-town guests, and even some of the in-town ones, were staying, Eunice said, "Why didn't you tell me Dianne was a teacher, like me?" Tomorrow a specially hired wedding bus will pick everyone up and drive them back to Collin's house where the wedding will kick off, and where, hopefully, at least a few women will be wearing black.

"You didn't care," said Jerome. He was polishing one of his wingtips for tomorrow with the hotel's little shoeshine kit buffing cloth. He loved free things. He puffed on it. "You didn't care until Dianne brought it up. She is the one who attached a monumental significance to it, not you. It seems a small matter. Obviously, my sister has nothing of substance to talk about if that is all she can dreg up. A woman that age working on her doctorate! What is she thinking? She will be retiring soon. It does not make sense."

"I like Dianne." Eunice was not all sure why she felt defensive, but she did. Or what her liking Dianne had to do with the issue. In addition to weak segues Jerome despised *non sequiturs*. Again, the shrug. A shrug is worth a thousand words, to Jerome. It meant *non sequiturs* are *verboten*. Not worth addressing. But what language was he speaking?

Suddenly, Eunice felt foolish in her satin teal peignoir set and her recently acquired Victoria's Secret Faux Boa Feather boudoir slippers she had packed in lieu of her old comfy mules that resembled, as Jerome had pointed out, dead rabbits.

Even she wondered where her next sentence came from: "I'm tired of using condoms," she said, and felt herself draw a deep breath, which was oddly painful. "We should know each other well enough by now. If you are so worried about STDs, then we can both have tests. We are monogamous, right?" And boldly, "We are long term, right?" She fleetingly thought of adding, and why do you make love to me but never kiss me, but she forbore.

Jerome stared at her. Even the unblinking eyes were the same. But her mother abhorred silence.

"It's not that." Jerome put down one wingtip and picked up the other. He looked at it appraisingly but did not resume his buffing. "It's something about me."

"Well, what?" A series of *maybes* hit Eunice. Maybe Jerome was so terrified of an accident he did not trust her birth control regime, or her. Maybe he thought she was ditzy. Or an entrapper. Or maybe testing and its resultant freedom would make them too close, too much like marriage. Or maybe, Eunice thought darkly and farfetchedly, it was some cultural idiosyncrasy, race snobbery, some kind of play of signifiers. One has sex, really, in the head, she'd read. What Jerome was doing with his symbolic wall was holding out for some other woman, more his intellect, an orphan with no animal companions. Who did not give a rip about sibling birth order and was interested in neither his dark nor trivial family secrets. But who was, most of all, Chinese.

Then Jerome said, ordinarily, "I already have an STD. The condoms are for you."

Long past midnight, Eunice sat at a computer in the lobby of one of the top 50 midsized hotels in the Hamptons, according to Zagat. She was wearing a raincoat over her peignoir like some weary, distracted female flasher, and while Jerome lay upstairs sleeping, typed a question into Google:

Should a man inform a woman he has an STD if he always wears a condom? So far, her efforts have been fruitless. It is as though no one else in the history of the Internet had ever had this particular problem. She does get some related hits: "STDs You Can Get While Using a Condom;" "When a Guy Doesn't Want to Wear a Condom;" "Should I Tell My Friend That Her Boyfriend Has an STD?" and one particularly fascinating, "How to Check If Your Husband Has Had Sex While He Was Out." She didn't peek at that one, but made a mental note for her sister, Martha, an RN, married to a congressman with five children, the Duggar branch of the family, in case it was ever an issue. As far as intel on unreported STDs and fair play? Zilch.

Then, in her mind, like a crazy person, she heard a voice. Martha's. Martha, even as a figment, was never one to stifle her opinions, much like their mother, but was kind about them and mostly only voiced them PRN, rather than nonstop.

Doesn't it strike you as strange, what you are doing now?

Eunice had to admit it was.

Martha believed Eunice had self-esteem issues. She had short listed the worst of Eunice's incriminating behavior:

1. Eunice gave up a PHD degree in mass communications with only 3 credit hours and the dissertation to go, because she felt obligated to come home to take care of her father who was dying of cancer and,

2. Eunice did not come home so much take care of her father but to protect him from her mother.

3. Eunice never finished her PhD in mass communications because after three years of bed pans, flying trips to the emergency room, and doctor consultations she did not want to communicate with anyone. Not a good reason.

4. Eunice mistakes manipulation for caring and chooses the type of men to support her illusion.

5. Eunice uses food for antidepressants.

Eunice did not put too much stock in Martha's list. She also felt a tad resentful Martha did not appreciate the fact that Eunice was for three years, as acknowledged by the final hospice situation medical personnel, The One. The One is the one who runs interference for the sick parent; The One is the one who insists on additional pain medications and on a Sunday, after pharmacy hours; The One is the one who tries to fix what she can; The One is the one who is holding the dying hand at the bitter end. Martha doesn't know (Eunice doesn't like to stir up the past) that her mother, despite the fact she came on at times like a Sherman tank, was useless in a crisis.

After the funeral, Eunice started all over with a new major, composition and rhetoric. During the years of taking care of her father she realized her own field of study, mass communications, terrified her. One of the reasons she had taken it on was that she thought somehow it would teach her how to communicate more fluidly. But there were other styles of communication much safer that did not involve addressing large segments of the population. Eunice has voluminous journals languishing in a secret place in the detached garage at home, written during her previous incarceration, when she found she had, if not a knack, a fondness for writing. (Much later, living with her mother again, she put a lid on the writing thing. It seemed dangerous. And after her father's death, her mother had become even more snoopy.) Her credit hours were elderly anyway, and she went back to Vanderbilt for a fresh start, stripped of most of her major credits, almost as a 28-year old freshman, and completely as a 28-year old virgin, a condition she mercifully discarded with her married composition theory professor her second year. As for number four of Martha's speculations about Eunice's choice of men, half of them, one of two, in all fairness to Eunice, did not represent a random selection from the general population of available men. Eunice had merely entered that relationship as a dalliance with the composition professor (why should he have a name?) but got hooked by the way he listened so intently. As for Jerome, Martha had only clapped eyes on him one time.

Martha's list also did not consider extenuating circumstances. She did not believe that when Eunice, at puberty, ballooned from 120 to 150 pounds that that phenomenon represented an insurmountable obstacle to a sex life, but was simply a matter of not trying. Martha believed 28-year old virgins were walking freak shows. The average age for losing one's virginity was 17 she had informed Eunice, oblivious to how it felt to be lethargic and lumpy and scared. The problem was, for a long time, even down to 118 eventually, Eunice still felt lethargic, lumpy, and scared.

The theory professor had a talent for making Eunice also

feel anxious, rejected, and stupid. Eunice had realized listening intently was his way to get ammunition. She finally broke up with him, or maybe he with her—it was all so confusing—when, on the advice of Martha, she had asserted her needs with confidence and clarity.

True, Eunice was a slow emotional learner. She did learn one thing during the years of her father's dying, and it was the one thing that allowed her to live in her childhood home with her mother: you can be a sponge, or you can be a mirror. Mirrors reflect the pain back to its proper owner. But where was her mirror reflecting self now? Determine your reality and stick to it, as Martha said. Now Eunice pictured Jerome, expressionless, with his unregenerate snobbery, standing in front of her. The devil in her made her put him half dressed in a Stanley Kowalski old man t-shirt. She addressed him: You feel I am too sensitive when you rebuff my interest in your family? You feel I am too demanding when I need to know you have an STD which could (coming from her new-found Googling) be transmitted to me despite those odious petroleum-based condoms? You see me as needy because Mr. Peepers died, and I needed something from you, just one thing from you?

Of course, silence.

At night the water looked broad and lazy. Eunice, wide-eyed, trying to trick sleepiness to come by playing hard to get, sat on one of the stone benches wedged up to the retaining wall at the breakwater, where in the darkness, the shore trees thrust themselves up into the night sky like those in Picasso's painting, but there were no stars. She glanced at the second floor, where Jerome, oblivious to her secret heart, was sleeping, probably soundly. It occurred to her that Jerome was depressed. All men are depressed, Martha said once. They just don't know it.

Eunice was depressed, and she knew it.

Some faint splash of a mysterious aquatic creature drew her eyes back to the waterscape, liquid and sky. In the dog days of August, the cloud shadowed moon looked wintry. Then a completely unexpected thing happened. She began to feel tears course down her cheeks. She had so forgotten how that felt her first thought was that she'd been suddenly bombed by mass tree pollen allergens. The waterworks were almost as startling as a voice coming out of the darkness.

"What are you doing here in the middle of the night?" Moving into the lamplight, Matthew, Michelle's churlish husband, appeared, the one who had sat alongside her at dinner, dismal and taciturn, for most of the evening.

Luckily it was dark enough he seemed to have noticed nothing. The last thing she needed was for her to be ratted out for sitting by the lake in the middle of the night, crying. She rubbed one cheek surreptitiously. Then the other.

"Good evening, again, Matthew." She was stumped for words. What did one say to someone after the witching hour beside a lake who had ignored her all through dinner and after one had discovered this someone's brother-in-law was a withholder of the truth and a sexual liability?

At dinner Matthew had sat on her left, Jerome on her right, and rebuffed her attempts at small talk, until she gave up and resigned herself to her position between two pillars of silence. (Luckily Eunice had not completely lost her old habit of being able to entertain herself with food. And soothe herself. *Maybe there was some truth in number five*. And food it was. If this were the meet-and-greet fare, what would the wedding supper be? she had thought greedily. There appeared a seafood salad of shrimp, calamari, scungilli, octopus, and mussels with lemon and olive oil; a main course of salmon (or steak depending on your checkmark) broiled and seasoned with breadcrumbs, garlic, lemon, and butter. For desserts a Lazy Susan spun exquisitely, with individual plates of fresh figs, not to mention the fancy cakes, and tarts, and macaroons towards which she had lingered on, but eschewed. She was not completely crazy. Finally, after one last piece of brioche she came up for air, stunned. If she had been alone, she would have had to have a designated driver back to the hotel.)

"I was kicked out. Were you, too?" He seemed to be a little more sober now than when she had seen him last, at least moving under his own power. Before she could imagine a reply, he said, "Why *are* you here anyway?"

At dinner, after a few drinks, Matthew had perked up, and began a kind of insider's joky banter with a mild, but sharp-eyed IBM accountant, Mr. Wong, who had once played golf with Tiger Woods' father. Later, she saw Matthew being dragged into the hotel, Michelle and Aaron supporting him under each arm. Jerome said not a word about it.

"I couldn't sleep?" she said, and realized she sounded as

though she were guessing.

"No, I mean, why are you here at all with old tight ass Jerome?"

"I should go," Eunice said. Apparently, he was still drunk. But before she could move, Matthew said, "Do you mind?" and bent down, blocking her on the way up, so that she could briefly see the top of his head with its bald spot like a vanilla wafer, and plunked down beside her.

"Don't go. I'm depressed," he said a little sulkily, and as though that should be enough motivation for her to stay. He moved over a few inches as if he were aware he might scare her away.

"As for me, I'll tell you why *I* am here." He paused briefly, seemingly waiting for Eunice to enquire.

Eunice could not think of any rule of etiquette that covered this situation.

"I am tired of loving a little porcupine. That's what she is you know. Oh, she looks gorgeous and smart and funny and you just want to grab and hug her, but when you try to get close to her--ouch. Porcupine. So, I have come out into the night. To contemplate my fate."

Eunice refrained from saying, I thought you got kicked out, though she could relate to the porcupine trope a little. Jerome often reminded her of an armadillo. But the last thing she wanted to do now was exchange animal metaphors. And the last thing she would have thought was that Michelle, anorexically slim and pre-emptively indignant, by any stretch of the imagination, looked huggable. Eunice would bet if there were any Tiger Moms in the crowd, Michelle would come the closest. Two kids in law school and one in med didn't just happen.

"I must go. It's late." She stood up.

"Not anymore. It's early now. Just tell me. Why are you with that pompous ass?"

"I beg your pardon?" The first insult she could pretend she didn't hear. It was after all a drunk speaking. And though that was precisely what she had been thinking all evening, to hear it a second time coming from someone else's mouth was disconcerting.

"How do you put up with it all? The silence? The lack of touchy-touchy? Does he ever compliment you? Does he ever say I love you? Just one time? Does he ever talk? He sat beside you all evening and didn't say one word to you."

"Neither did you." This was past rude and annoying.

"Hel-LO? I just got through saying I am depressed. Ok, why were you crying a few minutes ago?"

By now she should have been used to aggressive realism and be able to dish out some herself. The most she could manage was hopefully a haughty tone. "I wasn't crying. I have allergies. And as for Jerome, true he is a bit quiet. He is just Chinese. It's genes and conditioning, of which he has no control. Cultural differences."

"I beg your pardon?" Matthew leaned forward and turned an ear toward her mockishly as though he were deaf.

"You should know," Eunice was getting even more depressed. "A Peking University sociologist Xia Xueluan says that Chinese are not good at expressing positive emotions. In Chinese society, discussing any emotions is often considered irrelevant and meaningless."

"Chinese society? Jerome is from Long Island."

"He's almost first generation." Eunice said stiffly.

"Coming to America when you are three months old is not first generation."

"People are often unaware of how cultural ideas and practices shape emotions," said Eunice, with a little stab of panic.

"Well!" Matthew laughed. "Aren't we the little southern racist!"

"No, no." Eunice was flustered now. "There are actual studies…" her voice trailed off.

"Where did you find them?"

"I Googled them." Eunice felt her face burn. Such an awful man!

"You mean, in order to know what's up with other people's motivations, you have to… Google? Isn't that a little iffy?"

Matthew continued in his mirthful tone, "If you could see my face in the dark you would see genuine wonder. You think that's why those two, peas in a pod, are so cold? That's what keeps you going? What about All-American Collin? What about Dianne? She hugs complete strangers. It's our two ducks. And it ain't 'cause they are Chinese. It's because they're cold asses. My first wife was the same way. And she was one of those southern belles, southern, like you, honey chile."

"What about Daniel?" she said, inadvertently mimicking his anaphora. Daniel was the height of wall-offed emotions. But Matthew was right about one thing. In order to swallow what was bothering her, she was good at Googling explanations. She had always thought of it as objectivity though. Or open mindedness. Or survival. Oh, who was she kidding? If she were standing, her knees would have gone weak. Then Martha piped up: *Out of the mouths of drunks…*

"Daniel has Asperger's or something. Or he's just a weird genius. And he's so loaded and almost famous he can be anything he wants. Daniel could be Daniel if he were Prince of Wales."

Then Matthew pretended to be speaking, falsetto, to an invisible person. "Didn't you know your boyfriend was a jerk? Why, no, I thought he was just Chinese. That's rich! Wait, don't go."

Eunice had shot up and stood gazing away from him down the darkened lane with its uniform prefabricated cobbles. She felt shaky, crushed, and nettled if all those things could be present at once. She had an urge to go and find and eat every lost pastry on the Lazy Susan that had orbited by her that she had so foolishly ignored at dinner. Then a spark of Martha's DNA flashed in her, an urge to insult Matthew, or more rightly like Martha, to say something cogent and undeniable, but before anything came to her stunned mind, he said,

"I'm sorry. You looked like you needed saving. And I do, too. Twenty-five years, for me. Twenty-five years and not one *wǒ ài nǐ*."

He touched her arm, and Eunice bolted, her Victoria's Secret boudoir slippers slapping and sliding dangerously over the fake cobbles.

"How long will you be in Guiyang?" Michelle leaned over the aisle in the wedding bus filled with guests and addressed Jerome. Luckily, Matthew sat in the front, directly behind the driver, leaning forward, delivering directions.

Tomorrow, while the honeymooners were white water rafting in Colorado, a smaller rented van will take the immediate Lui family to West Egg, through Great Gatsby country, to the ancestral graves of their parents where they will pay their respects. And the next evening to a Broadway play. It would be a week's togetherness for the Lui family.

"I'm staying a month this trip," Jerome said, obviously having forbore to mention his extended plans to Eunice. Eunice smiled kindly at both the siblings. It was more polite than strangling them.

On her left, next to the window, Daniel had his face pressed to the glass. Eunice kept thinking she heard Daniel speak from time to time.

"Excuse me?" Eunice said finally. "Did you say something?"

"No." he said. "I was just reading signs."

A few minutes later, "Grindstone Coffee and Donuts."

"Motus Crossfit."

"Bike to Work August 2."

And even more softly, "New York State Experience. Taste It."

It was not near sundown, but right before her eyes, maybe because she had missed an entire night's sleep, the wedding party and guests seemed to morph into one huge mosaic. Or more closely, a salad… of Chinese, black, white, young, old, ancient, thin, obese, genius, Asperger's, toddlers, babies…the women dressed to the nines in black dinner dresses, and red gowns, and some as floral as her mother would have chosen. The men in Armani suits, and the Village artists in jeans, and the Episcopal priest in her chasuble. The groom sprung from mixed union, Irish Catholic and Jewish, and the bride from Chinese and WASP, and the happy couple themselves, harbored New York Yankee and Baltimore Oriole propensities, and the best man was a woman, and the maid of honor was a couple, and lesbian. Though she was the stranger, the only southerner, oddly, most of the kaleidoscope of faces looked benignly familiar. Maybe no one was a mystery. Maybe they were all just mere five-sensory humans powered by hard-knock experience that could not be Googled, processed, expanded, nor studied to form a substitute for instinct. The rain had backed off, the ground was spongy, the women's heels sinking into the turf, but the guests were all there, which for some reason reminded Eunice of the word *persistence*.

It was after five, the magic hour for heeding fashion advice, and the sun was still holding its own, as if inviting a last few minutes for basking. She knew that when she got home most things would be the same, the balled-up sock under her bed, the photographs on the baby grand, the curtains raised to a certain permanent height, the barely melted college loans… except for her journals and their rightfully earned realizations, unhonored up to now, pleading to be pulled from the fire, and evidence enough that a conglomeration of feelings and desires known as a Eunice Lynch was, after all, existent. And she knew, in the early morning, hours before daylight, she would catch a cab to the airport with her mad money, the one ancient rite from her mother's rule book she cared to keep.

One Day in The Life of a Former Good Ole Gal

At ten-thirty it was still so light on Regent Street that they could have read the *London Times* if they had wanted to. June looked at Havi's khaki trousers, woven leather sandals, and the open-throated, brooding blue silk shirt he had exchanged for the black suit and chauffeur's cap he'd worn all that day driving the Harcourt Holiday Global Tour bus around London. To June the crisp folds of his collar against his ebony throat seemed extraordinarily splendid. She suppressed a brief image of her husband Matt back home in Starksville, Mississippi, and the L. L. Bean catalogue clothes he had recently started buying, and the low-beam smile he'd worn as he waved good-bye to her yesterday at the Jackson airport. She was here to enjoy the moment.

June was also in London to have a holiday from her job at the Mississippi Power and Light Company and something her mother called *nerves* and Matt called *existential free-floating anxiety*. Just plain *fed-up* was what June called it—of the power and light company customers, of the same old everyday people at work, but especially of that group of folks she called the New People. The New People were the ones Matt liked to hang out with now that he had finished his doctoral degree and gotten a job teaching at Mississippi State. His favorite pastime had become drinking wine on the New People's polished hardwood floors between their woven art deco rugs and their sparse artsy furniture and talking shop.

If June has learned anything from Matt's recently completed Ph.D. in psychology, it was that not sharing feelings was considered maladjusted and if she prefaced her words with "I feel" Matt would listen to anything. He would also agree to almost anything including a vacation away from him and his friends, who were, at this moment probably drinking wine in their very own living room among the Early American and discussing other people's business in terms that June has found increasingly bothersome.

June had not been in London two hours before she had decided that the tour guide and driver of the Harcourt Holiday Global Tour minibus was the most interesting person she'd met in a long time. It wasn't just his accent, but the words he chose, the ones that no matter what seriousness he was explaining, seemed to make everything funny. She had asked him out after hours.

Now, sitting across from him later at Garfunkels, over coffee, June looked at the dark, fine hairs on Havi's arm, sighed, and told him that she was married.

"Aei-Aei. What sorrowful tidings," he said politely, and reached over and took her hand. "But you are most brave in venturing so far from home."

June hardly thought trekking around London in the red-and-green van with the tour group of elderly tourists she'd accidentally drawn for companions constituted bravery. Right now, she had heard more about gall bladder operations than she'd ever wanted to know. This was not quite what she'd had in mind when she had planned her separate vacation from Matt. But she had to laugh inwardly at Havi's response, permitting herself a smile as she gazed at a photograph, framed, hanging over his head. It looked like a picture of San Francisco's Chinatown.

"That is Soho." said Havi.

"It looks like Chinatown in San Francisco."

"It is often the delight of many tourists to explore that area. The conditions are not pleasant sometimes, but always interesting. Would you care to join me tomorrow evening in order to become bar-hoppers?"

"Sounds lovely." said June. She lifted her coffee cup.

"I will apologize in advance for the state of my abject poverty and the subway which will advance us to our destination."

June laughed out loud at his words. It was such a change from all the emoting and sharing Matt had tried to get her to do lately. "Oh, no problem. Thank you, Havi. I would be pleased to see Soho by any means." A twinge of something shadowy seemed to flash in his eyes then and she hastened to say, "I wasn't laughing at you—the way you talk is delightful."

"Whatever so, I am most happy to please you," Havi took her

hand and kissed it gallantly. The smooth skin around his

clear eyes crinkled slightly. "Tomorrow will be my most greatest pleasure." "Say ten or so?"

Havi clasped her other hand and they stood up. Then he walked her all the way home, by way of Piccadilly, past the Royal Academy, the Museum of Mankind, the store where the Royal family bought their groceries, on down June's street finally to her hotel opposite the headquarters of Guinness Book of World Records, where at the foot of the stairs he kissed her good-night, almost unamourously.

Half of June's problems in her old life could be traced to the New People, who seemed to go out of their way to make her feel dumpy and ignorant, even though she knows with her measly degree from business school she makes more money than any of them do teaching. But the women in the New People are a study—all rail-thin and never minding showing off their brains. The men spark Matt to question everything under the sun including and especially the authenticity of things. Authenticity is fine with June. It has something to do with asking yourself is this situation really what I want to be doing and am I saying what I'm really feeling? Is this moment really real? June feels real enough all the time except when she is drinking wine on one of those hardwood floors and makes a fool out of herself asking things like what existentialism is. Her teachers in business school were more interested in paradoxes of assets, liabilities, and capital than paradoxes in reality.

But it was those very peculiarities in Matt and his friends that allowed her to act on her feelings and head to

London. June's mother had said she wished she could be a fly on the wall when June told Matt she was going to London without him, with a perfectly good husband and a four-year-old Clinton to be considered. June had to tell her mother that that fly would have been disappointed. Matt had said barely anything sitting at the kitchen table, an empty pie plate from which he had just relieved of half a remaining Speedy Apple Crumb Surprise in front of him. He had just studied the empty plate, squinted a little like he was sighting down a fence row to see if it were straight and true, and nodded.

When June asked her mother if she would help Matt out with Clinton while she went to London for a weekend, they had been on their way home from delivering a check to the Delta Memorial and Vault Company (their motto: Preserving the Memory of Your Loved One with Dignity—We Serve All Cemeteries). Her Uncle Harvey had died, and the consensus for his monument—they didn't call them tombstones any more her mother had learned there—was HE IS NOT DEAD, BUT SLEEPING, an epitaph which made June, who had declined to vote, imagine the owner lying all disheveled in restless snoring slumber under the mussy dirt.

June's mother pressed her lips and started talking about flies and decent husbands but agreed to help. She did have to mention that she thought this was a strange way to spend the nest egg Uncle Harvey had left all his nieces and nephews. But Fay thought the world of Matt, as she often said, who washed his dishes behind him and had changed diapers and had stayed home studying most of the time in the last two years. Secretly June knew that Matt didn't do a lot of things naturally but read things out of books and acted accordingly. They were called humanists, some of them, the people Matt read, and sometimes he read out loud the parts which had startled him, written by a man named Havelock Ellis—who especially had interesting ideas about women—or those two Carl Rogers and Eric Fromm. And even when Matt had been squinting at the Pyrex plate and apple crumbs, June knew he had been thinking now what would old Dr. So and So say.

Matt had been the first man June had brought home that Fay had ever liked. Fay had approved of Matt's quiet slow manner and the way he had sat at ease that evening and studied books on mental hygiene while she and June had chatted. Later she had approved of the way he had split the cost of the babysitter for their dates (he had seen that in *Psychology Today*) and even took care of Clinton while June had classes (Bruno Bettleheim, *Love Is Not Enough*). June doesn't know for sure but from her mother's attitude she suspects that her own father was some kind of faithless charmer and that, if he hadn't gotten sick and died, Fay would have had a much different life.

And that was how June had come to be standing inside the main terminal of the Atlanta airport yesterday waving good-bye to her pale husband, and to Fay, who wore a sprig of nasturtiums, and to Clinton, who had decided to bawl.

Later, much later, June opened the door to her hotel room. Her roommate, Rosemary, the one she had met on the plane, the one she had chatted with, had seen the sights with all day through Westminster, the Tower of London, Madame

Taussauds, was dead.

June knew that she was dead by the way she was lying crosswise on top of the bed at the wrong end with one of her gold harem slippers dug into the coverlet and the other foot, bare, lying limp off the bed. Her head, too, was precariously on the edge as if the weight of it was delicately balanced by the rest of her. One good stomp and it looked like she would fall.

June felt the whole room tremble and a whirring sound caught in her ear like once when she'd almost fainted carrying Clinton. Just to be sure it really was Rosemary's death taking her for this wild spinning flight through space and not some midnight hallucination she called out, "Rosemary, Rosemary!" and the sound of her own voice plunged her back to earth.

Taking every ounce of strength she owned, June walked across the room and put her hand on the pink robe and gave it a little shake. When nothing happened, she pulled back on the shoulder gently. And just like in the movies, Rosemary fell around easily, and her arm flopped over and brushed June's knee where she was kneeling on the bed, and then June believed it. What was hard for her to believe was how long it took her to turn around and walk back to the door, turn the knob, open it, and shout down the empty hall. Then it occurred to her to use the phone and she moved in quick, controlled steps and picked up the receiver, "Call a doctor," she said after the bored voice of the desk clerk had answered, "My roommate is—is very ill." Then on afterthought she added, just to make them get the lead out, "She's had a massive stroke." Then she hung up and stared at Rosemary. Moving her arm had put her in an even more fragile position.

She took a deep breath and grasped one of the hands and the other wrist and hefted. Rosemary slid more on the bed but in a horribly unnatural position as though her lower half was sitting, and her upper half had fainted.

Just then there was a faint tap on the door. June got up and opened it quickly. Havi stood in the hall. She put out her hand and drew him into the room.

"I heard by the desk—" he stopped. "Oh, dear me. This is a most bummer situation," he said, seeing Rosemary's prone body. "Is she...?"

"She's dead," said June. "If a doctor is coming, it will just be to affirm it, I'm afraid."

They stood staring at each other, then back at Rosemary. Havi moved and put his arm around her. "Are you quite well?"

"Yes, thank you." It occurred to her she had said that almost as if it were a question at the breakfast table. She tried to shake a feeling that seemed to be coming on as if she were a bystander who had stopped to watch in sort of ironic observation.

Finally, the cartoon noise of the ambulance drew them to the window. On the well-lit street five floors below, two people in white jumped out of a van lettered in bold red, Damage Control Unit. Their uniforms brought to June's mind the Good Humor man and his ice cream truck back home and she had a crazy desire to laugh just like she used to get in church when she was a child and for no other reason than she knew she couldn't.

Then after they had disappeared under them to come into

the building, a black car pulled up and a short, chubby man Havi surmised was the doctor hopped out and disappeared too.

Soon the room was full. The drivers, the doctor, two people from the hotel staff, a few guests, a policeman in his upside-down fire bucket helmet. After a while the doctor gave almost an indifferent nod to no one in particular and turned to June.

"You are the roommate?"

She nodded.

"Family?"

"No."

"Ah, well then. I'm afraid I have the worst news. She is deceased. You must sit down if you feel faint."

"I see," said June, but kept standing. She noticed that he had looked at his watch as he had said the word *deceased*. Now he reached for a little pad from his bag. He took out a pen from his lapel.

"She has suffered a fatal heart attack. Perhaps I may call on you in the morning to give you a more a complete report? My office is near here, and I may need more information from you for the files as well." The doctor began scribbling.

Then he hesitated and stopped his notetaking. "Would you like a mild sedative?" He looked at her curiously.

"No, thank you," she said. She felt Havi's hand on her arm and saw the doctor's glance at it. Then he shut his bag with a brusque click and nodded, this time at the ambulance people. And while Havi talked in low tones to the desk clerk and the policeman, June watched the Good Humor men zip Rosemary into a black plastic bag, not unlike the clothes kind hanging in her closet.

At about five in the morning Havi and June sat on her bed, sharing a cigarette. Looking over at him June couldn't help thinking of that evening walk: a giant man on stilts outside the Guinness building, the shop windows, the traffic hubbub, the kiss downstairs, and then together with Rosemary's gold slippers and the flop of her arm things began to mix up so that one thing led to another, and before she knew it, she was crying. She wasn't as strong as she'd thought. Even when she had gotten herself into trouble as the saying went— she always pictured her boyfriend J.T. standing innocently by while she spontaneously impregnated herself—she hadn't cried much.

Then she felt Havi's arm around her. Sighing, she reached over and began unbuttoning his shirt. She took the cigarette from his fingers and stubbed it out in Rosemary's denture cup. Still

blubbering, she undid his belt, his khaki chinos.

And it was only afterwards June realized that for at least a minute or two the dissatisfaction that had plagued her for the last few months had dissolved.

"I have made you unhappy, have I not?" Havi was asking anxiously. June loved the combination of his jet-black skin and perfect, to her ear, English accent, and the occasional surprising American slang. It amused her like Charley Chan's son used to at the movies. Then Havi said, "Do you wish me to fuck out?"

"Fuck *off*," she corrected him gently, caressing his lips with her finger. "And no, I do not wish you to fuck off." She put her hand on his back and smoothed his foreignness. "This is nice," she said. It was already day out. Between the tied-back curtain, rain was falling.

Havi rolled over and got a cigarette and offered her one with great courtesy. She shook her head.

"Was she a long friend of yours?" he asked.

For a second June had no earthly idea what Havi was talking about. Then she remembered Rosemary.

June tried to think of the last thing she had said to Rosemary. After visiting Madame Tussaud's, Rosemary had fallen asleep in the adjacent planetarium show, and then afterwards had said she had no appetite for dinner. June thought of the last time she had seen her alive, sitting on the edge of the bed dressed in her pink tricot robe and metallic gold harem slippers as June were getting ready for her date with Havi.

"But Honey, do you think this is smart?" she had asked in her deep Tallulah Bankhead voice caused, she had confided some time that day to June, by years of smoking before she had, as she put it, gotten her heart. She had stared at June curiously.

Privately, June had hoped not, and it was by that question something had twanged inside her, as though the question itself was the answer to what she had decided to look for when she left Matt and Clinton for a little while. It was also an answer to questions that she didn't know she was still wondering about. For instance, why would sometimes, looking at Clinton, J.T. the first date she ever had, who was once known as the wildest boy in Starksville and who had made her life a living hell, come floating to her mind? Or sometimes just anything, an old song on the radio driving home from the Power and Light, a young couple holding hands might send her, make her think at completely weird times, of him and his Chevy which had leaked brake fluid all over her mother's yard and the careless way he used to spin out of the old gravel driveway so long ago.

June thought of Rosemary and how different she had looked compared to her own mother, Fay. Rosemary had been tall and lower-keyed, dressed in her Rosalyn Carter clothes, with a history of such tours behind her since her husband had died. She spent much of the day comparing London to last year's Hawaii. Fay, June's mother, was short and wore flowered dresses from TG&Y and was a little too much in awe of Matt for June's comfort. But there had been something similar in Rosemary to Fay, some core that seemed to hang June between Matt's new friends and some old disappearing way of life.

Suddenly she had a thought. She got up so quickly Havi rose anxiously on one elbow. "You are unwell?"

She didn't answer but began plunging her hand under the mattress. Havi leapt out of bed as though he thought the strain had finally driven her crazy, but by then she'd found it. She pulled, and a thick, black plastic envelope came out.

Inside was two thousand dollars in American Express checks and thirteen hundred in pounds.

Havi gave her a penetrating look as June slowly put only

the checks back in their typically southern hiding place and sat down again holding the wad of pounds. She knew that if any respectable thief in Starksville, Mississippi had decided to rob her mother, or any of her aunts, except for Aunt Zelda who believed in freezers, that the first place he would look would be under the mattress. Not that any huge savings ever went into places like that anymore. The last people in her family to completely forgo banks was her great cousin twice removed, Florence, who belonged to that generation of people who still said "Amen" aloud in church and "Tell it, Preacher."

Then June looked into Havi's guileless brown eyes and was struck by their beauty and the sheer practicality of their fucking.

The next day had dawned on a foggy sky broken with shafts of sun. According to the guidebook, June and Havi have entered a fashionable Soho restaurant. They had parked the car June had rented that afternoon on a street lined with rows of brightly lit cafe-bars and fruit and grocery stalls, their multi-colored interiors flowing, their Chinese proprietor's face appearing below the hanging plucked ducks and above and beside the live bamboo-caged chickens. Twanging Chinese rock n' roll had followed their steps.

Inside the restaurant they were received by a smiling, bowing Chinese woman and after removing their shoes had been shown into a small, private room dimly lit with a huge spherical lantern. The walls seemed to be made of white paper. A shiny black table was in the middle of the room and they had scooted down on cushions and were being served by another Chinese woman wearing a red and gold kimono.

She brought in a bottle of wine first, and two glasses, then a thin soup with floating dumplings. June noticed that her made-up face was as impassive as a glass doll's. She bowed whenever she left the room. Once she returned with another woman and between them, they carried an enormous bowl of shrimp that Havi called prawns and that seemed more like small lobsters.

Havi's face flickered in the light of the converted oil lantern hanging over their heads. "You like?" Despite the fact that he'd spent the day touring Windsor Castle while June had recuperated from the night's events all morning, he did not look tired.

"Oh, yes. Very much." said June.

At three o'clock she had gathered all Rosemary's personal belongings and the checks and handed them over to an official from Lloyds of London, who had made and had her sign an itemized list. Then after only a little thought, she had visited a beauty salon called Slick! and had her hair styled in a startling new way, highlighted with green steaks, and during the Happy Hour Cut (after 17:30) for only 16.95. (She is not completely crazy.)

Havi was not eating but staring at her.

"Why are you looking at me so intently?" she said.

"I feel most evil for the rented American Dodge Dart." he said.

"Oh Havi. Relax. Let go. You don't know the meaning of evil, I'd guess."

"There are many things I don't know, true."

During this time their table was being laden with bowls of rice, sauces with limpid swimming things, chopsticks, and teapots. June reached for her wine glass. June closed her eyes for a second and grasped around in her mind for techniques she'd heard the New People discussing. Distraction, she remembered. Reinforcement. Refocus of the internal state. "Where," she said, calling upon B. F. Skinner's carrot, "can we go next for noise and wild dancing?"

Havi brightened at that. He was awfully young.

Then he scratched his chin with his little fingernail and said, "What I think I feel now is most strange."

"Tell me," said June.

"That you are most wise. That the first time I looked into your eyes I was already beginning to learn from you. I knew you were a most excellent mind. Kind eyes. Perhaps a teacher, and a teacher of more than books."

"Is that why you went out with me?"

"Yes, I thought here is someone I would like to talk to about anything."

"Why are you in London? Where is your family?"

"I have come to London to earn money. Also, to improve my English which was learned only a little successfully from the Union Carbide fat cats I chauffeured in Cairo, and from my brother, whose education was prematurely ended by my father, at Berkeley University."

"Where's your brother now?"

"He is in Cairo with my old job. He was to complete his education, then help me through. Unfortunately, my father had only money for one." Havi's eyes glittered, but not bitterly, and he laughed. He held out his glass to be refilled by a hand from one of the almost invisible kimonos and said, "My brother is most delightful and amusing. But an idler and a wastrel."

"What a shame." said June. "Isn't there any money left for you?"

"I am afraid the most to show for it," said Havi, "is a spectacular sound system and many Elvis cd's."

June laughed and sipped her sake.

"I like your laugh." said Havi. He reached over and touched her fingers. Something in his eyes seemed to give way. "There is a thing in you that is strong, like my father's Mohammedan faith—a thing I have given up, but most wise, most wise—even, I think, even about the money found in the hiding mattress."

"Oh Havi," she said. "I'm not wise. Just realistic. Or maybe reality-oriented," she added, thinking of the New People.

"And your thoughts for me? Do you have any realistic thoughts for me?"

June lay her hand on the khaki thigh. "I think," she said finally, "that I don't know anyone I'd rather be with right now."

Later they were packed into one of the five lines of their third bar. They had to wait, drinking and standing, until someone moved from a table. On one side was a group of Australians who were getting to know one another and who all seemed to be named Sheila and Bruce. The rest of the people around them seemed to be a mixture of Indians,

Orientals, and Americans, the latter group who seemed to be traveling in small herds.

"Mervin—wait. There's a line." An American voice, a woman's, rang over a lull. A couple who'd just arrived began to squeeze backwards to leave.

"Always a que in Britain," another voice said. It belonged to a tall, bearded Brit in a muscle shirt on her left. And then as if that recollection seemed to make him angry, he called after the couple, "Not like in America." Then he looked straight at June and drawled, "Raight, sweetheart?"

June felt called upon to shout back, even though it seemed, strangely, none of her business, "Yeah, they should have more lines in America. Make like Poland." (It was the sake talking, she thought later.)

"See—I told you she was an American," the beard bellowed to an unseen friend and gave her a conspiratory wink. Then he reached over and slapped Havi on the back. "I'll have to buy you both a drink, mate."

Havi reeled against the slap but kept his feet, unfortunately stumbling against one of the Australians. One of them turned and struck out at Havi's head and connected with one of the Brits on the arm, but not the one who had caused the accident. There were some hard pushing and scrambling before the real punches were thrown. A glass crashed. A scream balanced in the air. June ducked, pulling Havi down with her.

"You are a most remarkable woman," said Havi after they had crawled on their knees between legs and toppling bodies and stood up off their knees outside on the street.

Two bobbies passed them blowing their whistles as June unlocked the car and they slipped in.

Hours later, June Caldwell stood in Soho, the center of London's vice and prostitution, half in, half out of a phone booth. The reason she was in such an awkward position was that the inside smelled like pee and the interior of an old, dead thermos bottle and she had to keep drawing her head out and taking deep breaths of air.

Suddenly, Clinton yelled in her ear, It's Mama. It's Mama, and she said, Hello, Sweetheart and How's Mama's big boy? back to him, trying not to read handwritten advertisements taped on the wall in front of her, such as, "May Lee, Exotic Dancer." And "Golden Showers, Special Rates."

Then Matt got on the phone and he said, how are you and I can't wait to see you and don't forget to bring Clinton home something, that's all he's talking about, and why'd you forget to call? Oh, never mind, don't answer that.

Finally, Fay got on the phone and asked her (of all things) was it raining there and said they hadn't had a decent drop since before she left and to be careful coming home on the plane and weren't you supposed to call last night?

When June hung up, she stepped out and took a big breath of air and Havi, who had been waiting for her, straightened up and smiled fondly, "Your family is well?" He was wearing a new black leather jacket with brass studs and knee-high boots which they had bought just that morning at the world-famous outdoor market on Petticoat Lane.

June herself was wearing a short mini-skirt of black

leather, a fur-collared 1920's short waisted jacket and knee-high German field boots. She also had a red beret from which stuck a ridiculously long feather. Not for nothing had she listened to the dark side of that man Kierkegaard as a sort of How Not To manual, she'd reasoned sometime that morning.

Soon June will climb aboard the red-and-white van that Havi will drive to Victoria Station, then she'll get on to a train for Heathrow. "I love you." Havi said it finally.

June forgave him. In the morning light he looked a little thin and tired but there was a look in his eyes that was bright and calm.

"I have corrupted him," she thought, wishing she had a few more days in town.

Last night, drunk, they had driven the car together, Havi steering, June operating the gear shift, until breakfast at the Continental Bar and a walk down Petticoat Lane had cleared their heads. Now Havi will take them with care and alacrity to her bed in the Garden Court Hotel. In three hours, her vacation will be over.

Twelve hours later, in Jackson, Mississippi, June Caldwell grabbed her bag and swung it up on her shoulder. On the TWA airliner which has just returned her to her old life, she had changed clothes, leaving a pair of German field boots in the lavatory for some future startled flight attendant, and washed the green streaks out of her hair with a wet comb.

In the lobby of the Delta terminal, her feet touching U.S.A. soil, she caught sight of her family.

The three of them seemed to be standing in the same

position as when she left them, with the same expressions, only Matt's face broke with relief when he saw her, Fay started waving her hanky, and Clinton punched an innocent, well-dressed man in front of him and started screaming, "There's my mamma. There's my mamma."

Back in London Havi revved up the tour bus. He had just had a good nap devoid of any dreams. It was not a necessary thing, but a good thing.

Part II
Men Dealing with It

Carrying the Fight

After his retirement, Captain Fox awoke each morning to a taste in his mouth reminiscent of some foul-tasting medicine of his childhood and to vague, distressing memories of which he had no image. His room, his house, felt cold to him even in the heat of the summer. In the mornings, he woke tired because, during the night, he squirmed and tossed as noisy as a squirrel, and it had become his habit to wake at one o'clock sharp and, for a few hours, read by the bed lamp, smoking sweet, air-cloying cigars.

Then during the day, he took frequent naps in the living room, a few in the morning and a few more in the afternoon. In fact, he had become so attached to the comfortable, dusky-rose Herculon that he once asked to be served his lunch there. In this spot, he had a perfect view of almost all his wife's comings and goings, which for some reason, he found oddly comforting. But as the summer wore on, at times it began to come to him that his wife's usual absent-minded face seemed to have taken on an unfamiliar demeanor to which he could not give name.

She would pass him, in his repose, thin lips pinched even thinner, shoulder blades stretching tight an old polo shirt of their daughter's like the taunt wings of a bird poised for flight. She wore jeans, like a teen-ager, and even the old woman slippers (worn because of her arthritis) and the severe bowl-cut of her gray hair did not belie the youthful, annoying boyishness of her figure. The wrinkles in her face seemed no more in number than in any other year, but to him, they were suddenly, strangely threatening. Even the awful macramé belt which had taken hours of her life seemed a reproach to him, for him, for Captain Fox had nothing to do.

One day after a discussion over the correct amount of salt required for stew she had remarked in a low, startling voice: "I know how to make soup."

"What's that?" asked Captain Fox, for unpleasantries other than from his own mouth rarely registered in his brain easily, and he was a man given to obtuseness when under subtle attack.

"I said," Mrs. Fox remarked, and again Captain Fox was struck by the nameless demeanor of her face, but the word *calculating* which came to him struck him as absurd. "I said, I know how to make soup. I know how to load the dishwasher, too, for that matter. I know, how, for God's sake, to take a cake out of the oven."

"My dear," said Captain Fox, who, true, had been generous with his wisdom and advise over the summer, pulled his thin frame to a sitting position, "I cannot presume to know what you mean," and he rose, forbearingly, and left for the bathroom, to cajole his daily bowel movement into cooperation.

After Captain Fox's retirement his usual bathroom upstairs displeased him, and it became his method to occupy the downstairs half bath, entered directly from the foyer, and at times he even left the door open and sat on the commode as though it were a modest, ceramic throne, and delivered insights and stock reports.

His wife had never admired this room, situated as it was near the preparation of food and where every sound in it was magnified and carried as far as the kitchen stove. And for a quarter of a century this bathroom had sat tidy and unuseful. But now after breakfast when the steaming coffee had warmed his bowels to the point of readiness, Captain Fox folded the *Wall Street Journal* under his arm and walked through the foyer as if he were going to work. And as Mrs. Fox gently clinked the breakfast dishes back to a sort of cleanness, Captain Fox rustled his paper and smacked his lips, making old-man noises and farting wetly.

At night when he awoke at one or drifting in and out of his naps, events of the past as well as the present stirred his hazy thoughts and they seemed more real than when they had happened. He heard odd conversations in which he had been a participant and he reflected on the things he'd said and on what he might have said. A particular conversation recurred—the one before his son had left home for good. He had not seen Robert in over ten years but at times his face stood out as clearly as a billboard stretched across the room. He had been carrying this sorrow with him for more than a decade, for with all his careful nurturing and loving propaganda, the boy had grown up to own a motorcycle, vote Independent, and eschew academia and the military as institutionalized enemies. But what hurt him most, what left him lying breathless and awed at the farthest level that psychic pain could go, was that Robert was a draft dodger living at an unknown address in Canada, unrepentant and ungrateful of proffered amnesty. At times when he thought of this his bowels moved inside him, fiery and unrelenting. At other times he ruminated on his wife's familial genes and their possible influences on his son: her family had been Bostonians, artists, and horticulturists. Sometimes he was of two minds, for if he had sent his boy to be killed, he would be in just as much anguish now. Perhaps it was better that his son was nameless and lost rather than dead, or even worse. Captain Fox had been illustrious in his own military career and a stickler for duty and that in itself would soothe him a little during those sojourns into the past. In the military when one is issued an order, it is necessary and dutiful to proceed according to direction; however, Robert's political insights into the Vietnam police action had been startling and filled the Captain with unease, making his own reasoning sound blundering and hackneyed.

"You are like a born-again preacher, Father. How can you parrot the same old, worn-out phrases — Allegiance, Duty. Liberty and Justice — the twins of political perversion. They are meaningless in this situation. There is no war, no fight to prevent the spread of communism. It's slaughter for the politician's pocket."

At these words Captain Fox's stomach turned so that he felt as if he were standing on his head, with all the red-eye gravy he'd had for lunch pushing at the back of his throat. "Son," he said as calmly as he could muster, for if he spoke too harshly, Robert would turn stiffly and leave, banging the old solid-oak door with an unbearable finality, "where would we be now if the valiant soldiers of WW I and II had retained your attitude? I'll tell you where," and his voice had warmed at the ensuing words, "likely as not we would all be subject to Nazi rule. You would be clicking your heels and saluting, 'Heil, Whoever.' I have told you again and again how devastated I was when these old ears heard the announcement that memorable summer day in 1940. Hitler's Panzer divisions had already overrun France and the Low Countries and were looking at the Channel with a gleam in their eye. This had to be stopped. And certainly, the American people were called upon to do their part. And when they called, I went without a backward look."

As Captain Fox was about to launch into his speech of the Advanced Naval Intelligence that he had been personally asked to attend by the Director of Naval Intelligence, he paused for a breath, and Robert extended his hand in front of Captain Fox's face. He had not wanted to hear about his father, his Citadel scholarship, the Pacific Fleet, or George Baille, son of his friend, a Georgian senator, who had been killed on the Gibraltar-Casablanca convoy. He did not address the subject of VJ Day. He apparently did not want a condensed run-down of the Marshall Plan.

"Father," he said, "there is no one talking but you." And he had left.

There were other things too that stirred in his mind, some having nothing to do with Robert and now that he was retired and had enough time to think about them, they seemed like fresh and urgent problems. He had been passed over for a department head position in the college he'd devoted himself to. He who'd received personal congratulations from General Samuel Adrian Buckley, commander of the Tenth Army. One of his daughters had died before she was a year old, and during her illness his wife had pleaded him to consult a non-military physician. He had several unpublished manuscripts on the devastating effects of peace on the economy lying dusty and unaccepted in an old desk drawer. And once he'd failed a driving test. It seemed everything had gone downhill after he'd left the navy and sometimes even the events in his life that he was ashamed of and thought he had forgotten floated up from the depths of his mind: he'd cheated on his wife three times and once with a Non-Anglo Saxon; he 'd concealed from both his wife and his mother a certain Christmas bonus; and he had lent money to a relative at exorbitant interest and once had even lied under oath.

All these things came to his mind without warning, like the remembering of an unpleasant dream the night before; and as the slow, uncompromising days of the summer dragged by, he looked into a mirror and saw his narrow, disciplined face had given some slack and made his big, bulbous nose stick out like a fist. And sometimes, he often thought, his wife's face, too, seemed to adopt a lean and suspicious expression and her eyes would narrow and half close whenever he spoke.

It was those tiny, busy-body flies that caused him to be left in the lurch. Mrs. Fox's habit was to leave the kitchen door wide open as she unloaded the groceries from the car; and as the flies buzzed in, numerous and merry, the ones already in would almost certainly never buzz out. Captain Fox had directed her in unpacking and bulging packages, feeling noble and forbearing for not mentioning that the interior had been exposed for perhaps three minutes to the onslaught of insects. But when Mrs. Fox began to use the old-fashioned screen-wire swatter (for according to Captain Fox it was the best kind because they could not see it coming) to alleviate the kitchen of these pests, Captain Fox roused himself from his post on the couch and watched her movements. These flies were of a Southern variety: small, business-minded, kamikaze-type insects, not in the least like their larger languorous cousins, a minority in town, and who buzz heavily after their snacks.

"My dear," Captain Fox stirred from the depths of his rumination, his voice modest and magnanimous, as Mrs. Fox in an absent-minded fashion, tapped unfruitfully about the kitchen, her thoughts on other things. "One does not address the fly like a golf ball. Aim, and then deliver the death blow, keeping the forearm firm but supple like a tennis stroke. Moreover, aim slightly in front of the animal's anterior, for when they feel the imminent swish, they take off forward as well as upward, like this." And he demonstrated their take-off with one hand as he took the swatter from her with his other and promptly killed three with two blows, like Till Eulenspiegal.

Absorbed as he was in the vendetta against the flies, Captain Fox did not at first receive the full impact of Mrs. Fox's next words, but then his timing faltered and as he swatted, he turned in surprise, and one graced fly zoomed exuberantly upward. "Do not think," she said coldly and loudly, "that I will remain another second in your presence," and she strode out of the kitchen.

"But where are you going?" He called uselessly, his words floating fearfully, even to him.

"Who are you calling?" he said softly, sitting suddenly on the bottom step, as he detected that the phone was being callously dialed.

"My dear," he began confusedly, after she had come down, and he had risen trailing her through the kitchen.

"I'm going," Mrs. Fox said distinctly. "I'm going to Constance." And in a matter of minutes, she was gloved and, on her way, to visit her sister who was living out her life, widowed and happy, in Jacksonville.

Now Captain Fox stood in the broad patterns of the evening shadows with the frozen foods becoming soggy in their containers and a milk carton glaring at him superiorly from the countertop. Already, he imagined a slight sour smell from the direction of the milk, but he only stroked his cheek in a confused fashion like someone who has missed the first part of a movie with a complex plot and wishes to get his money refunded. He thought of supper and at once could not remember what he had had for lunch or if he had had any lunch at all, and the result of his thought made his stomach growl and complain like a huge, hungry garbage compactor.

It was true, he had not had lunch, for Mrs. Fox was still not used to his being home at this time and often forgot him after suggesting several items which might be tempting to him but which he always declined at first saying, "I'll think of something a little later." For he had been like an old, finicky cat, and he only remembered what he wanted to eat after she had stopped asking. Now his hunger became a living thing, overpowering him and weakening him so suddenly that he was compelled to take deep, relaxing breaths. Ordinarily he had a nervous and mean stomach that would only occasionally tolerate fried or rich foods, but now he envisioned huge platters of heavily peppered catfish and white, billowy potatoes and new peas swimming in butter and cream. He almost heard the soft fizzle of frying chicken and he pictured his wife's crust, light and puffy and crispy golden. He wondered whether acute hunger could bring on a heart attack in a man his age. He moved desperately around, ignoring the sad groceries and when he could not find the mayonnaise, made a cheese sandwich with mustard. But the cheese was hard from lying unprotected in a loose wrapper and the bread, too, looked so suspicious and unappealing that he stood looking at it and a whimper rose in his throat and startled him. He did not know what to do.

As the days passed and the little house grew untidy and seemed to issue a disrespectful air from its very walls, Captain Fox began to make phone calls to his wife in Florida, upon one pretext or another, for he could not bring himself to ask when she was coming home or even why she left. "Where," he would inquire," is my old 1944 Navy annual, you know the one

General Buckley signed?" And of course, it was lying in its Saran Wrap in the packing case with all the others. "How long," he asked another time with a note of urgency in his voice, "is it prudent to leave chicken in the refrigerator before it is cooked?" "How much do we pay the gardener weekly?" he would ask, even though he could have just as well asked the gardener, long endeared to Captain Fox because of his impeccable honesty and hard work and who had been with them for over a decade. Across the miles on the other end of the invisible wire, his wife's voice sounded almost gay, if not distracted by some undisclosed pleasantries. And after they'd hung up, a heaviness would move through his heart and his eyes would warm and sting.

In the ensuing weeks, his insomnia plagued him, and his naps during the day became more frequent so that at times, on waking in a late afternoon, he did not know if it was morning or night. His whole life was askew. He lusted for his wife's cooking and his feeble attempts at recreating it left him anxious and almost as empty as before he had eaten. He searched the supermarkets for the dinner rolls that he loved — the kind with little round black seeds on the top that gave out a warm sour dough smell as they were cooking and the bottom crust which issued a buttery substance that practically fried itself to doneness. He thought of this bread at odd times during the day, but the grocery shelves rendered nothing, but Parkerhouse rolls, common sliced bread and buns. This bothered him greatly, for his appetite had suddenly come alive and insatiable, and he could hardly wait from one meal to the next. But his meals were unsatisfying and tasteless, and he began to live on great quantities of toast and honey. He saw himself neglected nutritionally and possibly failing in health.

Now it came to him that he needed new shoelaces, for the ones he had, had turned a faded black and the plastic aglets had long gone, and the business of the ends annoyed him beyond reason. He left early, after his early morning nap, to shop, and as he drove along, it occurred to him that he had not picked up the mail in the two weeks his wife had been away. This thought cheered him greatly, for he knew without doubt, that at least his *Legionnaires Magazine* would be there. At the door of the post office, he stopped and bought a newspaper, for suddenly he felt as if he were returning from a lost civilization, ignorant and starved for news. Before he folded the paper under his arm, he glanced at the headlines and realized that it was the 31st day of imprisonment for the hostages in Iran. He felt a slight twinge of guilt for having forgotten and at the same time a gratifying warmth of anger and duty. As he twiddled the dial on his mailbox, his fingers trembled with an imperceptible excitement for through its little glass face, he could see that it was quite full, and his *Legionnaires' Magazine* was peeping out modestly from under the other correspondence. He grasped it all carefully except for the magazine, which he folded neatly and stored inside his newspaper. Then he drove straight home, without once remembering the condition of his shoelaces.

At home, he set the coffee pot to perking on the stove and he turned to his mail and handled each piece with care. He placed the bills carefully in a faraway stack. He then opened and read with respectful consideration an advertisement for burial insurance and a magazine solicitation. Next, he folded each and put them all together in another neat little stack and sat looking at his *Legionnaire*, lying thin but promising on the sticky Formica. He rubbed his hands together with an almost lascivious pleasure, for it was his habit to save the best for last. And as he began reading, a little sigh escaped his lips. Why, it was almost time for the annual reunion of the Wisconsin crew. He realized with a shock of pleasure that he had completely forgotten it. He'd been secretly planning for months to attend, and he even had some plan, incomprehensible even in his own mind, not to ask his wife to accompany him until the last possible moment.

During the ensuing days, he moved with a lighter step and his days and nights righted themselves and no more did he awake at one in the morning, startled and confused. If he did awake during the night, it was for just a few brief mindless seconds, and he resettled himself comfortably on the greying sheets.

During the day he had much to do. He packed and repacked his bag as the trip lay in his mind like a bright promise. He burrowed in the bureau for Brooks Brothers shirts, still in their wrappers from the laundry and smelling slightly of cleanliness and good will. He gathered socks from the floor and waved them in the air and then mated them and packed them beside the shirts. And all the while the thought that guided him was not the reunion itself but its meeting ground in Jacksonville, where Mrs. Fox was visiting her sister.

He felt called upon as well to go outside and inspect the

drain gutters on the gently rotting fascia trim of their Cape Cod roofed house, one of the few in town. He also left elaborate and complicated instructions for the gardener, who came on Thursdays, explaining carefully that he would be away for perhaps a week. Finally, he called his daughter, and cautiously, without lying, he let her think that he was to fly home with her mother.

He bought a paper every day and kept abreast of the state of the world and the condition of the hostages. In his mind he kept a running dialogue with his wife about the affairs of the nation, and she nodded gently at his insights, as agreeably and pleasantly as when they first were married.

The day of his trip dawned bright and awesome. He assembled his luggage, considered calling his daughter to drive him to the airport, reconsidered, and called a taxi. He arrived at the minute and strode directly onto the plane. Within an hour, he was asleep, dreaming pleasantly of the lunch the stewardess had served: broiled chicken with broccoli and saffron rice.

At first the Atlanta airport, where he had to switch planes, overwhelmed him. He had two hours to wait for his next plane, but prudently he found his concourse gate and made a mental note of its whereabouts.

He took the moving sidewalk, and the recorded voice unnerved him, like the futuristic books of doom his son used to quote from and simultaneously raised his blood pressure. The people, too, seemed busy and alien to him. He wondered about their journeys and if it were true that all of them, as they appeared to him, were on a holiday.

Several incidents occurred that struck him as omens making the butter from his lunch became heavy and congealed in his stomach. First, he tripped slightly getting off an escalator and a bearded man with becoming streaks of gray around his temples had caught his arm briefly and said, solicitously, "Careful." Next, he bought *Time* and a *U.S. News and World Report*. Yin and Yang, his son had called them, and this thought was so startling that the clerk had spoken to him sharply, causing him to forget his change; but he had walked out so crisply and haughtily that when he remembered the money, he was ashamed to go back. And now without the few bills he usually kept in his pocket, he reached to pat his wallet, as was his habit when over ten miles from home and contacted nothing but folds of Dacron over his own narrow haunch. At first, his breath left him entirely, and he stopped and leaned against the cool wall of one of the tunnels in which he had been walking and rewalking. He folded his magazines under one arm and hugged himself with the other; and after fighting a great urge to cry, he persevered and straightened and began to walk with purpose, casting his eyes about for a security guard. But before he found one, a curious, almost psychic feeling pulled him, and he retraced his steps to the toilet he had used when he had gotten off the plane, for the round roaring holes in the planes made his very groin retract and this had been his first stop. And there, miraculously, lying behind a gleaming pipe, darkening slightly from the damp and shocking in its familiarity, was his wallet.

He made his way to his concourse again, but this time did not wander about anxiously but sat looking at the darkened sky and waiting. Presently he felt better and looked around him and discovered a quite pleasant young man beside him who nodded decorously over a paperback. As the deepening light changed, he stared at the monstrous glass walls and realized he was not looking out but rather at the reflection of himself and the young man, whose facial contours and ruddy coloring struck a vibration of inchoate recognition in his heart. After awhile he began to fall into a dreamy stupor much like the ones he drifted in at home on the rose-colored couch; and as varied thoughts entered and left his brain, he closed his eyes comfortably and relaxed, only occasionally peeping out from under his thickened lids to see the young man. He fantasized that this man was his son and they were off on a trip together, and this led to one thing and another back through the past until he saw his son — five years old, standing on a high diving board at the Y, shivering and skinny, with his arms wrapped around him in a little-boy fashion, and his nipples popping out on his chest like little blue buttons. He wrung his hands once and jumped. Then he was riding a bicycle, and he was twelve and his legs were fatter, but not much, and he pumped up a solid oak 2 x 6 leaning on a sawhorse for a perilous leap. Then he remembered a car, battered but redeemable, with only legs sticking out and some shy, skinny girl who handed him tools and understood his steel-muffled words. Next, he saw his son in tails, holding a frosty corsage, impatient but polite as his mother took his picture.

Abruptly, at the end of this dream sojourn, the thought of his wife appeared in a strange sort of fragile light. Then he could not control the images of the past that enveloped his mind; he saw her form and manner in odd slices of their life together, unrelated and absurd. Her ghost voice, unintelligible, murmured in his ear. Her eyes, seas of blueness and time, glistened once and were gone. He saw her hands strong and soft, caressing familiar objects which had no substance. He became faintly aware of vague pictures of her simple deeds that had no significance but seemed warm and pleasurable. Suddenly a thought came to him so alien and fierce that at first, he thought it was the voice of some passing psychic stranger: they had never hurt together. He could not fathom the meaning of this thought but at the same time it came to him that they never talked about Robert anymore, or their dead baby, or any of the dreads and emptinesses that had accosted their living. Somewhere something fearful yet familiar moved inside him and broke, and he was confronted by the sheer essence of his thoughts, naked and devoid of order.

Suddenly, there was a rushing sound in the air, and he realized people were standing and moving and that his plane had arrived. The intercom confused him for a second, for it announced the time of the next arrival but he moved with the sea and in front of him in the long line was the young man who did not, after all, look much like his on, and who, smiling, held his magazines while he searched for his ticket.

On this flight, he sat upright until the plane touched down in Jacksonville; and after a mindless ride in a taxi, he stared at the cab driver for a split second, confused and unable to speak, then suddenly and recklessly blurted out his sister-in-law's address.

Only Visiting This Planet

It was long after dark when his wife opened the door of her sister's home; and surrounded as he was by the gloom of the night shadows, the shock of the light blinded him briefly, then softened and gently silvered the outline of her hair.

Are You Decent?

"Is Mr. Wojciechowski feeling better today?" my wife said for the thirtieth time in two weeks. Then she laughed in sort of this guarded way, listened a minute, and covered up the receiver with her hand, "Of course you can. "

That meant in about twenty minutes we were in for another visit from the old gal we'd just two weeks ago bought the house from. Bought this house—sold our souls—it was no steal I tell you. I'm talking Garden District, landscaped, sunken-timbered, redwood molded. Upstairs, downstairs, two-and-a-half bathed, French doored. And the furniture. Except that was the problem.

Since Mr. Wojciechowski was going straight into the old folk's home, Mrs.

Wojciechowski was moving into a furnished apartment near her daughter, and since my wife fell in love with every stick of furniture here, we'd bought it along with the house, only every day, or sometimes twice a day, Mrs. Wojciechowski remembered something she needed and she called my wife, come over, and get it back. The blue rug in the upstairs bedroom that her daughter was really fond of. The table in the hallway she decided she just couldn't part with after all. Once she waited all afternoon on the patio for us when we had gone out of town. She'd wanted the lamp in the guest room. Mrs. Wojciechowski was here more than I was. When I came back from Alexandria yesterday, she had been standing in the azaleas, showing Maureen how to pinch back the buds for healthier shrubs.

My wife Maureen hung up the phone and turned around. "Well," she said. She had on that far-off, thinking look she has. That old woman, Mrs. Wojciechowski, was nobody my wife even knew real well. Maureen had seen the house in the paper, and this was after we had been arguing for six months about where we should live. We'd had this apartment in a complex with a social room and a weight room and a hot tub and sauna room. And no grass to fool with. Just concrete. About that time Maureen had been working in the Airs Above the Ground, this big flower shop that sold helium balloons. Maureen used to go about town dressed like a clown or a teddy bear or a Big Bad Wolf and deliver balloons and flowers. Sometimes she'd have to make up songs and sing them to the customers to commemorate a special occasion. But she quit that after her brother Robert died, got killed really, down in Lake Charles.

It didn't matter, her job I mean, because my territory had just been expanded and then lo and behold Robert had made his whole insurance policy out to her. Robert was a tool pusher, but he didn't get killed on an oil well. He got killed in this real freaky accident when he was off work trying to ride a green colt with just a halter. He had just slung himself up bareback, clutching a lead rope in one hand for a rein, and was going to ride across the highway to the winter pasture. He was going to turn the colt out in that, but a log truck happened by. The colt went blooey, wheeled around twice and went running blind into a second log truck just behind it. Hit the cab then and fell up under it. Which freaked Maureen out so bad she said she couldn't put on a clown nose or go around singing songs in a bear suit for a while. It just wasn't decent. Then not too long after that we heard about the insurance and then not too long after that was when Maureen started to get restless and suddenly, we have this $160,000 house. Maureen just chucks the whole $100,000 down and I get to pay the rest, which, what with interest and all, amounts to over a quarter of a mil.

Maureen moved over to the kitchen island over which hung a big bunch of brilliantly shining copper pots that she'd just prefer me not to use just yet. She bent over this cookbook that had come with the house. "Maybe we could have her for dinner," I said. She looked up from her book. She put her finger down the page to hold her place.

"Come on," she said. "She's an old woman. She'll get used to the idea after a while.

Eventually."

I didn't say anything. Then she told me again all about Mrs. Wojciechowski's stomach.

She had gotten her stomach after Mr. Wojciechowski had gotten his colon.

"Jesus," I tried to say politely. Outside, hanging on

hundred-year-old live oak trees are voodoo-looking contraptions, painted Crisco cans with peanut butter and honey oozing out of odd holes cut in them. Bird feeders. Another way Mrs. Wojciechowski had of controlling our lives. Maureen kept them filled because Mrs. Wojciechowski checked on them when she came over.

In a little while a fifteen-year-old powder blue Cadillac nosed itself into the driveway. Maureen stopped stirring whatever she was stirring in the copper pot on the stove and after wiping her hands on her pink gingham apron that matched potholders somewhere, she went outside to meet her.

I am just a drug salesman. I drive all over sixteen parishes to twenty-six different hospitals for Eaton Laboratories and talk doctors and administrators into buying new and different drugs and medical equipment. I do all right, but this new house payment has me permanently sober. It's like one minute I am thinking of ordering cablevision or having the newspaper delivered instead of walking down to buy one at the corner when I want and thinking how nice it is not to be strapped all the time, when wham, Maureen gets this money and suddenly, stupidly, we're up to our asses in debt. Since I was in the kitchen I poured myself a drink, what the hell, and went upstairs and sat on the side of the bed, on the candy- striped sheets that Maureen and I had got up out of this morning. Mrs. Wojciechowski's antique chiffonier gleams expensively beside the white curtained bay window.

No matter what I do, I don't feel at home. When we moved in, Mrs. Wojciechowski had left us everything, even canned goods in the cupboard, cereal, china, wine glasses, and cocktail napkins. In the refrigerator a pound of skim milk cheese, a box of opened prunes. A wilted stalk of celery for god's sake.

Maureen and I have been married five years. When we got married, she was a student in physical education and was about to get a college degree. But a friend of mine got me a job as a drug salesman in North Louisiana and we had to move. I was in a spot. I had lost everything and more on a drugstore I was trying to run near Covington. I had rented an old supermarket and hired two full-time pharmacists and was going to turn it into a giant super-store, but nothing came out right. I shudder now to think of those long, people-less aisles, the bills, the insurance, the W-2s, the worksheets and the debits and credits. I was glad to get this job. At first Maureen tried to finish up her degree but it worked out she'd have to put in an extra year transferring and all, so she took jobs: Kelly girl jobs, a receptionist for a urologist, car saleswoman, and finally the one at the Airs Above the Ground.

This bed was enormous. Mr. and Mrs. Wojciechowski's fluffy white bedspread was wadded up at one end and there was no Sunday morning smell of lovemaking mingling with the sheets. I set my drink on the nightstand— inside were two old, yellowed buttons and a half can of Prince Albert, along with our stuff Maureen had dumped in— and parted the curtains a bit with my finger. Outside Maureen was reaching up under the eaves of the gazebo and hauling down the potted ferns one by one. Mrs. Wojciechowski was standing nearby and fluttering her hands. Talking about the old days, probably. A squirrel banged down on top of a Crisco can behind the gazebo and hit the ground running. Around them the lawn was landscaped with shrubs and hedges. A white-shelled driveway was between rows of willow and made a half-circle around a clump of azaleas. It was the grounds of an estate. I laid back down on the bed, and Maureen appeared in the door. Outside was the sound of Mrs. Wojciechowski driving away with her ferns. Maureen's hair was mussed, and the color was high in her cheeks. "The ferns," she said. "For the breakfast room at the apartment."

"Ah, " I said. I got up. I went to her. I touched her breasts. "Let's go to bed, honey," I said.

"Now?" she said. She put her hands on my hands.

"Take your sweater off," I said. "Take your jeans off." I kissed her slowly and began to mess around.

"Duane," she said, but I kissed her again. I knew I could drive Robert out of her mind and decency and Mrs. Wojciechowski if I could just get her attention for a minute. Her eyes were close to mine, staring blue, and she wrapped her arms around me. She pressed her cheek against my neck. "Duane," she said, like she was remembering something. Just then tires scrunched the oyster shells in the driveway. The unmistakable sound of Mrs. Wojciechowski's Cadillac. The horn tooted.

"Oh, " said Maureen, lifting up her cheek. "Mrs. Wojciechowski must have forgotten something."

But I kept hold of her. I kept on holding her as if braced for a blow. Then the horn honked again, in that old lady impatient way.

Monday morning, I did not have to be in Shreveport until

noon. Maureen took her two canvas shopping bags she'd bought to save the environment from the pollution of the paper ones and drove off to Brookshires. I stayed in bed.

My phone began to ring downstairs on the first step where I'd left it. I got up and put on my flip flops and weaved across the room like I'd tied one on the night before. But it was just nerves and a headache and bad dreams.

"Hello," I said down in the foyer with this feeling that whatever I said next would be murderous and irretrievable.

"Mr. Higginbotham? This is Goodwill Industries. Do you have any donations for us today?" some young perky voice said. I closed my eyes a second.

I wanted to know how she'd gotten my name and knew where to call. I was relatively certain that something was being proven here. I held my breath and counted to five like an old yoga exercise I used to do. I let it out to five. After all, if you thought about it, it was not such a remarkable question

"Yeah," I said. "Twenty-three fifty-nine E. Jefferson Boulevard. Bring your biggest truck." The young voice said something else. I listened and nodded slowly. My heart expanded and hurt like it was growing wings. "Hurry," I said. "Please hurry." I hung up and stood there in my underwear and flip flops, watching the sun fall through the windows onto all the strange furniture, the rugs, the strange place.

Tabby's Blues Box

Owen lived in the most run-down house on Olive Street, which was saying a lot. It had boarded-up windows, and a sagging porch, and dozens of smelly cans of Nine-Lives on the railing where Owen fed his cat, Fur Face, every evening. On the front door he had posted an ingenious sign—WARNING: AIDS AND PITT BULLDOGS.

Owen didn't have Aids and he didn't have any kind of dog, but he didn't like salesmen or Jehovah's Witnesses or most people in general bothering him. Owen spent a lot of time fostering the myth that he was a crazed Vietnam vet who was prone to violence. He didn't want his daddy visiting him especially, because he might walk around in his sad-sack-of-shit way, and not saying it, but wanting him to go out and get a job. Owen got a pension every month. He didn't need a job.

When Owen first got home from Nam, he had gone upstairs and flushed his ribbons down the toilet. All of them. His daddy said, "You want a drink?" Owen never used to drink, but in Nam he'd picked up the habit. He had also picked

188

up another habit. This habit had inspired him to smuggle home some hash in a tape-recorder. It was a big one, a Sony with two speakers and in the speakers were two bags of hash, a half-a-kilo. Inside the deck were two more bags.

His daddy had wanted to toast Owen's homecoming, but he had sat there and cried instead. Owen said, "I'm not going to any of your poker games. I'm not going to sit around and play poker with you and your drinking pals." He had not seen his daddy cry since his mother had died. Then Owen said, "Hey, you got my tape recorder yet?"

And his daddy said, "Yeah, it's in the utility room." And Owen got a flat-head screwdriver and a pair of wire-cutters and went to the utility room and opened it. His load of the hash was there.

In a week he just left, moved out. He couldn't cope. He couldn't even know his little brother, and he had nothing to say to Shelby.

On the next street over from Olive was what was known as colored housing and just to keep busy Owen fixed his neighbors' cars. He did it to give himself something to do. He had an iron pipe slung between the forks of two pecan trees in his backyard, where he could even lift out a motor if he had to.

Right now, he was waiting for his friend, Rabbit, to bring him an ignition switch. He had the guts out of a Datsun 28Ozx, an old one, a '77, the one right before they changed the style and messed it up.

Rabbit showed. He owned the Z Owen was working on. He stuck his old-fashioned Afro in Owen's back door.

"Always afraid I'll catch you with woman in here, man."

Rabbit was always jiving.

"How much, Rabbit?" Owen said.

"Sit down, man. This going to be bad." said Rabbit. He plunked a sack on the table. "You can only get this here part from a dealer."

He counted out two dollars and thirty cents into Owen's hand, change from a hundred-dollar bill he had given him yesterday. Owen would get paid back in grass and gofer jobs.

A horn honked from outside.

"Got my sister to take me to work," said Rabbit. He worked at Hoogland's Nursery and Landscaping, which Owen always thought was a little ironic. He wondered if Rabbit was ever tempted to drop a few grass seed in with the petunias.

Rabbit was wearing a tie-dyed t-shirt and a string of beads to work that morning. He reminded him vaguely of the sixties, like maybe Rabbit was that far behind.

"If you bring me a filter, and a couple of quarts, I'll change your oil while I'm under there," Owen said.

"I'll send Little Sister back," said Rabbit, grinning. "I tell her you ain't high today." Rabbit also helped Owen maintain the image of psychopathic, dope-crazed vet. Rabbit opened the door. "LaShonda," he said. "She is."

"Send her right back." said Owen. Then he caught a glimpse of LaShonda through the door. She had gotten out and was leaning languorously on her car. She was wearing an Indian print dress and the sun caught a zillion little braids that flowed down her shoulders. Owen invited Rabbit and LaShonda over for a drink after work.

He spent the afternoon installing the ignition switch. He had never seen a Z that didn't lose its ignition somewhere along the way. Then he worked on a van with a faulty post-ignition shut-off jet. It was his day for ignitions. The van had been in his yard so long the grass had grown up around the tires, but he was taking his time with it. The owner was in jail for holding up a Circle K.

Next door, Mrs. Holly, who lived on Social Security, was watering begonias and watching him suspiciously. (She had lived in terror for years that the house next door would be rented to blacks, and then Owen had moved in. She'd heard rumors that he had killed babies in Vietnam and that he stalked high school girls at night. He had that awful sign tacked up. And the blacks came over constantly to get their cars fixed. Mrs. Holly's special blessing was that Mr. Holly had died before he'd had to live next door to that, and before Jesse Jackson had gotten so far.)

Owen took a break and sat on the railing of his porch, eating an orange popsicle. He was so quiet that Mrs. Holly must have thought he had stayed inside, and she even plunged through the boxwood once to rescue her elderly poodle who was sniffing around, and never saw him. In the past few years Owen only had Rabbit inside his house, a representative from the Veteran's Administration who was pretending to be some kind of Dr. Sidney Freeman from M*A*S*H by trying to get Owen to talk out his anxieties, and his daddy. His daddy had come twice since he had moved out, once after a storm to check and see if the wind had got him, and another time to bring him a package that had been sent to his old address. The sunsets

Owen saw from the porch blew his mind. If he didn't feel like working on a car, he'd come out and sit and wait for them, starting early in the afternoon. Waiting for the sunsets, he either read old *Mechanics Illustrated* or a book that came in a package by way of Shelby.

A nurse he knew in Nam had sent him *Sex Diary of a Metaphysician*. Whenever he read it, he started thinking about women. Owen had met the nurse in an unusual way. Or it ended up unusual. When he was in Nam, he'd gotten hit. It had been a minor wound, a flesh wound, as they say in the movies, but at first Owen hadn't been sure how bad it was. Owen had been about to get into bed with this whore when the shelling had started. He had slammed himself down just in time to meet a low-flying shell that had cut through the wall and was whizzing its way along the floor. It had grazed Owen all along his back and down his left leg and when it was over, and he had stood up, his pants had fallen off, like in a cartoon. Another funny thing about that was, for the life of him, he still couldn't remember how that whore had come out of it. He couldn't remember her at all. He had been dumped in a truck filled with other wounded soldiers and two nurses. They took him to a hospital and when one of them got to Owen, Owen had raised up one elbow and had said, "Never mind me. I'm ok." The nurse Shirley, had said, "Lay back down, soldier," and while she was examining him, meshing up his legs, his buttocks, pressing here and there to determine the nature of his injuries, a weird thing had happened. He'd gotten this terrific hard-on. "Huh? What's this?" Shirley had said. Then she gave him a good quick job with her hand.

When his scratch was all fixed up, he'd worked around the hospital for a few months, mostly taking the laundry over to the Vietnamese women who'd been hired to do that sort of thing and hauling off trash. He'd see Shirley sometimes when he came in and out and she'd always laugh and wave and give him thumbs up. When he got home, she'd sent him that book.

When Rabbit and LaShonda came over after work, they brought an oil filter, four quarts of oil, and LaShonda's boyfriend, Squig. They sat in a row on Owen's cracked, vinyl couch. Squig was a soft, overweight kid, with sloping shoulders like an up-side-down funnel. He was dressed in loud, shiny clothes. "This here Squig," Rabbit said, caught by some kind of secret joke or something. LaShonda, her legs crossed, sat back deep in the sofa between Rabbit and Squig. She gave off low-key, subtle rhythms. Owen couldn't see what a girl like that saw in Squig. He resolved to cut down on his reading. Squig went to college at Mississippi State because he got to stay with his grandmother free. He wore a comb on the back of his head. His comb and Rabbit's peg-legged pants clashed with LaShonda's presence between them. Squig had a beefy, loud laugh, and commanded a good space on the sofa, but he agreed with everything Rabbit said. Owen was drifting away from the moment, something that happened when he stayed around one or more people too long. He looked at LaShonda. What was she thinking? Did she think of anything? The most amazing thing about her was her hair, the cascade of miniature braids that started flat at her hairline, then flowed up and back suddenly and on and on down her shoulders. Her eyes were big. Her mouth was astonishing. The black, green, and red Indian print glowed between the dullards like an exotic bird. He imagined this finely boned woman would be capable of soaring into the air. She lifted her drink, she thumped a cigarette, she laughed. This amazing bird woman.

Fur Face bounded through an open window and froze. LaShonda coaxed him to rub against her legs. His small, hungry, green cat-eyes glistened.

LaShonda wanted to be a hairdresser. Squig wanted her to come to Mississippi State instead. He had given her silver and garnet bangles and a reversible paisley shawl which he bought with wages from his job as a bag boy at the A & P. LaShonda's father, a preacher, wanted her to stay home. LaShonda shrugged in a way that reminded Owen of New Orleans jazz. LaShonda liked cheeseburgers. She believed in Medjugorje. That was the biggest word Owen heard her say.

Owen went out and crawled under the Z. He opened the oil gasket. He banged his knuckle when the filter went in. Later after they drove away, he put *Sex Diary* in and turned on M*A*S*H. It was the episode where Radar gets a home movie from Kansas.

Saturday Rabbit rode over in his Z and brought Owen a stash. Then they sat in the kitchen and toked one. Pretty soon Rabbit said, "Squig gone. You got any plans tonight?"

Owen looked at him. Rabbit knew he did the same thing every night, and that was he smoked a little of the unremarkable grass supplied him and went to sleep watching TV.

"You come out with me and LaShonda and my main," said Rabbit. "Tabby's Blues Box—you ever hear of it?"

Tabby's Blues Box was this black night club on Lafayette Street downtown. Owen didn't say anything right away. He needed a minute to think about Squig fading into the sunset and LaShonda's unemotional, exquisite eyes.

"Come on, man," said Rabbit. Behind him, in the window, Fur Face made like a silent pop-up. He had a blue jay in his mouth. His eyes glittered like he was high on something.

"Shoo, you bastard," said Owen. Rabbit looked startled, then caught sight of Fur Face. "Bummer," he said, and laughed in quick, separate noises.

The cat jumped down and stopped to look at them, then carried the bird out and down the hall.

Owen took a deep breath. The air was flavored and sweet from toke and feathers and blood.

"What the hell," he said.

Rabbit's main squeeze wore a bright orange wig and her name was Princess. She had a sedated look on her face and weird eyebrows. Owen thought her eyebrows didn't fit her expression. Then he saw they were drawn on, two perpetually surprised arches like a McDonald's sign. He got into the back seat of her Ford Escort where LaShonda was. LaShonda sat on her side in some lavender gauze dress, that kind of deliberately, permanently wrinkled stuff. Owen could smell her pretty, tight hair from where he was. It smelled like lavender too. "Hey," he said. LaShonda looked at him and laughed. She raised one hand and let it drop. Princess's orange pile jiggled. She looked back and laughed, too. "Hey, girl," she said, looking at LaShonda and making her eyebrows go down by sticking out her chin.

Rabbit was wearing a fedora and a pink tie and a pin-stripe suit. He looked like a pimp. "How's the man?" he said. He leaned over for a brother handshake.

Princess wheeled around some corners until they were downtown, then turned onto Lafayette Street. They pulled past Tabby's Blues Box onto a side street. Two guys with tall, nappy-type hair were leaning against an old Chevy with a bashed-in rear. They lounged against the hood and passed a bottle. When Owen and LaShonda went by them, they checked Owen out.

Inside was a long counter and dozens of tables in a big smoky room. There wasn't even a stage but just one end of a dance floor where the musicians had set up. The musicians had long braided hair and little round sunglasses on like blind men wear. They were playing some hard-hitter, demi-boogie tune. After they sat down, Rabbit leaned over their table. "How you like this hip-hop?" he said.

A waitress came over. Rabbit ordered them all Ripple. Then he made Princess spread her fingers on the table and show them to Owen. They looked like little slender sausages, no nails. She said she'd been born three months premature, and she didn't have fingernails, or toenails, or hair of any kind. "Nowhere," she said and grinned at Rabbit. She gazed into his eyes and her lids drooped.

A wiry-sounding guitar struck up and Owen looked at the performers. Some lap-steeler had come on and had it going good. He had slick, shining black pants with studs down the side and a T-shirt that said "Free Mandela." Then a white horn player, and a drummer came on and started fooling around behind him. Owen looked back at Princess's fingers. Then he thought of something pretty weird he thought he had forgotten. Sometimes clean-up crews at the hospital in Nam were careless and the stripped sheets held bits and pieces of body parts. Then Owen would take the bag of sheets over to the laundry, and the Vietnamese-women would freak out when a finger or something would whirl around in the glass face dryer. Owen raised his wine and drained it. Then he ordered a round of decent whiskey and paid for everything.

"Not bad, or what?" said Owen to LaShonda, referring to the music. LaShonda gazed at the musicians and didn't say.

The group played three hard pieces, then the guy with the "Free Mandela" t-shirt came over. His name was Blue Romeo. His black, studded pants were torn in places. A thin, gold ring flashed from his nose. He thought he knew Rabbit from somewhere. Then he started staring at Owen. "I know you, chap?" he said. Rabbit and Princess went off to dance. Blue Romeo's eyes glittered like Fur Face's had when his mouth had been full of blue jay. They were slitty and red like Blue Romeo had crashed on something yesterday, but hard and shiny like he was on his way up again today. "No, I don't think so," said Owen.

"Don't mind if I join you folks?" said Blue Romeo, sitting down in Rabbit's chair. He kept looking at Owen. "You been together a long time, huh? This here's your wife?" Owen couldn't take his eyes off Blue Romeo's nose ring. It caught in the lights from the makeshift stage and flashed. The sound from the doo-wah behind him seemed to make it flash, like one of those sound-sensitive lights people hook up to their stereo systems. "You-all like this music?" said Blue Romeo. "How 'bout you, Whitey? Make you want to get your dick up, man?" Just then the waitress appeared and put a bottle in front of Blue Romeo. He unscrewed the cap with one hand and kept the other one on the table. "Know what I got under this here table, Whitey?" He went on conversationally. "I got a blade. But I'm gonna keep it under this table. For right now." He took a drink and peered at the bottle meditatively. A thread of cold ran up Owen's neck and he took some of his own drink. The whiskey ran over his tongue and down his throat tasteless as water. He said, "Say man..." and then he couldn't think of anything. Say, man, you high? You drunk? You want to leave us alone now? You want to get the fuck out of here? All he could manage was a hand, sliding faintly under the table to his pocket, where, ten years ago, he used to keep a side-arm.

"Now you thinking," said Blue Romeo, "you thinking I done got my ass in trouble bringing this black bitch to this here place. You thinking you goin' to have to fight that drunk nigger, ain't you? Ain't you?"

Owen looked around the room until he saw Rabbit and Princess. They had stopped dancing and were looking at them. Then they started walking over.

"Hey, Honkey, I'm talking to you." Blue Romeo laughed and the light on his nose ring jittered. "Cain't you talk?"

Owen took another slug of whiskey. The whiskey, bland in his throat, finally hit the back of his head, burned one deep, wild burn and shocked his brain into some kind of fast forward. He saw the next ten seconds like a speeded-up private movie in his mind: the way he would stand up, twist that gutter from Blue Romeo's hand, cut through the soft like it was cheese, blood spewing out familiarly, and into the air. Then would come that old satisfying jolt that made everything make sense for a few seconds. That good, deep feeling. That good old hard damn feeling. He saw LaShonda's mask giving way to a real face. He saw Rabbit and Princess arrested in their slow-motion journey across the room. But LaShonda pushed back her chair and stood up. She looked half-interested in what she was doing. "Chap," she said to Rabbit, coming up to them, "we better go."

Under the table, Owen's knees started dancing by themselves. He couldn't move for a second to get up and walk out the door. For a second, he couldn't budge for that, only for that movement that would take him up and into Blue Romeo's face.

Blue Romeo slid up and out of Rabbit's chair and Owen saw Rabbit turn square to him and freeze. "Don't do it, dude," he said to Blue Romeo in a pleasant, scared voice.

Blue Romeo had it half out of his pocket. Then he said to Owen, "Ain't you got no tongue, honkey? Where your wife? Huh?" He looked over at LaShonda. "What you doin' with him, Mama?"

"Blue Romeo!" said two musicians coming up behind him. They put their hands on his arms.

Owen stood up and felt for his wallet. He lay some more money on the table. He wasn't shaking any more. He thought of Blue Romeo's moving, churning, digesting guts, intact and functioning, and that seemed the most useless thing he could think of. He heard Princess say to LaShonda, "Girl, let's get."

LaShonda looked more like the princess. She moved across the floor and dancers moved out of her way. She moved in a deep, lavender cloud, undefined by Blue Romeo. She moved like she had already made some courageous escape.

Blue Romeo fixed his red, wild eye on Owen one more time. "Tell her I get her," he said. "Tell her I get her," he yelled.

"Stay cool, man," Rabbit said to Owen. Then they started out.

"I fix you, bitch," yelled Blue Romeo after them. "I fix you."

Outside Owen opened the door of the Escort for LaShonda. The two guys with the brown bag were still there beside the Chevy. Princess slid behind the wheel and Rabbit and her lit up a joint and cursed a little.

"Oh," said LaShonda. She took out a little gold compact. She looked into the mirror. Owen could feel his heart beating. He could feel Princess's and Rabbit's too, in a steady doo-wah rap. LaShonda's was holding a languid, ancient slow-beat behind his staccato, falling on a metal drum. Owen sat and listened to their triple rhythm, their melodic pulses in the dark.

Friendly Fire

Emmett said, "I'm in deep shit," but there was nobody there to hear him unless you wanted to count Fur Face on the porch rail, who'd just finished his Nine Lives and was cleaning his whiskers by the light of a half-assed moon. Emmett spoke out of his beer glass, using his deepest brain, the part that kept memories floating like preserved specimens in fluid. (Whoom, whoom, whoom, the sound of choppers on an early morning horizon. Fire. After-fire. Hums. Roars. Hatch doors. Wing lights. Ngu Tai. She so short she had to reach for him.) Being in deep shit with Daisy was like a helicopter crash.

Now here he is, in the night. The demilitarized zone. Daisy so young she knows nothing about it except in movies. Nobody bothered him until her. And Virgil, his brother! Spooking around. His own compound invaded. Changing his head. A search and destroy mission.

Fur Face finished cleaning his face and then happened off the porch into the night, cruising. A cricket orchestra cranked up. Daisy drove up in her round blob of a car with wheels.

"I wanted to see if the Health Department creeps had got you," she said. She was wearing a long scarf like an aviator and carrying a bottle of Tequila. Yeah, Emmett thought. Deep shit.

Daisy walked toward Emmett Rogers, out of uniform, who was not killed in battle, and who got up from his squat-sit, moved the lips of the face of the body he was inhabiting and said, "Come in. Welcome to my hooch. Come in."

The next day, Emmett took a deep breath and cranked up Daisy's bug. The interior smelled like alpine--because she had a little air freshener Christmas tree hanging from the rearview mirror—and toke. The stick-on clock over the radio said half-past eleven.

The motor idled high and whined a little like it needed a look. Maybe he should get out and set the idle. Maybe he should check the oil. His tools were metric. He had all day.

Emmett had this buzzing that started that morning at the back of his head and worked down his neck and into his stomach. He put his hand on the gear shift and stopped for a minute. Then he gave up and shoved the stick into first and pulled onto the street.

Emmett had not driven a car in five years since he gave his Volvo to an old army buddy Leo who had stopped by his house to crash for the night. Leo had been on his way to a detox unit in Mobile to dry out and Emmett had been afraid he was going to get rolled trying to hitch. His hands were shaking, and he said, "Two days. Two days. I already got it half-licked."

Emmett brushed his hair out of his eyes and adjusted the rearview mirror to suit him. Last night Daisy poured Old Crow over his stomach and licked it off. Duke Ellington on the c.d. player. Later she reached up and curled his hair around a finger and asked if he didn't want her to give him a haircut.

Emmett usually cut his hair himself, but it had gotten so thick on top he couldn't manage it. Fact is he needed a lot of things--a haircut, new shoes, clothes. A driver's license. A car.

One afternoon Emmett had been in the yard and Leo pulled up in the Volvo with a depressed-looking woman named Sheila. Sheila was medium-pretty and holding a fat, sleepy baby. Leo got out of the car and shook Emmett's hand. Then he told Emmett Sheila's husband had taken his charter boat out one morning several months ago and was never seen again.

Leo met Sheila at the detox unit in Mobile where she was a nurse's aide. Leo wanted to give Emmett back his car, but first he wanted Emmett to take them to the bus station. Leo's eyes looked calm and at the same time bright. He was on the mend he said. He said he'd turned his life around.

Emmett looked at the baby. It was the ugliest kid he'd ever seen. "Ain't he somethin'," Leo said. The baby had a wide, doughy face and big ears that drooped over at the top and three or four chins. The fat rings hung over his chest. "Ain't he somethin'," Leo said again.

Emmett gave them his car. He'd gotten used to being without one and he hadn't had a driver's license since before Nam. "Good-bye", Leo said and pumped his hand. Then he ran his hand through his hair quickly and got into Emmett's car with Sheila and the fat baby and drove away.

That morning, Emmett pulled up to a barbershop that he knew. He sat in the chair under a cape and let the barber crank him up to eye level.

"Ain't seen you in a while," the barber said. He was one of the guys Shelby used to play poker with. "How's Shelby?"

"Mostly off the sides," Emmett said. "But enough off the top it doesn't lay down so flat."

The barber said, "I'll do it," and shut up. He turned Emmett's head to the side and started-cutting.

Sunlight filled the little barbershop. Emmett was the only customer there. He folded his hands and blinked at the light. He looked down. His hands were prison-pale and moist. His fingers were long and lube grease lined the nails. Lockpicker's fingers, Daisy called them.

After his haircut, Emmett walked to a nearby shoe store. The clerk brought out a stack of boxes. Emmett put his foot up on the shoe stand and let him unlace his boots. In the summers the boots were hot and smelly.

The clerk wrinkled his nose and took a pair of beige slip-ons out of one of the boxes he'd brought out.

"Laces," said Emmett.

The clerk opened the other boxes and Emmett chose some black lace-ups. The clerk seemed huffy that Emmett wanted to pay in cash and not with a credit card. "I have to get change in the back," he said.

"Keep it." Emmett said and he put his boots under his arm. Outside the shoes felt springy and made him think of running. Looking at his new shoes, Emmett walked back to the car.

As he drove into the parking lot at K-mart, he looked at the people with packages and shopping bags hurrying back to their cars. They looked pissed off and late for something.

Inside Emmett bought three new shirts and a washer for his faucet that constantly dripped at home. The plumbing was old and everything in the house needed constant patching--the hot water heater, the washing machine. Most of the time Emmett liked the challenge of the place. But lately he had the feeling his house was crumbling at too fast a rate. He knew he should spring for some major repairs, but he just didn't have the heart. That was in his lease. He made all the repairs and in exchange for living there, unbothered, he had only to mail in one-hundred-and-five dollars once a month to Pioneer Realty. It was a good deal.

Emmett liked to think that his coming home from Nam had not made a ripple anywhere in the world. That he had not changed anyone's life or become connected with anything or anyone. Almost like if he were still in Nam, or dead or something, but he had the advantage of seeing the old town of his as it plugged along without him.

But then Daisy came.

Daisy and Emmett liked to go for drives, cook supper in Emmett's kitchen, or Daisy's favorite thing--watch movies. Home movies. The one thing Emmett couldn't stand was to sit in a movie theater.

Movie theaters gave him the shakes, so they just drove Daisy's bug over to Red Box and picked out something. Daisy liked chick flicks with happy endings. Emmett doesn't care what they watch as long as it's not a war movie. He's had enough of that stuff.

Daisy goes to community college when she is not working at her job as usher at the theater. This semester she is taking psychology.

Lately they've been going to places. Daisy is doing something she calls Emmett's desensitivity training, something she learned in her class. This meant going to places that might freak Emmett out because that would get rid of his fear, Daisy said. Like little places, then bigger and bigger places. Then one day soon bigger and bigger places with crowds.

Emmett had to laugh at her sometimes. Let Daisy be a mad scientist all she wants--except for movies. Emmett is positively not going to a movie theater.

The thing that's funny about Daisy is that underneath all that eye-shadow and Spandex beats the heart of a sentimental girl. Emmett thinks she's cute as hell, especially when she's all gussied up in purple hair spray and those weird gloves with the fingers cut out and half her nails gold and the other half black. Incongruous. Twenty-one down on yesterday's crossword puzzle. That would be the word for Daisy.

Emmett had to pick Daisy up at three. The clock on the dash said one-thirty. He should take a drive. Fill the tank before he picked her up.

Sometimes he looked at her and thought, who are you?

Watching her in the moonlight last night as it streamed across his bed. In the morning brushing her hair with his military brush and wrinkling her nose in the mirror. She was at least twenty years younger than Emmett. And crazy ideas! She wants to go to acting school at NYC. She wants to go to screen writing school in California. She wants to write television shows. She wants to be a real estate mogul. Right now, she works for her daddy who owns the Princess Movie Theater and goes to community college part time. She wants to be a psychiatrist.

When Daisy leaves him, Emmett feels uneasy sometimes. Inside him he had bits and pieces, like old shrapnel, of all the women he had ever known, and she made those pieces move and cut a bit and start him thinking. He thought of Shirley, and she reminded him of someone he knew in high school named Susan, and she reminded him of a girl named Martha, and on and on. He never been good at breaking up. But that was Before Vietnam as he puts it. He knows he's a lot tougher now. Or plain just don't care.

In Nam he learned not to count on anything ever being around. That was one thing he had got from there.

Sometimes the thought of Daisy just blew his mind. She lent him her car. She picked him up to buy groceries. She told him she was pursuing him. Emmett worried about something: if he pursued her back, what would happen? And what would he do with all the garbage in his head that has nothing to do with Daisy?

When he came home to Shelby, his daddy, and his little brother, he'd realized what a dangerous person somebody could be without even knowing it. For a while he couldn't sleep without his .45 and every morning he'd wake up and the clip would be missing. He thought he was losing his mind. Then he found out Shelby had taken the clips out. Shelby put them in his undershirt drawer, Emmett knew, because one morning, looking for a handkerchief, he opened his daddy's drawer and found five clips. Well, it was a crazy thing to sleep with a sidearm in his hand.

He decided to just go off someplace. Not be connected to

anybody. What if driving to work Shelby had a wreck thinking about Emmett's .45, worrying, not keeping his eyes on the road. What if his little brother came into his room at night and woke Emmett up out of a dream in the dark?

For a long time, Emmett felt like just talking to someone a few minutes might change that person's life forever. If you picked up a hitchhiker, you could set him down in another spot just in time for the next car which could have a wreck later on up the road, or you could put him in a place a mugger was ready to jump out from behind a lamp post. When Leo left with his car Emmett worried he was not protecting him after all but giving him a means to kill himself. But after Emmett saw Leo and Sheila and the ugly baby, he quit worrying. The only real thing wrong with Emmett, now that Daisy has got him stirring around a little more, was a recurring dream that woke him up at night in a cold sweat sometimes.

One Thursday, Emmett and Daisy sat on the porch watching Fur Face devour probably his millionth can of Nine Lives. It was 2:00 and they had just had lunch, hot dogs (split with cheese with bacon wrapped around them), and after that, love in the afternoon. And now a cigarette. It was really too hot to sit on the porch and smoke like that, but they were too hot and too lazy to go back in.

Then Daisy threw the cigarette half-smoked over the railing. It was really too hot to smoke, and if she didn't fill her lungs up with anything, she was able to smell honeysuckle. Old

Miz Shackleford next door, old nosy thing, at least had some kind of garden. She could see hydrangeas from Emmett's porch, mock banana, azaleas coming on, and day lilies. You could eat those day lily pods if you had a mind to.

"Jimmy Lee," somebody yelled from down the street. "Come on!"

There was a smack of a ball and bat and a few subdued shouts. Everything seemed lazy and drenched with summer.

Then Daisy said, in a voice like she had been thinking about it a long time, so that it made sense to her. "The first step is to get you over all your fears of spaces and places. In Psych 101 we just finished the unit on stimulus satiation and pairing responses. You just need a tad of operant conditioning."

"The first step to what?" said Emmett.

"The first step to your new life free of fear and stuff."

A few hours later, he was eyeing the glass doors of the theater.

"Daisy," said Emmett.

"Pairing responses," said Daisy. "We'll be pairing responses today."

"Shoot!" said Emmett.

"We're going to pair your fear response to theaters with a pleasurable response."

"What--" said Emmett.

"Anything," said Daisy. "Kissing, feeling, actual fucking. It's easy, doesn't require any special equipment. Absolutely free."

"Lord," said Emmett. "I don't even know if I can go in there, let alone get it, you know, up."

"Blowing, then," said Daisy. She pulled a wad of keys out of her purse, shook them out and stuck one in the door of the Princess Theater. "Come, come, come," she said to Emmett, swinging the door open.

Once Emmett had gone to a movie by himself in Washington, D.C. He had walked into *Heartbreak Ridge* on impulse and seen Clint Eastwood in that kind of camouflage that is only issued to Recons. Emmett really freaked. Clint Eastwood looked like the farthest thing in a black, black oven. After a few minutes, sweaty and sick, Emmett bolted.

Daisy shoved the keys into her purse and put her book under her arm. "Now, see? This isn't so bad. It's just a big old empty theater lobby." She looked at Emmett. The light from the Orange Smash machine lit up his face in a lurid glow.

The problem with Emmett was that he was real closed mouth about his problem. He was real closed mouth about Vietnam in general. The actual stuff that traumatized him. So, it made it difficult to pinpoint what she should be deconditioning.

Daisy had a real interest in getting him to conquer this last fear of theaters, an inconvenient habit for her travel plans.

"Here we go," she said, taking his arm and tucking it through her arm.

Daisy led Emmett through the lobby and into the dark, old-fashioned hall-way. "Ha!" she said. "Sensory deprivation!"

"Daisy," Emmett said weakly.

"Tick-a-lock!" said Daisy.

"But--"

"Tst! Tst!" Daisy reached under a curtained wall and

touched a light switch. The hall glowed dully then, and from the inside of the theater a few shards of light lit up the aisles. She led the way into the theater.

"Let's sit here," she said. "I used to sit here a lot and holler up at Lester to focus. That was on the old machine."

"OK," said Emmett after a few minutes. "That's enough. Let's go."

"Hang on," said Daisy, touching his arm. "I haven't even given you any reinforcement yet."

"Shit," said Emmett.

"Do you want to be a slave to your fears, your mind a machine that prevents you from relating fully to the events of your existence?"

"Yeah, I do, " he said. Emmett peered glumly into the muted gloom. Daisy was starting to sound like one of those headfuck books.

"What are you thinking about?" said Daisy. "Tell me. Would you like to, you know?"

"Hell, no," said Emmett.

Daisy put her hand on the back of Emmett's neck and began massaging it. "Well, see there. Everything's cool."

Emmett peered around the theater again, and really, he felt pretty ok. Little lights shot from the corner of his eyes though, red, green, mostly green. Daisy's hand on the back of his neck made his muscles twang like fiddle strings. What was he doing here? How had he let Daisy talk him into this? She was cute and everything, but shit, she got carried away sometimes.

Emmett stood up. "I've had enough," he said. "I'm going

home. You can come with me if you want, or you can sit here all night. It's your decision. Personally, sitting in an empty theater is a waste of time to me. I've had it." After that Emmett felt better and he turned to walk up the aisle to the door.

Sergeant Kirszner was slouching in the aisle, exhausted, unshaven, his eyes glowing under his helmet. "Hello, Rogers," he said.

"GAHD!" screamed Emmett. He leapt several feet backwards and crashed into somebody behind him. Emmett dived for cover.

"Rogers, if you don't get your shit together--" yelled a familiar voice. It was Taylor who was already there under a row of seats.

"Yi-yiiiii," yelled Emmett. He buried his face for a second, then forced himself to look up. Taylor was still there.

Then a rattle shook the ground. Emmett looked away from Taylor up toward terraced paddies, where a village was burning. He heaved himself up and charged forward, dived again. Then he lifted up on one elbow to try to see where he was, but he was knocked flat by a huge whiplash force.

"Hellllp!" That sounded like Kelly. Underneath the rows of seats, by light of rocket grenades, he could see the dirt kicking up. "We're fucked," he thought.

He remembered something. "Daisy!" he yelled. "Get down. Take cover!"

"Shhhhhh," said Zalinsky, putting his fingers to his lips.

Emmett stared. "Zalinsky?" he said. "Is that you?" Then bullets jitterbugged across Zalinski's chest.

Emmett started crawling away, but kept taking blows of

something, shocks, something to his back. Then he was in the safest possible place, the front of the paddy, shielded on two sides by dikes.

To his immediate left was Wallace, frozen, staring wide-eyed down the barrel of his machine gun.

"Wally?" said Emmett. Then he remembered something. These guys were already dead.

"Can you see anything?" said Wally, unfreezing a little.

"Wally!"

"I'm bleeding to death, Emmett," said Wally in a conversational type voice.

"Oh, shit," said Emmett. Then he tried something. "You got to get out of here. You got to go back, Wally. Where you came from."

But Wally wasn't going anywhere. He shook his head sadly at Emmett.

"You dead. You already dead, Wally," Emmett pleaded. "You dead." But then he had a thought. Maybe Wally wasn't dead. Maybe Emmett had been asleep and dreamed the war was over. Maybe he'd dreamed all that stuff about everybody being dead and how he went home, and nothing was real.

"Medic! Medic!" shouted Emmett. "Oh, Jesus, Wally. Oh fuck!"

Connors poked his head up from somewhere. "What the hell are you doing, Rogers? Are you crazy? You can't hide here."

"Emmett?" Connors' face twisted, melted, turned into Daisy's face. "Jesus, Emmett," she whispered. "Are you ok?"

Emmett's head cleared for a second. He raised up but that invited a burst of machine gun fire. He dug his heels in, scraped along the ground. He kept going.

He was making about a foot at a time. Bullets ripped the paddy to the right. Off target grenades.

"Come on, Rogers," said Connors. "You can make it. Push."

Emmett looked across to him. He dug in again.

"Push, Rogers, push," Connors called like someone in a rowing crew, setting him up a beat.

Emmett fixed his eyes on a little spot on the bridge of Connors' nose. Connors had this calming Texan voice. "Atta boy. Keep comin'."

Emmett was getting closer. Something was sliding underneath him, and he pulled on it. A cardboard box. White stuff fell out of it.

"Push!" Connors' voice was good and close. Emmett pushed. The spot between his eyes looked clearer. A piece of something. Dirt, maybe.

"You got it," said Connors, and two sets of hands, one pair black, the other pair white, reached down from the top of the theater seats to pull him out. A burst of fire, and the white hands disappeared.

The black hands kept pulling on him. They pulled him up. It was Johnson.

"Thanks, man," said Emmett. "Thanks," he said to the owner of the other pair of hands who had helped him. It was Wally lying flat out but smiling up at him. His chest looked like hamburger. Emmett looked at Connors. "Thanks," he said to him. Emmett noticed the little spot of dirt that he'd fixed his eyes on was not dirt but a bit of blood.

"What we need here, is a medic," Emmett said to Johnson.

"Forget it, man," said Johnson, and Connors took off his helmet and turned. Emmett saw the back of his head was gone and brains were oozing out from underneath his helmet.

"Oh, shit," moaned Emmett. He raised up on his knees and clutched his helmet. Then he leaped up and ran. His movement triggered an ambush somewhere farther up the hill. He hit the dirt again.

Emmett covered his head. They were always getting ambushed--they never struck first. Emmett had never even fired his rifle at a human being, only foliage and once at a hog that was snuffing around the rotting body of an old woman. He'd even missed the hog.

Emmett strained his eyes into the dark. He thought he saw a flash of something like an animal, a hog, disappear behind a row of seats. Emmett was disgusted with himself. He couldn't hit shit. John Wayne wouldn't have missed. But then, where he thought the hog had disappeared, a Charlie got up, dusted himself off, and walked away.

Emmett started crawling again. He felt shells cut near him, but he couldn't tell what direction they were coming from.

"No, not that way, to the left," said Johnson, in front of him now, beckoning. One of his eyes was hanging by a slimy thread down his cheek.

Johnson was right. The shelling to the left of Emmett stopped and he could hear shells pinging in his right ear. But there was no hope. He figured tanks were the only thing to save them, but who ever heard of tanks in Harrisonville? Not Harrisonville. Danang. What was he thinking?

Then Emmett saw jets streaking down off the crest of the

tree line, rolling in right toward him, before they let the napalm go. "Johnson, over on," he shouted, but Johnson had been hit when Emmett wasn't looking. He was lying on his side making deep, chesty, constricted gurgles.

Emmett jumped up, tucked his head, and started running.

Suddenly he found himself being propelled against a hard, slick wall. Somebody grabbed him. He screamed and gave up.

"Emmett! Emmett! Stop it! Stop it!" yelled a woman's voice. Ngu Tai? Emmett gulped in air. He turned his head. An orange light bathed the woman's face, a face which was not Ngu Tai's.

"Holy shit," said Daisy.

Vaporizing Cassini

J.P. said, "USS Nimitz and USS Roosevelt UAP encounter videos have now been verified as real by the U.S. Navy. The US Army has just signed a CRADA deal with the R&D study of UAP material recovered from the Roswell UAP crash, according to the web media. And the Pentagon report came out this morning."

"Meh," said his wife. She was a tall, good looking woman in running shorts. She had just finished her morning stint of 5 miles. She had long legs, cropped hair, and large hands, like she could make good fists if she needed to.

"The assessment says that the lack of 'high-quality reporting' on the events 'hampers our ability to draw firm conclusions about the nature or intent of UAP.' In other words, they still don't know what the UAPs were, though the report suggests a range of possible explanations. The most intriguing was 'Other.'   I think this is good news. They are at least admitting they can't explain the phenomenon." True, the report was not exactly what he had hoped for, but it opened the door for possibility. Made UAP reporting respectable. Personally, J.P. prefers the older term, UFO.

J.P. was already shaved and dressed for the day. He was sitting at the kitchen table, which will become Jill's laptop computer table after he leaves. Since Covid, Jill, a Burger King insurance adjustor, works from home. Even after things lightened up, Jill continued to work from home because the people she saw every day were jerks, she said. Jill says whatever is on her mind. J.P. sometimes gets the feeling Jill has run out of patience, with her job, and with J.P.

"There's a connection between alien appearances and farms across the world. They must be studying our agricultural capabilities. Not to mention all the sightings at missile bases and power plants. They're studying every detail of what holds our society together—energy, weapons, food."

"Take the garbage to the street when you leave. Don't forget." She kind of shook out her hair. By that J.P. meant she ran her long fingers through the short sweaty strands and fluffed them up. When they met, she had long hair, almost to her waist, but she cut it one day, on a whim. She poured herself a cup of coffee.

J.P. has a right to talk about UAPs, as they call them now, because he teaches astronomy at a local state college. And he has an especial interest. When he was a child, four or five, he actually saw one suspending benignly in the afternoon sky while he was standing near his parent's strawberry patch in Folsom, Louisiana. It suspended, but back then J.P. didn't know that word. He also didn't know about flying saucers at all, so he couldn't have made it up off TV. The thing suddenly disappeared. He had the feeling it took off at tremendous speed. Today he would say - zero knots to light speed.

As usual, Jill did not have anything to say on the matter.

At one time, J.P. thought he might have Asperger's, or at least be on the spectrum. He made it through college with flying colors, but he was bad at business deals. He was also directionally challenged, he couldn't stand collars on shirts, and he couldn't stand socks, and he saw significance in numbers on license plates, like 911. Or 606, their anniversary. Not long into their marriage, Jill gave him a test off the internet, but halfway through she abruptly aborted it.

When he was in college, he worked out another explanation. Maybe he had been looking up in the sky as a four-year-old, waving goodbye to the spaceship that had dumped him off as an experiment in the yard of a small-town southern family with a strawberry patch and a house with a balloon mortgage. He had worked out, more whimsically than seriously, that the aliens, of which he was one, had implanted false memories in him, and in the family, that they had had a baby four years before, and had implanted memories in the whole town for that matter. When J.P. lived in a college dorm, and he would find himself alone in the TV room in the basement, he would become so uneasy he would leave. That was after he had read his first UFO abduction story, an old one from the sixties. Back then Betty and Barny Hill were big in the news, though most people thought they were crazy.

On that Friday of the week, garbage day, Dr. J.P. Melrose came into the classroom a few minutes early as was his custom. He spoke to the few students already there, and he opened his laptop and began pulling up his materials for the class. A conspicuous noise interrupted his search for a particular power point. Raymond Carter had entered the room and dropped his books loudly on one of the tables near the back of the room. Raymond Carter was one of those perplexing students who loved to argue, was fairly intelligent, who wrote soundly if not imaginatively, but was rarely guilty of doing the day's reading. He was a journalism major and UAP skeptic and he was taking Astron 101 to fulfill his department's requirement for an easy science class for all majors.

"Sir?" he said, picking up on the previous class's discussion as if there had not been a day's interval and the roll had been called and announcements deployed, "I happened to catch the Pentagon news release this morning, and one of the videos. The navy's radar imaging to observe the UFOs seemed to be on par with the Ghost Hunter shows, and, as usual, the footage is only at night. Isn't that a little suspicious?"

The class stopped checking their phones and texting and arranging their notebooks. Most of the students were not astronomy majors either, but like Raymond, were picking up a required science. At least Raymond's forays into skepticism if not annoy-the-professor chatter served to keep their attention.

J.P. did not say, "For every hazy video, the government has 100s more that are sharp and clear."

J.P. did say, "That's a false equivalence. There are incidents of the same caliber that happened during daytime that have never been declassified."

"Funny that the actual footage is so grainy, like a

prerequisite for photographing UFOs requires somebody's grandmother's Polaroid." His response evinced a few snorts.

"Filming something a mile away moving hundreds of miles per hour in unpredictable directions will not look as defined as filtered selfies."

The class looked elated that once again Dr. Melrose was being distracted from one of his boring lectures to his nattering on about UAPs. Just for that, J.P. decided to give them a pop quiz at the end of class.

J.P.'s defense of UFOs had earned him a reputation as a fun teacher, but his colleagues' opinions were less than admiring. Luckily, this small-town college valued popular teachers because it translated into money. And J.P. is a full professor, so he has all the rights and privileges of a secured position. Once his full professorship was bestowed, he had not held back on his UAP opinions.

Jill was another matter. When they were first married, Jill had listened skeptically, but fondly amused or so he liked to think, to his theories. But lately Jill and his department seemed to be on the same page, as if he were another beautiful mind, a John Nash, a little "tetched" as they said in Folsom. J.P. feels as though he was on the brink here with the release of heretofore classified information and that it was just a matter of time before he will be in everyone's good graces. The Pentagon was actually saying it could not identify 438 of the suspicious objects. Even Raymond Carter and his comic relief needed to step back once this monumental fact sunk in. He was a little disappointed the Pentagon stopped short of saying extraterrestrial. And he was a little dismayed Jill did not share his enthusiasm. He blamed the government and their weasel words. Tonight, he will pull out the full nine-page report which he had printed out this morning and go over it word for word. He will show her the videos.

J.P. cleared his throat and said, "Ok, let's get started. Today's lecture is on Saturn." There were audible groans.

"Saturn is the most elegant planet in our solar system. It is famous for what?"

"Its rings," said a handful of disaffected voices.

"Yes, for its bright yet eerie rings. This gassy giant has over sixty natural satellites in orbit around it. It also has one artificial satellite: the remains of NASA's vaporized *Cassini* spacecraft. In this module we will explore the weather observed in the atmosphere of Saturn, and the strange organizations that develop within the rings. We will also explore its wide assortment of moons – Titan covered in fog, two-sided Iapetus, wild Prometheus, and Enceladus and its icy plumes."

It was a good lecture, he thought later in the confines of his office. An elementary lecture, suitable for layman, for students needing a science requirement. In this course, he tried to make the history of astronomy take up as many classes as he could, and he steered away from anything that smacked of math. He chose words such as "elegant" the way the late great Carl Sagan had intrigued housewives and children with his passionate diction.

That was back in the 90s, the early 1990s, as Voyager I headed into the unknown, described on *Cosmos* in Sagan's boyish baritone. If he were alive today! How intrigued he would have been. Three decent videos from the Pentagon and the nine-page report!

For more than a decade, the U.S. Department of Defense had been quietly cataloging and investigating scores of bizarre encounters—most from the U.S. Navy—of ships and fighter jets tangling with, or being tailgated by, unidentified flying objects.

For the past three years, Jill had been evolving into an unidentifiable phenomenon. It is his passion for UAPs that is her biggest turnoff J.P. believes. Things had gotten so bad that J.P. was actually counting on the Pentagon to redeem him to his wife.

On September 15, 2017, right in the middle of divorce discussions, initiated by Jill, her father was diagnosed with a slow growing brain cancer. J.P. remembered because it was the same date the Cassini spacecraft plunged into Saturn, becoming part of the planet it had been orbiting since 2004. The intentional plunge into the planet had the goal of ensuring that Saturn's icy moons – in particular ocean-bearing Enceladus – would not risk being contaminated by microbes that might have remained on board the spacecraft from Earth. J.P. was moved to tears, something that rarely happened to him, but it had an unexpected perk when already in a rare emotional state he held Jill, devastated, and she, though shocked, mistakenly thought his subdued sobs were for her father.

Cassini was launched when J.P. was in the seventh grade. He had grown up with its discoveries, and its well…courage. At the end of the voyage, out of fuel, Cassini hurled itself into the hot gasses, pointing its antennae at Earth as long as it could. It was gone in 85 seconds.

All plans for divorce came to a halt after Cassini's vaporization and after his father-in-law made his announcement. Instead of splitting up, Jill proposed they stay together until after her father's death. She could not stand disappointing him. J.P. saw it as a reprieve, as an extended time in which he could win her back. But things did not change. He failed to convince Jill that his UAP theories were valid. He continued to remain clueless about what he should say and how he should act and be a husband. Getting ready to go home, he remembered he had not put the garbage on the curb.

As he was piling books and papers into his briefcase, the phone rang and a young man's voice (at first, he thought it was a student) was introducing himself as Randy Whittier and speaking about the Pentagon's report in the NY Times, and the unveiling of the videos. It was a local TV station. "We'd like to interview you, Dr. Melrose, live. The program airs at 6. We'll highlight the Pentagon report and show one of the videos. Then we'll cut to you and get your drift."

"I'll do it," J.P. blurted out. He was interested. He was more than interested. "I'll be there." Now, J.P. had the opportunity to connect with Jill in a spectacular way. To make UAP reporting normal. He decided to stay in his office until it was time to go the TV station. He called Jill but she didn't answer. He texted her a message to turn on the news at six and turned off his phone. Texting was better than speaking. Speaking was better than not speaking. Over the years, accompanied by great drama, he had learned to let Jill know if he would be late. And he had learned the monumental importance of remembering birthdays.

A year into their marriage, Jill announced she did not want children. J.P. had acquiesced without argument. In fact, if he let Jill make all the major decisions they got along well, up to a point. Then came the complaining she felt isolated and lonely. As far as the baby, only Jill's parents were disappointed in their decision. His own folks seemed relieved.

With plenty of time to spare, J.P. headed out. At the TV station he was ushered into a waiting room and offered coffee. He was almost an hour early. He went into the little bathroom of the waiting room and looked into a mirror. Maybe he should have gone home first. He looked a little seedy as Jill would say. He needed a haircut and his plaid shirt looked tired.

Eventually a young woman dressed like a bank teller appeared in the door. "Time," she said. They walked down the hall to the studio. Randy was talking to a camera man and when he saw J.P. he waved him over to three director chairs. In one of them sat Raymond Carter. "I think you two know each other. Raymond's doing his internship with us. I thought it good to have the both of you, the skeptic and the believer, making comments, so I talked him into being interviewed too. Sorry, this is so last minute. But we had a spot."

"No problem, boss," said Raymond. Then he grinned at J.P. "Dr. Melrose, long time no see."

J.P. nodded and climbed into one of the chairs. He could handle Raymond. He handled him every Monday, Wednesday, and Friday.

"So cute," said the bank teller woman, "a professor and

his student."

After local news, the camera J.P. and Raymond were sitting in front of started blinking and Randy spoke in bowel deep tones:

"Late last year the Senate passed a bill that required U.S. intelligence agencies to share what they know about 'Unidentified Aerial Phenomena,' or UAPs, the present term for UFOs. That report was released just this morning. Happily, for both sides, believers and skeptics, it doesn't confirm the existence of alien spacecraft. But it doesn't rule them out either.

"The report states, 'Some UAP appeared to remain stationary in winds aloft, move against the wind, maneuver abruptly, or move at considerable speed, without discernable means of propulsion. In a small number of cases, military aircraft systems processed radio frequency (RF) energy associated with the Unidentified Aerial Phenomena.' According to the Pentagon UFOs remain unidentified and mysterious. The strange encounter with the UFO you are seeing in this clip is one of more than 140 that US intelligence cannot explain. This one was observed by 2 Navy jet fighter pilots off the coast of CA.

"We have here tonight Dr. J.P. Melrose, Professor of Astronomy at Northeastern University and our journalist intern, UFO skeptic, and student at UNE, Raymond Carter. First, Dr. Melrose, can we have your opinion?"

"Well, my happy opinion is that the report takes us one step into the realm of conversation outside of the crazy factor, if nothing else. Over the years pilots and others have seen things which are clearly impossible within our world but have been afraid to share that information for fear that they would be laughed at.

"It gives permission to start looking for them in a more concerted way, using things like artificial intelligence and pattern recognition, taking radar data from all over the country and trying to look for anomalies rather than just relying on what amounts to gunsight data from military aircraft. That is all I hoped for at this point."

"But do you think they are real, Dr. Melrose?"

"What is it you are asking? Is it something created in the visible world out of delusion? Is it something other countries might have created, you know, China or Russia? I think if China or Russia had this technology, we would know about that by now. So, I am a guy who has seen a UAP, myself." J.P. stared into the camera a second for effect. He felt a surge of relief. "OK, I can tell you right now that I am enjoying some validation knowing that this is not just something that I imagined, but I am not here to talk about what I saw."

"But what are its intentions? Suspending the old explanations of swamp gas and weather balloons for the sake of argument. What if it is Russia or China, or even both?"

"Russia or China is the new swamp gas. Over fifty of these things were tracked on radar swarming U.S. battleships. A dozen swarming the USS Omaha at one time. No foreign government could have built or financed a fleet of these things, waiting secretly to unleash them to use for global domination."

"Mr. Carter? Want to weigh in?"

"It's funny how people can extrapolate stuff." Raymond

glanced at J.P. amusedly. "To understand the videos, all you need to do is ask any fighter pilot familiar with advanced camera systems. What looks like great tremendous speed and impossible maneuvers is just a common optical illusion caused by the effects of the state-of-the-art technology." of glare filters."

"Well, that's a relief," Randy said. "I hope you are right. Anything else?"

"Terrorism is losing its appeal. How is the government supposed to justify a defense budget now? I'll tell you how. Space Force—"

"And define Space Force for our viewers."

"Space Force is a new branch of the Air Force designed to develop the use of space for military purposes. And the spacecraft they are so concerned about are complete illusions, or easily explained. Erratic dots of light! And tell me why supposed aliens would put lights on their spacecrafts emitting in our light spectrum which would be visible to humans?"

"Dr. Melrose, any last words?"

"Over 8 million species exist on earth. The universe is infinite and so are the probabilities of a species to evolve like us. Humans on Earth are just 315,000 years old according to new calculations, and we only now can break the sound barrier. Imagine species starting before us, their technological abilities.

"The report is important because it opens the door for a serious look at UFOs. Specifically, it encourages the U.S. government to collect better data on UFOs, and I think the release of the report increases the chances that scientists will try to interpret that data. Historically, UFOs have felt off limits to mainstream science, but perhaps no more. I am satisfied." J.P. realized he'd used the older term.

"Mr. Carter? Last word?"

"Perhaps these videos were designed to push us into lockdown and destroy freedom. Make us so desperate to get back to normal we'd do anything, even take an experimental Covid vaccine."

"You both have raised some interesting questions."

J.P. knew he had won. Disavowing the science of Covid vaccines made Raymond look like the kook. He felt almost happy. If only he knew what happiness actually felt like. He will know when he sees Jill.

Jill met him at the door. "Where have you been?" Her hair was plastered to her head as if she had been swimming. Her healthy skin looked as though it had developed a mineral deficiency since that morning and her eyes were red and foreign.

J.P. had forgotten to turn his phone back on in his haste to get home. "I was at the KNOE studio. Being interviewed about the Pentagon report."

Jill said raggedly, "My father's dead. Emergency surgery. A myocardial infarction on the table."

"Jill." He reached for her. He knew that was the thing to do.

She shook him off. "You have to leave. As soon as you can. No more, J.P. You can come to the funeral if you like. I don't care."

"You did not see my interview?"

"Are you crazy? I was at the hospital. Are you crazy?"

J.P., have you had enough?

J.P. had pulled over and parked on their now dark street after he realized he didn't know where he was going.

The question came from somewhere deep in his brain. But the metal voice did not sound like his own. J.P. got out of his car and leaned against the door. He stared up at the night sky. Some cool light was emanating behind the clouds. Interesting, but he remembered he had just lost Jill. He stared up at his old friends, the stars and planets. Dark energy was pushing them away faster and faster. Every night he looked up he knew he was seeing less. Like looking at himself and Jill.

It's time to go home. This time the voice was coming from the long shadows of the trees lining the street.

He came out of the shadows of the cypresses the city had planted so long ago they had some height and substance. Behind them, glittering between tree trunks and gnarly cypress knees, was Bayou Desiard which wound through his neighborhood and on past his university.

"Henghist?" J.P. said.

He shook his head slightly, trying to remember why the intruder seemed familiar. He was stocky but not fat, not muscled, and medium height. Extra bulk but more solid than flab. He had a military crew cut. He was wearing one of those one-piece jumpsuits that old men favor, but he wasn't old. The jumpsuit was metallic.

J.P. said, "How did I know your name?"

You have been screened off with clouds. Now you are not.

He seemed to be looking at J.P. respectfully with his large eyes in his narrow gray face. At that second J.P. felt the same sensation he'd had from his one sky dive. He'd drifted too far, and mesmerized by the landscape, had opened his chute a few seconds late. When he returned to regular speed the tremendous opening shocked him upright. He crash landed and broke his ankle. He had scared Jill so bad she made him quit, not realizing the whole experience made him feel normal, with something that could only be called fear.

He knew he was facing an alien.

You were put here to explore.

Explore what?

Extreme loneliness.

How did you get here? J.P. thought. Extreme loneliness? Was that the heaviness?

Then he thought, *how far is your planet?* Primitive vocalizations seemed odious and unnecessary. *Do you have weapons? Has your planet run out of resources? Do you wish to adopt Earth's technology?* J.P. remembered from his research that light gray color was more benign than dark gray. Henghist's face glowed lightly.

J.P. knew diverse species existed in all shapes and forms from vegans to carnivores and cannibals, but with always the possibility for sensate evolution.

J.P. was given to believe wherever Henghist was from, his planet had no need for Earth's primitive technology, carcinogens, litter, petroleum guzzling carbon monoxide belching vehicles, and disposable polymers.

Jill's form appeared a brief second. *Keep your head on straight* she thought to him, looking at him not unkindly.

I will.

Behind Henghist, behind the cypresses, a familiar craft lit up the bayou and lowered gently down on the dark water in its own pool of liquid light. It was elegant.

How do I know this is real?

Do you know what euneirophrenia is?

Yes. The peace of mind that comes with having pleasant dreams. Yes.

How else would you know that word? A metallic chuckle.

You have you-yesterday, you-today and you-tomorrow amongst your parts?

Yes.

What is it called?

Perdurance.

The water in the bayou turned translucent, then waxed turbulent, and a faint hum began.

Biryena B' parmeta U' hona--?

U' shart awi min oudaleh B' roukha D' akhunawoota, J.P. finished.

Is it possible to construct, in the precisely meticulous framework of algebraic QFT, a theory in 4-dimensional spacetime that includes interface and does not rely on perturbative methods?

No, it has not been possible. It has been possible to do so only in 2 dimensions. J.P took a deep sweet breath. *Ok, ok. All right then.*

Let's go.

Jill appeared one last time, jogging past them in her running shoes down the line of cypress, her long legs and ponytail flashing in the craft's gentle blinding light.

Even in the Dark

They were driving through Texas toward the Louisiana border to get home when his wife spotted a woman and a little boy walking along Hwy 90. It was almost dark by then and his wife's head jerked around as they passed.

"Stop-stop-stop," she half screamed.

Leonard could tell who they were as they flew past even in the dark. Mexicans or Guatemalans, illegal.

He had just picked up his wife from her parents' house in Beaumont that afternoon. She left him three months ago but had a change of heart and called him to come get her. It wasn't exactly a dream come true, but he was glad to have her back.

"We've got to go back, Leonard," said Gina. "It's getting dark. What are they doing out here?"

Gina used to be an RN. It made her sensitive to others' pain, most of the time. Not his, especially, but little kids, and lost dogs, and orphaned baby birds. When Gina was sixteen, she was knocked up by a gang rape, a fact that defined her life thereafter, and eventually his too. Whether she will admit it or

234

not, everything Gina did was to make up for that, not the rape, but the baby. Of course, she gave the baby up. Back then, that's what you did.

"We can't, Gina. We have to get home and let Maggie out to pee." Maggie was the three-year -old black Schnauzer Gina surprisingly paid eight hundred dollars for after their old dog Fresco died, instead of getting a pound puppy like they always agreed was best. In addition to that breeder's fee, there was the tags and license and the twice-a-year shots and the chip. When Maggie escapes the fence and runs down the street, Leonard just sees $1500 darting in and out of the parked cars.

"Go back, go back, Leonard, please? They could be in danger on this dark road."

"You know they probably came through Roma. You know they are illegal. They have come this far. Let's not get involved. We could be liable." He knew that wasn't true, but he said it anyway.

Gina had long frosted dark hair that she kept in a ponytail, much too young for her age, but Leonard didn't mind. She still turned him on. Gina had always run too fat, but sexy fat, with her wide chocolate gelato Italian eyes and big breasts. Last year Gina stepped off the curb on one of her long walks to lose weight to wave at some friends going by and wham, a drunk driver hit her and flung her forty feet through the air. A drunk driver in the middle of the day. She was hospitalized for months. Leonard was sure during that dark time he was going to lose her. Now Gina didn't drive because she was afraid she might faint from one of her dizzy spells she got now.

Gina started to say something and instead looked at herself in her window's reflection and shook her head. Leonard knew he had not really won.

"Jesus," Gina said, "it's like we are still where we started three months ago." Gina used to try to find things to laugh at. Not now, though.

They had a strong case and were offered over $115,000 because the driver was so falling down drunk and therefore it wasn't all Gina's fault for stepping in the street. CT scan showed 14-15 herniated disks, broken collar bone, broken hip, both wrists fractured, concussion. The state of her claim was still open because they had to get an entire new lawyer to work on the case because the first one didn't do jack squat for her in terms of receiving income from the case. A hundred and fifteen thousand would not have even paid for the medical bills for one day. Luckily, she had good hospitalization from her former nursing job.

"Are you sorry you called me now?" Leonard said.

"Not yet," Gina said. But even in the dark, Leonard knew she didn't smile.

At first, Leonard had been in shock when Gina left. She called her mother, who arrived, apologetically, to drive her to her parent's house. He hadn't seen other women in the last three months, until last night, before Gina called him to take her home even though some of Gina's own friends had come over under the guise of casserole delivery. The casseroles were appropriate even if the intentions were not. He had felt like she had died, and he was in mourning, and eating funeral food because it had come as the biggest blow in his life outside the accident. Leonard was also scared shitless when her duplicitous friends showed up. Not only were they two faced to Gina, they were full of scary rhetoric. They were not real Me Too people, but they knew the drill. Despite his caution, last night was a mistake.

Ever since the accident, ever since she had come out of the coma, Gina said and did things that surprised him. Little things, like the expensive dog, and suddenly liking sweet potatoes which she had always hated. Until this big thing. Until they had a blow up about What To Do With The Money. Their lawyer thinks they are looking at close to a million dollars once he takes his cut. The drunk had excellent insurance if not good sense.

Leonard believes they should retire to Florida so they can fish and lounge on the beach and Gina can forget about her traumas. Gina used to love deep sea fishing when they were first married.

Gina thought they should start a foundation for rape victims with the money. She had thought about it a lot. The mission of the foundation will be to start a "comprehensive" treatment for victims of rape, sexual assault, and sexual abuse, including medical care and other support services. They had been arguing over money they hadn't even received yet.

"You see," Gina had said, brutally, "there is no we. This is money I will have earned with my suffering. Why do you keep saying, 'we?'"

"Sickness and health," Leonard had said, "good times, bad times, blah blah." And he had suffered plenty sitting out her coma for weeks, thinking the worst.

Right before the accident, Gina had become enamored with the Me Too Movement. It was as though she had waited most of her life for it. It helped. It did at first. But…Me Too started taking over their lives. Gina made FB friends all over the world and real live friends right here in town, and, true, it seemed to help the *thing*. By the *thing* Leonard meant that dark past heavy *thing* that hung over her that started so long ago when she was a teenager on her first date, a teenager who drank too much, and had the misfortune to be raised Catholic, which kept the pot quietly stirred. Gina's new friends encouraged her idea for a foundation. Leonard just wants Gina to forget.

And the Me-Too thing was good in the beginning for a lot of women, but listening to his unmarried and divorced buddies, Leonard was glad he was married no matter how hard it was. Everyone was so offended about everything nowadays and someone could be deemed a perv just for approaching a woman for a legitimate date. Leonard would not say this to Gina, ever.

Now Gina was taking a deep breath in the darkening car. And just as she was saying, "I'm going to ask you one more time to turn around, Leonard," a Border Patrol SUV appeared around the next curve, its lights flashing, and shut down their argument.

At home, in bed, Leonard spooned with Gina in the dark

room. It was dark but he could see a little. Maggie was curled into a ball at the foot of the bed and Gina had one foot on her and was gripping his arm, a grip that loosened little by little as she drifted off to sleep. They had not had sex since before the accident.

Leonard was warm and cozy under the covers. Both didn't mind devastating their utility bill by turning down the thermostat so low it made the room frigid as a winter's night, and then huddling under their comforter. They both happily agreed to that arrangement. Once in the military on maneuvers he was buried in snow all one night. The only thing sticking out was his glasses frosted over with clear ice. Snow doesn't keep you warm like they say. He liked to think about that time and then feel his nice warm covers.

If anyone had asked Leonard what he wanted out of life three months ago, he would have said, "To be a good person." But Leonard knew he was not a good person, and he will never be one now. He was like those psychologists who say they got into their professions because they wanted to help people, and then they do one of their own tests on themselves and find out that they are the psychopaths.

Just as he was drifting off to sleep, Gina stirred and said, "Honey, did you check the doors? Is the system on?"

"Yes," he lied. He did not check the doors because the doors locked every time they were closed. The security system was on because it was always on. But Gina made him check them, anyway. Not every night. Just when she was feeling nervous.

"Please? Again?"

Leonard got out his nice warm burrow and put on his flip flops. Maggie looked up but then laid her head back down. She was Gina's dog. He stumbled his way around in the dark into the living room.

He opened the front door and slammed it hard. He knew she was listening. Then he went to the back door and slammed it.

From the kitchen he could see his neighbor's house. Someone was up and their kitchen light mirrored his own. He knew it was Margaret, sleepless, wearing her oversized T-shirt, and her furry house slippers. Since her husband died, she couldn't sleep, not because she missed him, but because she said for the first time in her life she knew she was going to die. Her husband's sudden death made her think about God and heaven and hell and what's-it-all-for kind of things. She had not loved her husband much, Patrick, who left her for months at a time traveling all over the world for his computer company, but she'd respected him.

Those two had been their new neighbors for over six months, but outside his saying "Welcome to the neighborhood" to Patrick and "How're you?" to Margaret when he'd set off one morning to walk Maggie, there had not been much interaction, until yesterday, when she'd shown up at his door with Maggie in her arms. Since Gina had been gone, Leonard just let Maggie out to pee by herself and sometimes forgot her. Nobody else on the street was up. It was too early.

It was then it happened.

Her house seemed more appropriate. Leonard locked

Maggie up and followed Margaret.

Afterwards, Leonard held Margaret, and he told her how she was safe inside her house and she was too young to worry about death. But he knew even as he said it, it was not true. Young people died all the time. The Mexican mother and her child might be dead now having gotten into the wrong car at the wrong time. Mothers and fathers, both, leave their babies in hot cars. Children wash up on shores. Young people with their whole lives ahead of them get cancer.

He'd held Margaret the way he used to hold Gina after she would relive the moment the nuns took her baby without her getting to hold him, and her mother grabbed both her wrists and said, "Now, Gina. We already settled this. You know it's for the best." When he heard that story for the first time, he vowed to be a good man for the rest of his life. Now he has lost even that.

Leonard stared out his window at Margaret's light still burning. Her voice seemed to be coming to him from a great distance. "There are things we never let ourselves think about," she'd said. He could not remember what he replied.

He knew Margaret was not thinking of him. He knew she would not rat him out, make demands. He knew she wouldn't accuse him of assault. Of cancelling her. He knew she would make herself some chamomile tea and take some Unisom and go back to her king-sized bed without even a Maggie there for her. And in the morning, she will sense Gina, and if by chance they meet, she will barely nod.

And then he walked down the hall back into the cold bedroom.

Fishing Trip

When he finally got home, Lynda was sitting at the kitchen table with Lyn, their son, and after one look at their faces, he knew he was ass deep in trouble. Yes, they named their son after Lynda, a name as close as they could get, Lynden. That was because Lynda's mother and grandmother and great aunt had all died of breast cancer, and she was making sure if she was next, she was remembered.

Same names, same expressions, looking at him in sorrow and disgust. And anger, the kind you put a lid on and try not to yell because the issue is so important.

Like him, Lyn was still wearing his fishing clothes, old overalls, the ones he always wore to the camp, the ones he had put on so early that morning before he got in the Woody with Richard. Lyn at sixteen could be the quarter back, the hunting and fishing ad guy, the drag racer, the guy who knocked up his girlfriend senior year, and with his perpetual petulant expression and a few tweaks to his wardrobe, the Gothic Columbine Killer. Lyn was none of those things. Lyn was a straight A student who played guitar and dabbled in writing music. He had loads of girlfriends, none of whom he clicked with.

The fishing trip was cooked up by Lynda so that Lyn at some point could tell Richard that he was gay in a bucolic neutral territory, he guessed. Richard had always known Lyn talked like there was music in his voice and he walked like he was listening to a beat. Why couldn't they leave it at that?

"You let him walk six miles home?" She didn't seem surprised. "You stayed at the camp all day, and he walked home?" Then she says Richard caused her anguish, and he caused Lyn anguish. They, as though they were one person, felt humiliated and exposed.

At some point he stopped listening. Their faces reminded him of his mother's soap opera characters, the ones she talked about as though they were real people, the ones he glimpsed when he went to visit her and the actors' tense lines were exchanged in the seconds before he turned off the sound so he and his mom could visit, and there was nothing left but watchful expressions and silent-movie lips.

Finally, Richard said, "It's okay, Lyn. As I tried to tell you at the camp. I've known for some time. I'm okay with it. But do we have to say it out loud?"

"Yes, because otherwise it just means you tolerate me," Lyn said. He touched his sunburn face. "If you already knew, why didn't you tell me you knew? If you already knew, why when we passed those girls playing volleyball in their bathing suits today did you say, 'Hey, check that out'? Why did you always say things, like when you find the right girl, blah, blah,

blah, all my life?"

Richard turned to Lynda, "How long have you known?"

"Six months."

"Why didn't you mention it to me?"

"Because it was Lyn's call. But how did you sense it and not me? I'm his mother." She turned to Lyn. "I'm your mother."

"I told you, first Mom. Close enough. But telling him was a lame idea. Now he is telling us he's always known I am gay but wants us to pretend I am not. So fucked up."

"Every hear of 'don't ask, don't tell.' Works beautifully in the military." Richard remembered he'd left the bait box in the Woody. He mustn't forget to take it out. And the ice chest full of water and no fish. A day shot.

"What did you say to him today? How did you get separated? And why? How could you have handled this more badly?" She seemed to like the idea of her role as the hip accepting mom of a gay son.

When Richard was sixteen in high school a confession like that would have gotten your brains beaten out.

Richard said, "He just stalked off. I thought he would be back."

Lynda put her hands on Lyn's shoulders. "What did he say to you?"

"He said he always knew. He thinks he has gaydar. He made the 'don't ask ,don't tell' stupid-ass remark. He said, you can't be gay during this election because I'm voting for the Trump/Pence ticket."

They both should have known that was a sarcastic joke, but Lynda said, "Are you insane? Have you completely flipped?"

Richard knew what came after coming out. Jeffrey at work had been passed over for two promotions. His daughter was black, lesbian, bi, questioning, trans. What do the bullies probably say when she goes to school? Hey, get her. She's all five of them. Richard knows all the lingo because Jeffrey is his office mate and old fishing buddy, and he has been in on the drama from day one. At first Jeffrey, whose background was old time black religion, and her mother, tried to pray the gay away, then they suggested she find a skinny, unathletic boy, and when that didn't work, they sent her to conversion camp—putting all the lesbians together in a remote area— where she found her girlfriend. Then they passed her around Christian therapists. They were the ones ending up converting because the therapists were mean, and his daughter started freaking and taking drugs. So, they are in P-Flag now, and instead of being Richard's fishing buddy, Jeffery marches with his wife in Gay Pride or goes to how-to-handle-it type meetings. Saturdays shot.

Gay beats drugs any day. But the rednecks at work hold the keys to the kingdom.

Richard tried running defense, "Maybe pointing out those volleyball girls, I was telling you I was keeping your secret."

"How did you know, though?" Lynda said. "I am his mother."

"Maybe telling you when you find the right girl, meant

nothing is set in stone. You are young."

Lyn said, "Maybe you were just saying it's not okay to be yourself."

"It's okay to be yourself," said Lynda. "I am your mother, and I am telling you it's okay. Your dad is mixed up." Then glaring at me with her plastic pride expression, "I won't have you passing judgement on him, do you hear?"

Despite everything, knowing what is in store, Richard said, "I am just being practical. Remember Aunt Patti? You don't know the whole story. She came out to Grandpa and he kicked her out of the house and she slept on other people's couches until she died. You know she killed herself? That was the reason." Now that he has dredged up that, he won't sleep tonight.

"This isn't the Dark Ages anymore," said Lyn. "Things have changed now."

"Not as much as you may think," said Richard thinking of Pence and all the Adam and Steve bumper stickers on the trucks at work. At work he refrained from discussing politics.

After Patti came out, he had tried to work two jobs to get himself an apartment so he could save his sister. He was only seventeen, one year older than Lyn. But he wasn't fast enough. "People can be mean."

"So now you are saying I'm weak and can't handle anything."

"No. Don't exaggerate. Why do you have to come out now?"

"Because he has a boyfriend now," said Lynda. She smiled smugly. "That is one thing I do know."

Richard stared at her. She was a tall, cold, but talky woman, accented by blonde-white hair completely dyed, and her signature red lipstick she'd worn for decades. It occurred to him she had always given him the feeling she was looking for something to judge. He had always forgiven her because of her small town Southern Baptist upbringing, maybe one step away from Westboro, which she at times tried mightily to minimize. For a minute he felt sick and crazy.

No one had talked about Patti for decades. The past had a film over it and the things he remembers was that nothing ever really happened to him. They happened to Patti. Suddenly he burst into tears, like a girl.

They went into shock, all three of them. Richard pressed his palms on his eyes to stop the flow and when took them down, he saw the anger slipping from Lyn's face.

Richard got up slowly, delicately.

"It doesn't matter, Lyn," said Richard. He put both arms behind his head and clenched his hands together and squeezed his head with his elbows. "Really it doesn't matter one way or another."

Lyn stared at him as if he had turned into a stranger before his eyes. Neither of them could look away. Finally, Lynn said, "You're scared, aren't you?"

"I was waiting for you. I thought you'd be right back. When you didn't show I thought it better if I drive home and check on you."

He had driven slowly, thinking he'd spot Lyn sitting by the road, exhausted, but his slowness gave Lyn enough time to get home before him.

"I'm smothering you, aren't I?" said Lynda. "Is all this my fault?"

"I have to go," said Richard. "I need to drive."

He walked out of the door into the overgrown backyard where the afternoon sun made it look like a tangled meadow.

Lyn followed him. "Dad," he said, "I'm coming with you."

Lynda was following him.

"Can I go?" she said. "I'm his mother."

Southern Landscaping

Understandably, Malcom Barlow couldn't fathom why his wife was on the roof. So, he asked her.

"Darling, what are you doing?" An academic question.

Everything had been going well up to now. Diane had been released just this morning after her usual ten days of detox, stabilized, with new experimental prescriptions already called into the pharmacy for drugs which ultimately never worked but always gave Malcolm a polite hopeful window of time, until things proved differently. Their efficacy should kick in in about two to four weeks, the doctor always said ("It's all hit or miss. Nobody knows how these things work.") after the drugs from the detox had worn off. That was always the plan.

Diane was gazing up at the six o'clock afternoon sky in surround sound by the crickets and frogs cranking up. They lived in a choice part of town, bordered by the park in the back, this side of Ballytore Road, and it was empty and shady and wet smelling. The cypresses were a hundred years old and the cypresses shared their space with magnolias and live oaks

249

dripping with moss, and in the spring a conglomeration of pink, white, coral, and red azalea blooms which brought out the denizens with their kids, and dogs, and poop bags to trail around the old mossy brick paths. Fall was the nicest when everything was preparing to die.

"Getting away from the voices," she said.

Malcolm simply must take down that trellis. Or plant it with thorny roses instead of the jasmine.

So, it had come to that again. High on the roof there, far from Malcolm sans glasses and with his myopic eyes, she looked like a teenager again with her dark loose hair and flowy sun dress and legs still lovely catching the afternoon sun.

"You know they are not real," Malcolm said. "Do you want your ear plugs? Do you want your headphones? Do you need your white noise?"

Their daughter, Julie, had come up with the white noise idea to keep Diane's voices at bay. Julie was better with Diane than Malcolm. During her teen years she kept them hopping with her woman's rights, animal rights, veganism, and ecological concerns. Once she wrote a letter to Obama that earned them a visit by the CIA. Most families, in his day, just worried about a daughter getting pregnant, or not being asked to get married, or both, not a daughter who talked like a man, and knew her own mind just a bit too well. She'd bombarded them with lectures inspired by the act of merely raising a fork full of roast beef to the lips or buying a new Mercedes. Like a hippie from his day. She was a good kid though. On weekends she worked in women's shelters and homeless kitchens. Malcom inwardly shuddered at times, at the thought of the kind of nerdy social working New Age type men she might bump into and marry. He suspected she had a secret boyfriend.

Malcolm, who ran Southern Landscaping with the ruthlessness of one who could only have been born into hard scrabble and worked his way up the food chain to a hard-won dominion, was frequently struck dumb by his daughter and her penchant for argument and consciousness raising and climate rallies. He, who allowed only one chair in his office for visitors, who frequently commented to his employees, "I'm running a business, not a charity," who could be heard to shout, "You know how long an hour is? It's lunch *hour!*" to some hapless employee sculking in two minutes late, felt helpless around his daughter, his gorgeous tall daughter, who never wore make up, and who could make him feel like a Philistine in his own home. As far as Diane, Malcom was an enabler, so he had been told. Which means everything you do in kindness is wrong.

Julie believes his landscaping business, with its five different locations, that paid for everyone's cars and a quarter of a million-dollar plantation style mansion, green house, and swimming pool was immoral. His business, envy-inspiring lawns, tiered rock gardens, living ornamental walls that earned their bread and butter, was just land that customers could have used to grow food for the homeless. Bizarre.

In his day, women like Julie ended up working in Margaret Sangers, or Edna Gladney's, and wore tennis shoes with long sad skirts. And never married.

"Darling," he said, "Aren't you going to come down?

We'll go out to dinner."

Diane was staring in the direction of the trellis, fascinated.

"What do you see, darling? Do you see things? Tell me. It's just in your mind, you know."

Then Diane looked down at him, as if noticing him for the first time. "Tiny chickens dancing, people running with bright colored flashing lights around them, dog barking, my mom's voice."

"Your mom's dead, my sweet. She's been dead for twenty years. Come down and we'll have dinner."

"Sh-h-h!" Diane said over her shoulder. "Go away, pleasssse."

Malcom glanced at his phone. Julie should be coming in from class soon. She would know what to say to her mother.

His brothers' wives practically slept with a dust cloth in their hands. They had completed Master Gardener classes. They drove, maybe not Mercedes, but late model Hondas. Why couldn't Diane be like them? Even sober, even before the voices, Diane never fit in with them. She wanted to finish her art degree when they first married, but Malcom discouraged that. Even back then, she was fragile.

Julie's cousins were all married and soccer moms. Why couldn't his daughter grow up to be like them instead of this woman about to graduate with a useless degree in Environmental Science? And with a social conscience. He had no heir to his kingdom. She will sell it and give the money to charities. This strange child who looked at her father as a person whose heart beat faster only when thinking of Southern Landscaping. Who had called him a capitalist when she was thirteen years old.

"You son of a bitch," said Diane. "What do you have against me?"

"Sweetie," said Malcolm, "please come down. Do you want me to come up? Do you want the ladder? I'll get the ladder and come up." He was not sure the trellis would hold him.

"That's right. Mess things around. I've done enough for you."

Malcolm hustled to the garage and careened back with the ladder. He laid it on top of the trellis. "Dear? I'm coming up."

"If you come up, I'll jump. Don't come near me, you filth!" Then she took a step nearer the edge.

"Wait, darling. Don't move. Just stay where you are."

The hedge stirred. Mrs. Kaufman from next door in a sun hat and holding rose bush trimmers was peering through the hedge. "Shall I call someone?" She and her husband were retired, both bankers, no children. Living in heaven, unaware. But they were aware of the Barlow family problems.

Still, Malcom was embarrassed. "No, thank you." They were making a scene.

"There is your whore!" said Diane. "What?!" She turned her head to the left.

"Ok, stop lying. I want a divorce."

Mrs. Kaufman was seventy-two years old.

"Please leave us alone, Mrs. Kaufman," Malcolm said. "But thank you.

"Dear, we are making a scene. Just sit down and I'll come

up and get you."

"I will jump. I will jump. I will jump."

"Diane, look at me. Sit down and look at me."

Then Diane did look at him, almost as if she were asking for help, and said, her voice rising, "They tell me to jump."

Julie slid up the drive in her Toyota Hybrid. She got sedately out of the car and reached for her backpack. What a CEO she would have made.

"Your mother—" Malcom began.

"Mama," Julie interrupted him, "stay back from the edge."

Diane moved back and made a shooing gesture at her imaginary friends. "It's the voices again, Julie. They're telling me things."

"They are not true things, Mama. Come down."

"How?" said Diane. "I can't see for the shadows. The shadow people."

"Go to the trellis. That is where the ladder is. Daddy and I will stand right here and catch you if you slip. Don't try to talk. Just come down. Slowly. Now."

"All right," said Diane. "You know things I don't. You know what to do. All right."

Acknowledgements

The author wishes to thank the State of Louisiana Board of Regents Support Fund (BORSF) for providing time for just writing.

"Are You Decent?" *Strictly Fiction II,* anthology, Potpourri Publications, Prairie Village, KS, 1995. pps. 79-84.

"Carrying the Fight" *The Wolf Head Quarterly*, Duluth, MN, Summer, 1997, pps. 11-23.

"Foreign Travel" *The Cotton Boll: An Atlanta Review.* Atlanta, GA. Vol. 1/No. 3. Fall, 1986. pps. 63-72.

"Only Visiting This Planet" *Southern Review.* Vol. 24/No. 4. Baton Rouge, LA. 1988. pps. 914-923.

"Tabby's Blues Box" in slightly different form. *Louisiana Literature.* Hammond, LA. Spring, 1990. pps. 40-48.

"The Not-So-Chinese Wedding" *Running Wild Novella Anthology*, Running Wild Press, Fall 2012.

Dorie LaRue is the author of two novels, Resurrecting Virgil, and The Trouble With Student Affairs; and three collections of poetry, Mad Rains, An Enemy in Their Mouths, and In God's Due Time. She obtained her Ph.D. in English at the University of Louisiana. She lives in Shreveport, Louisiana, and teaches creative writing at LSUS.